War Machine

War Machine

A YELLOWTHREAD STREET MYSTERY

WILLIAM MARSHALL

HAMISH HAMILTON
LONDON

The Hong Bay district of Hong Kong
is fictitious, as are the people who,
for one reason or another, inhabit it.

02218048

First published in Great Britain 1982
by Hamish Hamilton Ltd
Garden House 57–59 Long Acre London WC2E 9JZ

British Library Cataloguing in Publication Data

Marshall, William, 1944
    War machine.
    I. Title
    823'.914[F]   PR6063.A68

    ISBN 0–241–10823–3

Photoset and printed in Great Britain by
Redwood Burn Ltd, Trowbridge, Wiltshire

Night-Jar

At 4.15 a.m. at the seawall on Beach Road, Detective Inspector Auden screwed up his face and listened.

Nothing.

There was a storm building up somewhere out in the South China Sea and he flexed his shoulders under his shirt as the air around him built up and became sticky and close.

Still nothing.

He screwed up his face and cocked his head to put his ear in the direction of the sea. There was a dull roar of thunder a long way out and, somewhere off to his right, the sound of a small outboard motor as a fisherman in one of the western inlets of Hong Bay either went back to his boat after a long night or started off from his boat for a long day, but apart from that...

... nothing.

In the open back of the Army radio directional van, Corporal Tong pulled back his earphones, rubbed at his ears with his fingers, and catching Auden's eye, shook his head.

Persistent reports of gunfire ...

Fifty yards away, walking the deserted sidewalk by the seawall, Detective Inspector Spencer asked The Fireworks Man, 'Anything?'

The Fireworks Man said quietly in Cantonese, 'I can't hear anything except the water.'

Spencer glanced at his watch. There was a crackle from his walkie talkie and he put it against his ear to hear what was being said to the RD van from the Water Police.

Sergeant Lew of the Water Police, a hundred and fifty yards out in the harbour, transmitted in Cantonese to the Army Corporal,

1

'Nothing. How about you?'

The Army Corporal looked at Auden and shook his head.

Persistent reports of gunfire. It was 4.18. Auden said, 'We might as well pack up. Tell Lew—'

Lew's voice said, 'There! I heard it! It's coming from—did you get it?'

Auden looked at the Corporal.

The Corporal shook his head.

Lew's voice said between bursts of static, 'Sorry. It was thunder. I should have been counting the time between the lightning and the rolls. The storm's about two miles out. My coxswain tells me the time's right for it to be thunder.' The sound came rolling in across the miles and rumbled over Beach Road.

The Fireworks Man said to Spencer, 'It's thunder.'

There was another explosion and then another.

Auden said to no one in particular, 'Thunder.' He saw Spencer approaching him and he went forward to meet him to decide to call it a night.

Night noises. Things that went bump in the night.

Auden called out, 'Bill, this is a waste of time. It's probably just a lot of little lonely old ladies ringing up to get attention.' He looked out at the dark sea and wiped his face with his hand, 'It's a waste of time. It could have been anything.'

'Two nights in a row?'

Auden said, 'It's almost half past four. All the reports were in by three both times.' He looked at The Fireworks Man, 'It could have just been some idiot with a few fire crackers.' He looked up as another roll of thunder crashed above him, 'Summer's the time of year for thunder. It could have been—'

The Fireworks Man heard it first. The Fireworks Man said suddenly, 'That's a gunshot.'

And then another. The Fireworks Man said, 'That's not fireworks, that's a gunshot!'

From his van, the Army Corporal called out, 'Sir! Gunfire! I can hear it in the phones!'

Lew's voice was on the R/T. Lew said from his boat, 'Shots! I

2

can hear shots!'

Auden yelled to the Corporal, 'Where?' The muffled cracks were echoing across the water, coming from—from where? Auden called, 'Where are they coming from, the sea or the shore?'

The Corporal said, 'The sea! They're coming in from the sea!' He snapped the radio link open to Lew on the police launch.

Lew was saying, 'Fifteen ... no, twenty degrees ...' He realised the link was open, 'They're coming out to us from the shore!'

Auden wrenched the microphone from the Corporal's hand. Auden said quickly, 'Are you taking fire?'

'No, we can just hear them. They're not aimed at us. They seem to be coming from—from where you are.'

'The Army says the shots are coming in from the sea!'

There was another shot, and then another. The sounds seemed to be echoing above their heads. Spencer said urgently to The Fireworks Man, 'Come on, you're the expert on explosions. Where are they coming from?'

'I'm the expert on fireworks and they're not fireworks.' The sounds seemed to be ripping directly above The Fireworks Man's head. He had done his work. The sounds were not fireworks. It was thank you and goodbye time.

Lew's voice crackled on the radio, 'No, they're hitting Lamma Island. The sounds are travelling across the Channel and bouncing off Lamma Island and then they're—' Lew said, 'No, the wind's changed and they're—and the sound's echoing off—' Through the link Auden heard Lew's coxswain shout out something in rapid Tanka and then Lew cursed, 'They're changing direction! The wind out here keeps changing and the sounds are—' There was a fusillade of shots, 'It's impossible! First the sound goes one way and then the other!' Lew said, 'They've got to be coming out from the shore! Are you getting any muzzle flashes?'

Spencer had a stopwatch in his hand counting the seconds between the shots. They were coming bang—pause, bang—pause—exactly one and a half seconds apart. Spencer said urgently to The Fireworks Man, 'Are you sure they're shots? They're regular.'

'No, I'm not sure they're shots, but they're not fireworks!' At seventy one, he was too old to duck. The Fireworks Man said, 'They're shooting at us!'

At the van, Auden had his hand on the Corporal's shoulder. On the roof of the van the directional antennae were turning first one way and then the other. The Corporal said in protest, 'They're moving! The shots are moving!'

Spencer said, 'They're only one and a half seconds apart. They can't be moving.'

'I tell you they are! I'm catching the echoes. They're moving as far as three miles apart. They're muffled. It's almost as if—' The Army Corporal said with an odd look on his face, 'As if they're being broadcast.' The Army Corporal said desperately, 'Look, I need at least two other vans to triangulate this and at least—'

At sea, Lew said, 'I just had a clear sound. It seemed to be coming from somewhere behind you, high up.' He asked again, 'Are you getting any muzzle flashes?'

Auden scanned the area behind him with night glasses. He glanced at Spencer. Spencer was still timing and counting. So far, there had been twelve shots in eighteen seconds exactly. Spencer said, 'It's like some sort of machine. It's firing every—'

Auden saw only lines and lines of skyscrapers. Back from the sea shore, Hong Kong was lit up at its usual level of Gone With The Wind premiere intensity and if there were flashes they were invisible in the brilliance.

Spencer said at his side, 'What are they shooting *at*? How many are there?'

Lew's voice cut in on the radio, 'Did you hear that one? I heard it clearly. It must have been straight on in my direction. It sounded like—'

Auden demanded, 'Where the hell are the bullets going?'

Lew said, 'It sounded like a blank. It had that softer slower sound to it like the blanks you use at gun handling practice.' Lew's voice said suddenly, 'Something just landed in the water beside us!'

Spencer's stopwatch was going tickticktickick...

Lew's voice said quietly, 'It's sunk. Whatever it was, it's...'

From the shore, everyone around the van heard the dull thump, then rushing across the sea, unfettered and unmuffled there was a sharp detonation that rolled and echoed with the thunder.

Lew's voice said curiously on the radio, 'About fifty feet away. Deep. Something deep in the water's just—' Lew said in very rapid, furious Cantonese, 'Sir, under the water—and there was a brilliant white light!' Lew said incredulously, 'I think it was a fucking *depth charge!*'

The Fireworks Man, looking hard at Spencer looking out to sea, said anxiously, 'Inspector? *What the hell's going on?*'

There was a silence.

At 4.20 a.m. on an oppressive Summer's night, for the third time in succession, that was what everyone wanted to know.

Hong Kong is an island of some 30 square miles under British administration in the South China Sea facing Kowloon and the New Territories areas of continental China. Kowloon and the New Territories are also British administered, surrounded by the Communist Chinese province of Kwantung. The climate is generally sub-tropical, with hot, humid summers and heavy rainfall. The population of Hong Kong and the surrounding areas at any one time, including tourists and visitors, is in excess of four millions. The New Territories are leased from the Chinese. The lease is due to expire in 1997, but the British nevertheless maintain a military presence along the border, although, should the Communists who supply almost all the Colony's drinking water, ever desire to terminate the lease early, they need only turn off the taps. Hong Bay is on the southern side of the island and the tourist brochures advise you not to go there after dark.

Persistent reports of gunfire.

At exactly 4.21 a.m. and thirty seconds, with the expenditure of precisely one hundred and twenty three rounds of ammunition, the shooting stopped.

Out to sea where the underwater light had been, the water stopped foaming, and, receding into ripples, became again eternal and undisturbed.

1

Out of a clear blue sky...

On the fourth floor girders of a half completed building across the street Mr Muscles was at it again. It was a little after 7.15 a.m. and Detective Senior Inspector Christopher O'Yee, in the peak of condition and almost at the stage of being able to hold his first cup of Yellowthread Street police station coffee in his hand without trembling with the effort, said in shaky admiration, 'Yep, he's definitely working on his gastrocnemius with side benefits to his planters and biceps femoris.' He looked at Detective Chief Inspector Harry Feiffer working on nothing more spectacular than the monthly crime reports and said in explanation, 'Calves, feet and rear thighs.'

Feiffer said, 'Oh.'

Through the open window of the Detectives' Room, O'Yee could see Mr Muscles' chest rippling through his Tee shirt as he moved on from his gastrocnemius and, flexing his glinting chest expanders, decided to have a quick go at his serratus magnus. O'Yee said, 'You know I've watched that guy. He gets over there about 6.30 and he goes through his exercise routine for about an hour, then he goes down to the ground, waits for the other rivetters to turn up at the time clock and then, when they take the elevator cage, he runs up the stairs.' He shook his head and sipped at his coffee as Mr Muscles stopped for a moment and flexed, 'And then he does twice the work of any two men.' Mr Muscles was a squat Southern Chinese of, to say the least, healthy appearance. O'Yee said, 'What do you think he's up to?'

In the last three years, let alone the last month, the total haul of illegal firearms was two pistols, one rusty revolver, a sawn-off shotgun, a starting pistol and two cap guns converted to fire live ammunition. And no live ammunition. If there was someone running around at night shooting off at least half a dozen rifles and a hundred and twenty three rounds of ammunition at a time then he hadn't found them lying around on the street. Feiffer said without interest, 'I don't know. Maybe he's found an undetectable way to commit suicide.' And according to the phone-in reports of the night, not only had the half dozen guns and hundred and twenty three rounds of ammunition come from nowhere, evidently, they were also being fired from nowhere. Reports of the gunfire ranged from Hop Pei Cove to the west as far north as Singapore Road and then east out to the New Hong Bay Cemetry. Feiffer said wearily, 'If he succeeds let me know and I'll join him.'

'People like this guy don't die, they live to be six hundred and three.' O'Yee looked down into the black glutinous swamp Constable Yan had the gall to call coffee and then to his cigarette in an ashtray by the window. O'Yee said, 'Do you realise that while we're standing around here letting our systems go to hell that guy is up there getting *fit*?' Mr Muscles stepped into his expanders and made a straining motion like a bird pulling a difficult worm out of the ground. O'Yee could almost hear the creak, 'Your body is like a finely tuned watch. You should look after it.'

There was an ordnance map of Hong Kong on Feiffer's desk. He put it on top of the monthly returns and looked at it for a moment. Feiffer said with a groan, 'I even went so far as to ring up the Hong Kong representative of the Chinese People's Army to ask him if there'd been manoeuvres on the border and after he'd got over the shock that I knew his secret number he said he didn't know and gave me the secret number of British Intelligence so I could ask them.'

'... mind you, my grandfather lived to be eighty nine and he used to drink like a goddamned fish and smoke eighty Burmese hand rolled cigarettes a day.' O'Yee looked down at his ashtray and took up the cigarette, 'His theory was that it wasn't good for you to be too fit. You know, like a racehorse. They're always shooting them because they get so delicate.'

Feiffer said, 'Like a finely tuned watch.' He looked at his own and found it had stopped, 'When are Auden and Spencer due back on?'

'At nine.' O'Yee said, 'They've gone out on their own initiative to the cove to have a look around for spent shell cases.' The body-builder, having dealt with the gastrocnemius and biceps femoris had moved on to doing neck exercises, ' Do you think we ought to get up earlier and jog or something?' O'Yee said, 'Mind you, I had a friend in San Francisco who jogged and he got a heart attack and died.' Mr Muscles was building himself up into The Incredible Hulk. O'Yee said, 'I don't cough or anything in the mornings, do you?'

Feiffer put the map down and lit a cigarette.

O'Yee looked at Mr Muscles.

Feiffer said, 'Hmm.' He took up his coffee and tried it again. Once you got used to it it wasn't too bad at all. O'Yee said, 'No, it's all in the blood. My grandfather lived to be eighty nine years old and the only reason he isn't with us still is that he tried to cross a road outside the chest hospital when the brakes weren't working properly on his iron lung.'

The storm had passed over a little before dawn and it was a lovely cool morning and if anyone was ever going to die of anything, today was just not the day.

7.21 a.m. As O'Yee turned away, across the road Mr Muscles began flexing his way down the steel stairs to the ground floor to await the arrival of his less energetic, elevator-riding colleagues.

There was a temporary supply shack near the stairs on the third floor and, with a flourish, Mr Muscles leant his still glittering chest expanders against it as he passed.

Coming from under the door of the wooden shack there was a faint stream of black oily smoke, but Mr Muscles, grunting and groaning, had his fist in his face to exercise his triceps and forearm extensors and totally failed to notice it.

*

9

There was definitely something black, sludgy and infinitely horrible moving along in the dark on the ground behind him. In the bowels of the Hop Pei Cove storm water drainage system, Auden stood up to his gumbooted ankles in slime and God knew what, up to his nostrils in stench, up to his spine in cold shivers, shone the flashlight quickly into the mire behind him and said, 'Yugh, it's moving!'

Spencer said, 'It's only a rat. They're harmless.' He shone his own light down into the slowly swirling water and saw that it wasn't. Either. Spencer said in a gasp, 'God, it's alive!' He flashed the light upwards as something oozing disengaged itself from the roof and fell in a twisting motion onto his boot and then breast-stroked away, 'Ugh! Whatever it was, it was—' He backed up against the wall of the giant drain and at least half a dozen other things went squelch, whistle, plop, scuttle, flurry as they unglued themselves from the material, went flailing down through the fetid air, hit the water and sank and then—snakes alive—got up again and dashed off. Auden said, 'Oh Christ—' He reached down for his Colt Python in its shoulder holster and had a horrible picture of blowing down one of the walls and releasing into the world— Auden said, 'Christ, Bill, I'm beginning to wonder if this is a good idea!' The Senior Inspectors' Examining Board interviews were only a week away. Auden said quickly, 'No, it's a good idea! It shows initiative getting up early and coming in here on our own time and—' The light illuminated something from an alcoholic's nightmare. Auden said, 'God! What in hell's name is that?'

Whatever it was was swimming purposefully in Spencer's direction. The tops of Spencer's gumboots were open where he had tucked his pants into them. The thing's beady eyes battened on them and thought it had found the Ideal Home Exhibition. Spencer drew back his boot and kicked it to the next stand.

The next stand was Auden's boot bungalow. Auden said, 'Ahhggh!' and stomped on it.

It was a great life in the exotic East. Auden said, 'Right, first principles. If the gunfire can't be located because it's travelling all over the Colony then it's clear that it isn't being aimed in any particular direction. Right?'

It was a lizard with wings. Definitely. Spencer stepped back. His flashlight battery dimmed for a moment and he panicked. Spencer said, 'Right, Phil! Right! Right! Whatever you say!'

Auden sidestepped the flying lizard. The lizard galumphed into the water and didn't surface. 'I didn't say it, we both did. We came up with it in concert.' There was plenty of Senior Inspector's gold braid to go around. *Wasn't there?* The lizard still hadn't surfaced. Where the hell was it? Auden said, 'So therefore, the shots weren't aimed at anything. Right?'

'Right!' Spencer peered down into the mire, 'Because they were blanks.' Spencer said tensing, 'Right!'

'Right.' Where was it? What was it doing down there? *Where was it going?* Auden said, 'And since the shots seemed to bounce off the islands and the islands are just a little above sea level, then the shots had to come in a straight line from the shore here to—' It surfaced. Auden saw its head. It had turned from some sort of lizard into some sort of bat. Auden stepped back, 'So they're probably shooting from cover at sea level and since there are buildings everywhere in Hong Kong from any point in a straight line to the harbour they have to be either shooting from a beach—'

Spencer ducked. There was nothing there, but he ducked. 'Right! And we know the Water Police would have seen the flashes if they'd been shooting from a beach, so they're— They're shooting from in here, but they're not aiming outwards, they're just standing in here in the drains shooting blanks along the pipes and the noise is being projected outwards.'

Auden said with feeling, 'They must be mad.'

'And since no one's reported any lights they stand in here at night in the darkness.'

Auden said, 'They must be completely around the fucking twist!'

Spencer said, 'So all we have to do is wander along the three or four miles of interconnected pipes along the beach front until we find some evidence.'

11

Auden said nothing.

Spencer said, 'Even if it takes all day.'

Auden swallowed. In the enthusiasm stakes he was not going to be found lacking by the Examining Board. Auden said between clenched teeth, shining his light onto something bubbling, 'And night.'

Spencer said, 'Right.'

'Right.' From the dark recesses of the far end of the pipe something groaned. Whatever it was, it wasn't human.

There was a silence. Spencer said, 'Mind you, Phil, if they were ejecting their cartridges straight into the ooze then we could be just wasting out time and we'd be better off getting the Sub Aqua Squad in here with metal detectors and underwater—'

It groaned again. It wasn't much. Just something minor. A Minotaur maybe or a Cyclops getting out of bed and reaching for the morning papers, or— Auden, stepping backwards, said, nodding, 'Or firecrackers. I mean, The Fireworks Man could be wrong and they could have been firecrackers and all the burned paper, by now, would have just floated out and—'

Spencer said with a disappointment in his voice, 'In which case we would have seen it at one of the entrances and the case would have been solved.'

The news in the morning's paper obviously didn't suit the Cyclops. There was a retching sound followed by a long drawn out gurgling.

Auden said, 'Exactly so.' He was about to say, 'Lead on.' Senior Inspectors didn't say "Lead on", they led. Auden said to the Examining Board as they gasped at his dedication and sniffed at the stench on his clothes that five hundred years in a non stop Chinese laundry would only faintly begin to remove, 'I'll go first, shall I?'

Squelch, whistle, plop, scuttle, flurry, scuttle, whistle, plop, squelch—ROAR! . . . gurgle.

There was plenty of gold braid to go around.

Auden said, stepping back, 'I know, let's split the difference shall we, and go together?'

Team spirit.

Auden said to the Examining Board, 'I'm all in favour of that.'

How he was going to spot ejected shell cases in opaque muck by dimming flashlight with his eye tightly shut he had no idea, but he thought, as did Spencer, that if he got really lucky, somehow he might manage it.

Something wet brushed against his leg on its way to Spencer's gumboot and Auden opened his eyes to see what it was and wished he hadn't.

*

In the Detectives' Room, Feiffer stubbed out his cigarette in frustration and said, 'Damn it, Christopher, it's impossible. There just aren't that many unlicensed guns in the entire Colony!' He had a copy of the Anti Triad Squad's report for the half year and he held it up and waved it in O'Yee's direction, 'Even the Chinese secret societies haven't got half a dozen guns and a hundred and twenty three rounds of ammunition. And as for brilliant white lights or depth charges or whatever it was that landed near Lew's launch—'

O'Yee said, 'It's kids. It has to be.'

'Kids doing what?'

'Kids being kids.' O'Yee had his second cup of Yan's invigorating coffee. Even if life was short that was no reason to deny yourself its little pleasures. Even if the pleasures made it short that was still no reason. O'Yee said, 'Just kids. The Policeman's Friend. Just put down "Kids" in the report and the crime computer will gobble it up, think about it for a while and then spit it out in the Minor Juvenile Disturbances column.' O'Yee said, 'It's not as if anyone's actually shooting *at* anyone. Just put it down as kids.'

Feiffer looked at his watch. It had started again of its own volition. He hesitated.

O'Yee said, 'Look, Harry, it's been going on for three nights now. It's like lights in the sky. It's just one of those things you can't explain and if you could it'd turn out to be something so bloody stupid that you'd wonder why you bothered about it in the first place.' O'Yee said, 'Put kids.' He asked, 'Can you smell this coffee?'

'Another Constable Yan Special Brew?'

'He's improving. After the first mouthful your stomach doesn't even clench.' O'Yee moved back towards the window and glanced across at the rivetters standing chatting to Mr Muscles. It was a beautiful day. What could possibly happen?

He was getting nowhere. Feiffer said, 'Yeah, why not?' "Kids". He looked down at the map with all the crosses reporting the sound of gunfire in the night. Feiffer said, 'If there was anything else happening we probably wouldn't even bother with this sort of thing, would we?'

O'Yee said, 'No.' He went out to have a word to Yan to get the percolator and his his magic recipe working again. O'Yee said from the door, 'Did I ever tell you about my grandfather? He was eighty nine when he died and he'd be with us still if his kidney machine hadn't caught fire on his way out of his girlfriend's house.'

Feiffer looked down at the map.

O'Yee went to get the coffee.

Across the street, Mr Muscles' colleagues took the elevator and Mr Muscles took the stairs.

*

There was a round area of scorched greyness on the ceiling of the pipe where all the ooze, slime and primeaval swamp seemed to have been cleaned away in a single stroke.

Spencer shone his light up to it and tried to stretch up to get a better view. Auden said, 'What is it?'

'I don't know.' Spencer shone his light along the roof and saw another cleared patch a few feet back in line with the first.

And then another.

The patches, like the footprints of a giant roof walking spider,

14

marched away into the darkness.

Auden sniffed. The faintest smell of something different was there. Something that reminded him of—

Both he and Spencer flashed their lights down into the ooze simultaneously and there, a little beneath the surface, like a single golden eye, something glinted at them.

*

Mr Muscles, grinning, made it to the third floor supply shack first. He flexed, waved to his colleagues in the elevator, reached down for his expanders, and called out abruptly, 'Hey! The shack is on fire! There's smoke coming out!' He looked at his expanders in horror, 'The shack's burning and all my copies of *Asian Bodybuilder* are in there!' The door to the shack was shut.

Mr Muscles called out urgently to the foreman as he stepped out of the elevator and came over, 'Quick, bring the keys! All my stuff is in there!'

On the second floor some of the rivetters had already begun work and the foreman waved to them to compliment them on their industry and, reaching into his back pocket took out his ear protectors to insulate himself against the noise.

Mr Muscles said, 'Hey! Hey! The shack's—' He tried the door but it was solid.

Mr Muscles yelled at the top of his voice, 'Hey! All my bodybuilding stuff is in there!' The smoke was coming out in increasing volume. From inside the shack there was a thump.

Mr Muscles yelled out, 'Hey, there's someone in there with matches or something and he's playing with my equipment!'

There was a hissing sound from under the door and then suddenly, another.

Mr Muscles yelled out at the locked door, 'Hey! *Hey*!!' He yelled, 'Hey! You'll smash all my—' The rivetting was pounding in his head. Mr Muscles yelled, 'Hey! All that gear cost me—' The rivetting was going non-stop. Mr Muscles shrieked in desperation, 'Hey! Stop! *Stop*!'

In the briefest of brief pauses in the rivetting, from inside the shack there was a single click and for one glorious, wonderful moment, Mr Muscles thought that whoever was in there had had second thoughts and was going to come out and—

8.11 a.m. At the third floor shack Mr Muscles pounded on the door and yelled, 'Hey! *Hey*—!!'

*

In the drains, Auden turned a corner and said in a gasp, 'My God, the place is full of them!' He had the brass cartridge case from the mud in his hand and as he shone his flashlight into a glittering garden of the things, he dropped it back into the slime and turned his light upwards. The long pipe stretched two hundred yards in a straight line towards Hop Pei Cove and on the ceiling of almost every one of those yards there were the spotless giant spider's footmarks where the muzzle blasts from the guns had scorched away the slime of decades. The cartridge cases were everywhere, in piles, in lines, forming half completed circles and rectangles and, in one or two spots, poking out from the mire like volcanic islands. Auden said, 'My God, Bill, there must be a thousand of them.'

Spencer had one in his hand. He turned it over. The top of the long open necked object was pleated. Spencer said, 'They're blanks. You can see where the neck was turned in by a machine to close it off.' He held it out in his palm for Auden to examine as he bent to pick up another, 'They're all blanks. Every one of them.' He looked up at the marks on the ceiling, 'They must have held the guns at an angle and blasted them off in the direction of the roof.' He got up again and scraped at one of the scorches with a case. A fine rain of burned cordite came down. The scorch marks, as far as he could make out, all seemed to be the same size, 'They must have walked backwards and forwards with their rifles aimed up at the ceiling just banging away until—'

Auden said, 'Until what? Until they ran out of amunition? And then left?' Auden weighed a dozen of the cases in his hand, 'There

16

must be a small fortune in brass in here and they just left it?' He dug around in a mound. Every one of the cases was a blank. Auden said, 'These are definitely rifle cases. I can't make out the headstamp, but they were definitely fired by a rifle.' He heard Spencer say, 'One ... two ... three...' and he glanced back to see him picking up cases and examining them in the light, 'What are you doing?'

Spencer said, 'Four ... five ... the same again ... six ... seven...'

He was examining the different firing pin and extractor marks on the cases. Auden said, 'How many guns do you think there were?'

Spencer's voice had gone quiet. He was still counting. Spencer said, 'Ten, eleven...'

'But they're all bloody blanks! What the hell for?' Auden said, 'Kids. It's got to be kids. Who else would—'

Spencer picked up another few cases from the mound and looked at them. He found something else among them and he brushed the mud from it carefully with his finger. Spencer said softly, 'Phil—' He held the object out for inspection and looked up at the muzzle blasts on the ceiling.

Barring one, there was no conceivable reason on Earth why anyone would spend his nights in a storm water drain firing blank cartridges up at the ceiling and leaving the empty, valuable cases where they lay.

That one reason was that he was practising for something and that as well as having an unlimited supply of blank practice rounds for the purpose, somewhere, ready for the proper occasion when he was good enough, he also had an unlimited supply of—

Auden said in a gasp, 'Oh my God—!' He took the object from Spencer's hand and peered at it in the light to make sure there was no mistake.

There was no mistake.

Spencer reached down into the mud and brought up a handful of cases.

They were all live, not crimped, but loaded with long pointed

17

bullets.

There was a slapping sound as something crawling along the roof decided to let go its slimy hold and fall directly into Auden's gumboot, but in the interval between letting go and landing Auden and Spencer were gone, running through the slime into the open air for a telephone, and the creature, falling onto a mound of cases, dislodged them and was buried under their weight.

*

The foreman had gone. The elevator was going all the way down to the ground and in the rivetting he could not hear Mr Muscles' shouts. Mr Muscles heard a clicking sound in the shack in a pause in the rivetting and he put his ear hard against the woodwork and heard another and then another. The smoke smelled of burning rubber and the door was solid and immovable.

There was a window on the other side of the shack, but it was on the side facing the street and he could not get to it.

Mr Muscles tried to look through a crack in the wood, but he could see nothing.

The smoke was increasing as if something inside the shack was burning through. Mr Muscles got down on his haunches and tried to look under the door jamb.

The smoke was thick and rubbery and he got up again and put both his mighty paws on the door itself and began straining. Mr Muscles said over and over, 'You bastards ... you bastards ... I'll show you what a strong man is...'

He heard a click and then a sort of snapping sound as something inside the shack gave way. Mr Muscles said between sobs, 'Oh, no, please, please, don't—' and at that moment the rivetting stopped and from inside the shack there was another, louder snap and a click and as the window facing the street was blown out in a shower of disintegrating spinning glass—in one and a half second measured volleys—the shooting started.

*

18

On the phone, Auden yelled above the noise, 'Live rounds, thousands of them!' He shook his head to clear the noise and thought it was the sound of the rivetting being carried to the Station by the wind, 'Guns! They've got at least ten or eleven of them and they—'

O'Yee's voice shouted back, 'Do fucking tell!' The bullets were flying in the window and ripping into the masonry behind him. He saw Feiffer on the floor reaching for his revolver and he got down as a bullet smashed into the desk above his head and sent a shower of flying splinters into a filing cabinet and scarred it from top to bottom. He heard Auden shouting, 'What? What are you saying? I can't—' and O'Yee screamed into the phone, 'We're taking fire!' The last remaining shards of glass in the window jamb went and showered the room with shrapnel. O'Yee yelled, 'We're under—' He looked and the phone was flying outwards and upwards and disintegrating into bits of coloured airborne plastic. O'Yee fell backwards with the receiver still in his hand. He saw Feiffer look up and he went towards him yelling, 'Harry, keep down!' as Feiffer ducked a bullet that gouged out a corner of the desk and span it across the room.

The firing was non stop. Feiffer shouted above the sound, 'It's coming from the building across the road! I can see the muscle builder! It's coming from the supply shack on the third floor!' There was a series of heavy thumps as the shooters raised their elevation and ripped bricks out of the outside wall above the Station window, 'I'm going to try to get to—' He saw O'Yee staring at him with the telephone receiver still in his hand, 'Get on to the Emergency Unit and get some counter-sniper gear up here!'

The firing lowered again and blew the entire window jamb out spinning into the room. In the street Feiffer could hear the screaming as people ran to escape. Feiffer yelled, 'Use the bloody telephone, man! What the hell do you think it's for?'

It was for scrap. O'Yee held the shattered instrument up and then brought it down again as someone took it for a moving target and missed it by a millimetre.

19

O'Yee saw Constable Yan standing at the door of the Detectives' Room looking down stupidly at the remains of the coffee percolator in his hand. O'Yee said, 'Yan—!' as a hand from behind swept the smashed percolator onto the floor, span Yan around and shoved an Armalite rifle into his arms. It was Constable Sun. Sun yelled at Feiffer and O'Yee, 'You stay here! We've got a clear exit out through the charge room onto the street!' and then as if by magic another Armalite appeared and he slid it hard and fast across the floor into Feiffer's grasp.

Feiffer yelled, 'It's the supply shack on the building across the street!' and Sun yelled back something in acknowledgement and shoved Yan hard in the middle of the back to get him moving.

At the shack Mr Muscles shrieked, 'What are you doing to my gear?! What are you bastards doing to my *equipment*?!' His great muscles were shaking with the effort on the door and he got his shoulder against it and roared with the exertion as he applied every ounce of his strength to get it open. The shooting was roaring and echoing in the street. He saw people running.

The door to the supply shack flew open. Mr Muscles said, 'Oh, no—!'

He looked down to the street and saw two uniformed cops scurrying out of the Station with rifles in their hands. Mr Muscles said, 'Oh, NO!' and in that instant all the noise stopped and there was only a gentle click, click, click sound coming from inside the shack.

He saw the cops looking up at him with their rifles raised and Mr Muscles, his hands all empty and gentle, held out his arms like a Buddhist priest about to give a blessing and said with a curious look on his face, 'No, it's—' It was all too much to understand. Mr Muscles half turned his body slowly and pointed into the interior of the shack.

Mr Muscles said . . .

There was a single click and then the faintest of popping sounds and Mr Muscles said in a sad, lost voice, all his work over so many years all gone for nothing, 'No, it's just not fair . . .' and then, in one single roaring, flaming, vapourising explosion, he, the shack, and everything around it for a distance of thrity feet was gone forever.

*

8.21 a.m.
Out of a clear blue sky.
In the charge room of the Station a telephone began ringing insistently, then, after a little while, stopped as the caller decided perhaps he would try again later.

2

On the third floor of the half completed building, the Government Medical Officer, Doctor Macarthur, took an elbow from his collected exhibits on the laid out door of the shattered supply shack and asked the foreman evenly, 'Is this him?' The elbow had half the forearm attached, the forearm flexor muscle standing out on it like whipcord.

Feiffer had his hand on the foreman's arm, steadying him. The foreman said, 'Yes.'

'And this?' Macarthur lifted up part of a shoulder, 'You can see the development of the deltoid—'

The foreman nodded. 'Yes.'

Feiffer said quietly in Cantonese, 'Take it easy.'

The foreman nodded. He had a cone shaped roll-your-own cigarette in his left hand and he pursed his lips and looked down at it and thought that if he put it anywhere near his mouth he would throw up. Doctor Macarthur moved back a little of the burned and ragged skin around the muscle with a probe, 'The level of development suggests—'

The works foreman said, 'Yes. He was a bodybuilder. He was going to enter the Mr Asia contest in Macao in the—' He closed his eyes and Macarthur withdrew the probe and the skin flopped back like a piece of wet canvas. The foreman, nodding, looked at his cigarette. It had gone out. The foreman said again, 'Yes, that was him.'

The door had mounds of human tissue and bone laid out on it like a giant jigsaw puzzle. The awful stuff covered every inch of it and spilled over onto a section of planked flooring. The foreman said with an effort, 'I'm trying to be helpful, but I don't know any of the others.' He turned to Feiffer and saw the man smile at him encouragingly, 'If you had a face or two—'

Feiffer shook his head.

Macarthur selected something else. It was part of a lung.

The foreman said quickly, 'I don't know.'

'The development is good.'

'I don't know.' The foreman said again, 'I'm, I'm trying to be helpful, but I—I really didn't know him that well. I—' He put his hand to his face, 'I—I couldn't recognise his lung.' He looked at Feiffer, 'Could I?'

'No. It's all right. That can all be done at the Mortuary.'

'I won't have to—' The foreman said, 'His name was Shuk. He was a good worker. He wasn't a special friend of mine or anything, but he worked hard and he was—' Down in the street, Inspector Sands of Ballistics was using a portable jack hammer to break bricks out of the Station wall in order to collect spent bullets. The foreman said, 'I've checked and all my workers are accounted for.' He went to indicate the human debris on the door and found himself pointing at what looked like a severed penis, 'I just don't know who all these other—who these other people *are*!'

Feiffer said, 'And the supply shack door was locked?'

'Yes! No! It was just a shack for keeping things in and for people to cook themselves up a meal or—' The foreman said, 'It must have been jammed or—' His hand indicated a human leg, 'Or one of the people inside must have held it closed.' He saw Auden and Spencer pick up something from a truss section on the floor that looked like a length of sausages. They were human intestines. The foreman said, 'All I heard was him yelling something at me and then the shooting started.' He became aware of an awful smell coming from the remains, growing in intensity like bad meat. 'He got the door open and then he saw your policemen in the street and he held up his hands to show he wasn't one of them and then—' The foreman said, 'I've seen a few industrial accidents in my time, but—but in those they always had the faces left.' He got the dead cigarette up to his mouth in a trembling hand and drew in on the extinct tobacco, 'I've never seen people blown up before.'

23

He looked away down into the street, 'I heard one of the cops say he thought it was kids. Was it?'

'We don't know.'

The foreman said, 'I've got children of my own.' He shook his head, 'They just went mad and started shooting with guns and then—and then they accidently blew themselves up? Or what?' Spencer came over and put the plastic bag containing the intestines on the plank near the door. He had something else in his other hand. It was a shoe. The foreman said quietly, 'I don't know!'

Feiffer asked, 'Is that the only one?' and Spencer nodded and went back to where Auden was looking at something between two girders. The foreman said again to the shoe, 'I don't know!'

Macarthur selected a section of white cranium and turned it over in his hand. The scalp still had a few tufts of black hair adhering to it. Feiffer said quietly before he could show it to the foreman, 'All Chinese have black hair,' and Macarthur, pausing for a second, said, 'Oh, yeah,' put it down and reached in under the mass and brought out a hand.

The hand still had a digital watch strapped to its wrist. The watch was still going, flashing its little seconds light like a pulse. The foreman said, 'I don't know! I just don't know! Is it one of the kids'?' He looked at the giant wrist, 'It's his, isn't it? And the pieces of skull, they're his too. Aren't they?'

'Yes.' Feiffer indicated part of a leg. 'And that?'

The muscles were like whipcord. The foreman said, 'Yes!'

'And that?' Part of a back, with the latissimus dorsi like a great—

The foreman said, 'Yes!' His body was shaking from one end to the other. He felt his mouth tighten, 'And that—' He nodded at another section of chest, 'And that's him too!' The remains covered the entire door. There was enough there for twenty humans. The foreman looked at the dozen sections of cranium laid out like a half done jigsaw puzzle at the top of the door, 'And that, that's him too! And that! And that! The foreman said with his breath coming in short, sharp gusts, 'It's all him, isn't it! All of it?

24

All this—this is all just one person, isn't it? There isn't anyone else. This is all that's left of just one person, *isn't it?*'

Feiffer said softly, 'Yes, we think so.'

The foreman saw Spencer lean down to get something adhering to a girder. When it came up in his hand it was the colour of vinegar. The foreman yelled to him, 'Yes! Yes! That's him too! What the hell's that? His heart or his liver or his—' His hands were shaking uncontrollably. The foreman yelled, 'It's all him! There isn't anyone else here! It's all just—*him!*'

Macarthur said, shaking his head, 'There isn't anything else.' He looked up at Feiffer, 'That's all. Leaving aside the face and part of the stomach we've got everything.'

The foreman's eyes were full of tears. The foreman said on the edge of hysteria, 'He doesn't need his face. What does he need his face for? He's dead. He's just butcher's stall offal. He doesn't need a face. Only people need a face and he isn't a person anymore, is he? He's just—' The foreman said desperately, 'What am I going to do? I've got a wife and children and I can't tell them I stood here doing this!' By the smashed cranium there was a mound of grey jelly. Brains. The foreman, gagging, said, 'Oh, no!'

Feiffer turned the foreman around to face him, 'You're sure you didn't see anyone else around the shack either before or after the shooting started? Anything? A shadow? Anything at all?'

'The door was shut! He couldn't get in! If anyone had come out he would have seen them!' The foreman said, 'I know it's true, but I just can't believe it.' He put his hand to his forehead and tried to form words, 'I know there's only one man there on the door because you've told me, but I—it looks like so many—' He put his hand to his own stomach, 'All that, inside—all that—' Auden and Spencer stopped for a moment at a girder and exchanged a few words. The foreman saw them shaking their heads. The awful thing in the plastic bag was bouncing a little against Auden's leg. The foreman said, 'But if there was no one inside the shack and when the explosion came the only person who was—was hurt—was—was—him, and this is what it did to him—'

Macarthur said quietly to Feiffer, 'It looks like you've got a

25

sniper on your hands who knows how to set up remote controlled gunfire. Maybe two or three.'

'Yeah.' The thought had occurred to both Auden and Spencer. Feiffer saw them pause to look upwards to the other floors and then unbutton their coats to have quick access to their revolvers. Feiffer said, 'Yes, it definitely looks that way, doesn't it?'

The foreman's eyes were staring at the pile of remains on the door. Trying to comprehend it, he shook his head. The foreman said, 'What can I tell my family?' The smell was rising, clogging his nostrils. The foreman looked down again at his cigarette, but it was out. The foreman said quietly to Macarthur, 'Sir, if this is just one man—all this—'

Macarthur said, 'Yes?'

The words cascaded into the foreman's mind like a torrent and then tumbled over and over. Everything he had ever been told or thought he knew or had seen on television or at the movies or read about, it was all—

The foreman said in a shriek, *'My God, what must a war be like?'*

He was about to find out. Far across the girdered and planked third floor on the east corner of the building there was another, identical supply shack with its window facing directly at him.

There was the faintest of snapping sounds and then something inside the shack began hissing softly.

There was another snapping sound and then another, and, too far away on the floor to be heard, the hissing increased serially and urgently in volume.

It was 12.06 p.m. and the sounds were, as they had been planned to be, dead on time.

*

They fazed him. By the shattered hole in the wall that had once been one of the Detectives' Room windows Inspector Sands of Ballistics turned his collection of shell cases, cartridges and spent bullets over in his hand and shook his head. He rattled the objects together in his hand and pursed his lips.

They fazed him.

He looked again and went through the objects in a logical order: six undistorted fired bullets from the Station wall, all in good condition, jacketed and with firm deep striations from the lands and grooves of the barrels that had fired them, (he separated one of the bullets and felt its weight—about 125 grains), four empty blank shell cases from the drains, (he took one up and flicked at the spread open crimp with his thumbnail), and finally, two live, bulleted rounds also from the drains, bullet weight about one hundred and twenty five grains, in perfect condition, commercially made, and without the slightest trace of identification anywhere on or about its entire length.

Sands looked at the silver primer at the base of one of the live cartridges.

It was an axiom that every commercially made cartridge had its calibre, nomenclature or at least date of manufacture on its base.

He shook his head.

These had none.

There was a blue band painted at the base of each of the blank rounds, but what it represented, Sands had no idea.

He thought he knew just about every round for every gun that the mind of man had ever thought of, but he had never seen one like this. He had a pocket micrometer in the top pocket of his coveralls and he took it out and measured the bullet.

About seven millimetres.

Maybe it was a wildcat round loaded by some enthusiastic home gunsmith. If that was the case the enthusiastic home gunsmith would have had to have used a standard cartridge case and neck it down and the standard cartridge case would have had markings on it.

He looked at one of the fired blanks. The star crimp at the neck that had been forced open by the charge of powder was black and scorched with the blast—the bang when it came must have been of tremendous power.

Why? For a blank round?

Sands looked up at the half completed building across the street

27

and watched absently as Auden and Spencer stopped by a girder to talk. Sands' mind was far away, flipping through cartridge manuals, getting nowhere.

If only he had got to see one of the rifles before the explosion in the supply shack had turned them into dust. Sands said to himself, 'Fuck it, what are they?' He looked again at the blue bands on the base of the blanks, 'What the hell are they *for*?'

Nobody made cartridge cases that looked like this anymore. Even the design: the straight sided cylinder neck narrowing gracefully to the bullet was inefficient. Everybody knew these days that the best design for a rifle case was straight sided and—

Sands said suddenly, 'These days!' He looked up at the building, 'These days!' He saw O'Yee coming out of the Station with a pair of binoculars to scan the third floor and Sands said louder than he had intended, 'These days, Christopher! *These days!*'

The blue band around the base of the blank....

Sands said, 'These days ... these ...'

A single blue band around the base of an unmarked cartridge ... His mind went flick, flick, flick through a thousand pages of technical manuals in an instant.

He found the right page. He found the right reference, the illustration. He found ...

Sands said jubilantly, *'Right!'*

The full implications of his discovery struck him and he said in a gasp, 'God Almighty, it isn't possible ...'

O'Yee was scanning the building with binoculars, one hand a little inside his coat where his shoulder holster hung, and before he put down the glasses and saw him standing there, Sands slipped the cases and the bullets into a plastic evidence bag and, determined to say nothing until he was absolutely sure, stuffed the bag into his pocket along with his micrometer and went back to examine the walls minutely for more bullets.

*

In all the western movies, they always said something like, 'Quiet? Yeah, it is. Too quiet.'

It was. There was something strange and a little uncompleted about it, something—

By the main door of the Station, O'Yee scanned the ground floor of the half completed building with his binoculars and then moved to the elevator. It was up, on the third floor: he could see the cables hanging down below the cage, slack and waiting.

Auden and Spencer were in the centre of the floor, poking at something with a steel rod. They came up empty. He saw Spencer shake his head and look around for somewhere else to search. There was no wind: the air was still and silent. A faint pall of smoke hung over some of the girders and billowed lazily from the west to the east corner of the building.

The crowd behind the cordon was beginning to break up and from behind him, O'Yee heard Sands chipping away at the bricks, not with his pneumatic drill, but with a little hand held bit head.

On the third floor, the foreman had evidently fallen silent. He was looking down at his shoes, hanging his head, quiet and thoughtful, and Feiffer a little way from him, was writing in his notebook and alternately nodding to Macarthur.

From where he stood O'Yee could hear no voices and he had the feeling that, somehow, up there, now, there were no voices to be heard.

'Yep, pard, jest too quiet.' Outside the town, in the cut away shot, he could feel the distant rumbling under his feet as the cattle milled and grunted as the prelude to a stampede.

He was being stupid.

Nerves.

He put down the glasses and turned to go back into the Station and stopped at the front door.

The front door was full of ragged bullet holes and there were long strips of wood hanging down, about to give way at the slightest touch.

Something ... He had seen the building every day for the last month in one stage or another of its construction and there was something just not right about it.

He turned back and looked up to where the supply shack had been.

That wasn't it. It was something else.

All the workmen had gone. Each of the other floors below the third was empty and skeletonised, like a deserted ship's engine room.

But there was something.

Something...

He heard Sands curse softly to himself as a sliver of brick cut his hand and O'Yee shook his head and said softly to himself, 'No, you're being stupid.'

The next thing would be astrology.

He said aloud, 'No, there's something wrong. I can feel it.'

But what?

He turned again and glanced at Sands to see if he was watching him making a fool of himself.

It had been kids. Kids with guns had gone mad and blown themselves up and killed someone and that was—

O'Yee raised the binoculars and scanned the second floor.

Nothing.

Something.

He scanned the third again and saw the tableaux of Auden and Spencer in their little knot and then Macarthur, Feiffer and the foreman in theirs.

He could almost smell it. It was...

O'Yee yelled suddenly, *'Smoke!'* He saw Sands spin to see him, 'Smoke!' O'Yee shouted, 'There's another supply shack up there and it's in a direct line and it's smoking!' He saw something at the window of the shack flash and then shatter and then—he saw Auden and Spencer look up, in direct line. O'Yee yelled, 'Smoke! It's smoking! It's happening again! The first one was a come-on bomb!' He saw Sands running towards his Ballistics truck to get a weapon and O'Yee reached back into the Station behind him, got an Armalite from just inside the door and pulled back on the cocking handle in a single motion, 'There are more of them in the

30

second shack and they're—'

He heard the first shot roar out over the third floor. He saw—

It was happening in slow motion.

He saw the flash, the smoke, the muzzle blast as the window disintegrated fully in a single blast of light and motion. He saw Spencer look up and then to one side. He heard him say—

He saw Auden look down at his chest. He saw—

The shooting began in a single uninterrupted burst as the machine gun inside the shack began working.

He saw Spencer say—

He saw Auden fall.

He saw him die. He saw—

O'Yee and Sands had their Armalites up simultaneously.

He saw bits flying off the shack as the bullets went in.

*

Spencer yelled, 'It was a blank! He wasn't hit! It was a blank!' Feiffer saw him on the floor reaching for Auden and drawing his revolver with his other hand as the bullets ripped over his head and ricochetted off girders in a shower of sparks. Macarthur was standing over the door with his mouth open and Feiffer yelled at him, 'It's happening again!' and wrenched the man to the ground. He looked around for the foreman and saw him a little ahead behind a pile of girders, keeping his head down. It was a medium machine gun: the bullets came out in an uninterrupted stream and sparked off the girders like bombs.

Auden was on his back, rolling around trying to unlimber the barrel of his giant gun from its holster. His shirt was still white. There was no blood on it. Spencer yelled out as Feiffer got up into a crouch and then ducked again as the fire seemed to swivel back to him, 'It was a blank! It blew the window out! The first round was a blank!' He was shouting something else, but the firing drowned him out.

The sound was shattering. Bits and pieces were flying off the roof of the shack as the fire came up from the ground. Through a

31

hole in the planking Feiffer saw O'Yee and Sands standing side by side in the middle of the street spraying automatic fire up from their Armalites. The clip came out of Sands' gun as he fired the last burst in the magazine and he had another one in and was firing back before Feiffer even saw him cock the bolt.

People were scattering in the street. Feiffer heard shouting and then a car horn blow. There was someone on a bullhorn warning people in Chinese to get out or get down—Yan, or Constable Sun—and then there was a fusilade of poppings as they got their revolvers up and shot rapid fire into the shack.

It was a machine. They had found only one body. It was some sort of machinery. Auden had his big gun out and was banging at the shack and shaking with the recoil. Feiffer saw one of the big bullets strike the corner of the shack and rip an entire plank out with the concussion. The firing was going on in an unceasing burst. Spencer had his gun out, trying to get a bead on the window as he rolled to avoid the bullets.

Feiffer shouted, 'There's no one in there! It's a set-up! There's no one in there!' as a stream of bullets from the shack passed over his head and whined off metal into the air.

The foreman got his head up and looked back. A shower of sparks hit him in the face and he got down again, shaking his head and yelling something.

Feiffer yelled, 'Don't fire! It's a set-up! There's no one in there!' The shooting from the street had assumed war battle proportions. There must have been at least half a dozen Armalites and revolvers all firing at once. Feiffer yelled above the din, 'Don't shoot! We want what's in there before it—' and then a line of bullets ripped up a plank by his hand and traversed without pause in the direction of Macarthur and the door.

Macarthur shouted, '*Jesus!*' and got himself down with his hands over his ears. A bullet struck his long silver probe on the planks and propelled it like a lance into the air.

Feiffer yelled, 'Stop firing! We have to—' The machine gun stream seemed to move away. The gun inside was evidently jumping wildly and spraying in alternate directions. He got up

32

and crouched to run. He saw the foreman shouting at him, but there were no words.

The firing from the street was continuous.

The foreman yelled, 'No! No one else! No one else!' and rolled to one side as a stray bullet from the street ripped through the plank he was lying on and made it jump.

The machine gun had stopped. There was only the firing from the street. Feiffer got up and yelled down, 'No! Cease fire! There's no one in there! *Cease fire!*'

The shooting stopped. The foreman was on his hands and knees saying over and over in Cantonese, 'No . . . no . . . What can I tell my family? No . . . no . . .' He saw Feiffer getting into a crouch to run past him for the shack. The foreman said, 'No! No! Not twice!'

There was smoke coming from the shack. The foreman saw Feiffer coming towards him and stood in his way like a blocking forward. The foreman said—

'Get out of the way!'

'No!' The foreman screamed, 'No! Not twice! *No!*'

The shack was smoking heavily. A black oil spume was flowing out of the smashed window and through the holes in the wood.

The foreman yelled to Auden and Spencer, 'Get down! Get down!' He saw Feiffer almost on top of him with his gun drawn and he reached out and caught the man by the shoulder and dragged him down. The foreman yelled, 'No! I'm not going to let it happen twice!'

The smoke from the shack became a cloud. Feiffer wrenched at the man's grasp and ordered him—

Auden and Spencer were on the ground.

Auden said, 'Christ, it was a—I thought I'd been—'

The foreman, holding Feiffer in a grip of steel, was shaking with purpose. The foreman said between clenched teeth in a supplication to the gods, 'No . . . no . . . I need to have something good to tell my—'

The explosion from the shack came in a single overwhelming roar and scythed down every single stick in its construction to the ground.

The foreman, totally deafened for the instant, said, 'I just—' No sounds came out. He saw Feiffer's face an inch from his own. He was shaking his head and saying something over and over. Whatever it was it was in English and the foreman could not make it out from the movement of his lips.

Feiffer said in English, his eyes looked as if they still had not quite comprehended, 'Thank you. Thank you . . . very much.' He was gasping for air.

'All right.' The foreman, still deafened, failed to hear his own voice. The foreman, looking at what lay on the door behind him, said louder in case no words were coming out, 'All right.' The foreman's eyes were filling with tears.

At last, he had something to tell his family.

The foreman, patting Feiffer on the shoulder over and over and staring back at what was left of Mr Muscles on the door, said over and over with the tears streaming down his face, 'All right. All right. *All right!*'

*

In the street, O'Yee said in the sudden stillness, 'Christ. Holy mother of—Christ Almighty!' A phone rang in the charge room of the open Station and he went in, rubbing his forehead and put the Armalite by the charge desk, and took up the receiver.

There was a pause and then a giggle and then a voice said something barely audible in Cantonese.

O'Yee said, 'What?'

The voice said again, slower, 'I have a divine mission to eradicate all the uniformed forces of colonial repression in the world and I have now made a beginning.'

The hot weather brought them out like beetles.

O'Yee heard giggling in the background.

O'Yee said, 'What?' A heavy black pall of smoke was drifting in through the Station door.

Out of a clear blue sky . . .

Far away in the mountains, O'Yee could still hear the echoes of the gunfire rolling and echoing like thunder.

He was trembling.

O'Yee yelled, 'You stupid, time-wasting—*fucker*!'

12.47 p.m.

He slammed down the phone and went back outside.

3

There was a ragged coolie wandering about on the roof of the Hong Bay fishmarkets looking for somewhere to put down the load of bamboo scaffolding he carried and have an afternoon sleep. At 2.06 p.m. the sun was over Hanford Road on its way towards Wharf Cove in the west and the coolie shaded his eyes and looked up at it. He wore an enveloping cotton labourer's veil over his head and shoulders and he put his hand inside the veil and rubbed at the back of his neck where the bamboo lay. The roof of the deserted fishmarkets was flat and covered in seagull droppings and the bones of long dead fish and the coolie looked down to place his sandles carefully to skirt them.

The load looked heavy. He rotated his shoulders and shifted the weight a little as he walked. The bamboo poles were tied together in a bundle with rattan and the coolie rotated his shoulders again and shifted the biting knots on his collarbone.

He walked to the edge of the roof and looked down two storeys into Cuttlefish Lane. The street was full of traffic and people going about their business and he felt alone and above them. He could smell the sea and the suds the filleters used in the markets to wash down their boning boards, and the disinfectant the floor cleaners had used to hose down the floors and steel tables before work ceased punctually with the last basket at noon.

Across Cuttlefish Lane, a parking warden was clearing a waiting driver out of the driveway to an ambulance sub-station, not being obnoxious about it, but from the gestures he made to the driver, firm. The parking warden waved his hands: he was not going to give the driver a ticket this time, but NO PARKING AT ANY TIME also meant NO STANDING and the traffic warden

36

pointed to his watch and indicated that it also meant 'No hanging around talking to Traffic Wardens hoping your passenger will come back before you have to move on'.

The traffic warden put his fingers to his forehead and then waved whatever the driver said to him away. There wasn't one he hadn't heard twice already ranging from 'My little girl had to find a toilet and she'll be frightened if I'm not here when she comes back' to the standard 'I had a blackout and I thought I'd stop for a while because I was becoming a danger to my fellow drivers' to the highly exotic, 'Someone slipped me curare and the only thing I can move until it wears off is my mouth.' The traffic warden, seen from the roof mimed, 'No,' and made a few well meant remarks concerning the driver's responsibility to his fellow parents, black-outers and curare victims to ensure that they could be reached by ambulance in other NO PARKING spots.

The coolie looked at the doors to the ambulance sub-station. They were closed and there was no sign of an ambulance through the glass windows. He listened. No sirens. The coolie unlimbered his bamboo and squatted down with the veil still hanging over his face. He touched his fingers to his lips and watched as the car pulled out of the driveway watched by the traffic warden and the traffic warden drew a deep breath, congratulated himself on his maturity in not losing his temper, and looked down the street for more evil-doers.

The coolie undid the rattan around one end of the bamboo sheaf and looked again at the sun. It was directly behind him. The coolie put his hand under his veil to his neck again and felt the warmth coming through the cotton material onto his fingers.

The coolie's left eye was blinking a little. He put his hand onto the lid and wiped away perspiration and the tic stopped.

He heard a siren a long way off. Traffic was flowing freely up Cuttlefish Lane and spilling out onto the two way lanes in Canton Street going either in the direction of Yellowthread Street, or, to the south, down to Beach Road and the shoreline.

The coolie sat back on his heels and reached down to the bamboo.

He pulled out a long, well polished rifle and held it below the level of the cement railing that served as a rain run off for the roof. He looked behind him. The roof was flat and deserted.

He took out something resembling a squat metal cup from inside the bamboo and affixed it quickly and efficiently to the rifle with a wing nut.

He took out a piece of chalk from his trousers pocket and still squatting, his eyes flickering back and forth from the roof to the traffic warden and the ambulance station, wrote in a series of grass characters *Divine mission to eradicate all the uniformed forces of colonial repression.*

It interested him not at all. He had promised to write the words and he had.

He looked down at the characters with a faint derisory sneer and, putting the chalk back into his pocket, reached inside the bamboo sheaf and took out a single black cannister that fitted exactly into the cup on the muzzle of the rifle.

The knuckles on his left hand began to tingle and he put the rifle and the loaded grenade down onto the roof and leaning forward a little, rubbed at the knuckles with the palm of his other hand until the tingling stopped.

It was 2.07 p.m. on a beautiful, warm, balmy day. Inside the sheaf of bamboo poles there was one more object and the coolie took it out reverently and, like a priest kissing a holy item before dispensing a blessing, put his lips to it and closed his eyes.

It was a brown, cotton cap, heavily sweat-stained with a single star on it as its insignia.

The coolie drew a calming breath.

Just one, single inch...

Lying down full length behind the cement railing, listening to the far off siren, a blue banded blank cartridge on top of the others in the magazine of his rifle, he chambered it, and settled down to wait.

*

It was impossible. *All of them? All of them* had been... At a reloading bench in the shuttered Police Armoury at Headquarters, Inspector Sands read the words again in the reference book spread out open in front of him and said aloud, 'All of them? Every last one?'

It was impossible.

It was true.

It was in front of him on the page in black and white, complete with photographs and drawings. Sands said, 'All of them? Every one?'

Sands shook his head.

It was impossible.

He looked at the pile of cases from the drain and the bullets from the walls of the Station and picked them up one by one and measured them with his pocket micrometer.

He looked down at the figures and dimensions laid out in the technical manual in front of him.

'*Hong Kong Shipment.*

These weapons, all of which were ...'

The words swam in front of his eyes.

Sands said aloud in the empty room, 'Jesus *Christ*! All of them?'

It defied comprehension.

Sands said, 'Jesus Christ in Heaven!'

He reached for the phone and began dialling the number for Yellowthread Street as rapidly as his trembling finger could find the numbers.

*

In Cuttlefish Lane the ambulance driver turned off his siren and flicked his indicator lever to signal a left turn into the double doors of the sub-station. A little known fact was that, by and large, the only time ambulances used their sirens was when they wanted to get back to the station for lunch or out of the station to do a last call before going home. The ambulanceman smiled to himself and, as he saw the driveway approaching, turned off his flashing

39

lights as well.

He was doing O.K. It had been visiting day in the bronchial ward and he had scored two cartons of cigarettes from the visitors' gifts confiscated by appalled elderly Sisters and Matrons, one bottle of brandy from the fruit basket in the alcoholic ward, and since it was Monday, his usual tame undertaker's retainer of fifty Hong Kong dollars to continue telling him the names and addresses of DOAs before the opposition found out.

The ambulanceman had a long standing arrangement with the parking warden to keep the driveway clear and he saw the man doing his duty for him and slid one of the cartons of cigarettes and the bottle of brandy under his seat so the usual daily pay-off would stay at reasonable proportions.

It was definitely the ambulance driver's winning day.

He felt like a game of Chinese chess. He thought he might ask the traffic warden in for a while.

He reached the driveway, pressed a button on the dashboard of his ambulance and the big double doors opened automatically to let him in. He saw the traffic warden turn in his direction and start walking towards him.

The ambulance driver waved, drove in with the doors still open, and getting out and walking around to the back of his vehicle, opened the back door wide to let the smell of his last passenger out.

The ambulance driver had the carton of cigarettes in his hand. He broke open the seal, ripped the foil from the first pack with his thumbnail, and taking out a gold cigarette lighter, lit a relaxing smoke and began walking towards the warden to discuss chess and corruption.

On the roof of the fishmarkets the coolie took his veil off and put it in his pocket.

He blinked.

Just one, single inch...

His hand touched the stock of the rifle.

*

40

On the phone in the Detectives' Room, Feiffer said incredulously to Sands, 'What do you mean, "all of them"? How many are there?'

He saw O'Yee look over.

Feiffer said in disbelief, '*How many*?! It's a *what*?'

He said softly into the phone, the smashed and still smoking building across the street visible in the hole in the wall where one of the Detectives' Room windows had been, '*Oh, my God!*'

*

It was happening. At last it was happening. It was happening. He saw it. He felt it. He knew it. It was in every part of his body, tingling, shivering, building up, roaring, *increasing*... The coolie said, 'Yes!' He felt the trigger break and then the concussion, the thump as the stock of the gun hit hard in recoil against his shoulder. He saw the flash, the smoke, the black apple-like object go sailing free and fast in a parabola down into the open back of the ambulance. He saw it disappear into the blackness. He saw the faint light coming through the windows of the ambulance—the ambulanceman half way along the street with the traffic warden turn and mouth something in surprise—he saw the objects in the back of the ambulance: cylinders, a stretcher, some sort of white box, something made of stainless steel, something...

The coolie, frozen in time, began shaking. He felt the rifle come snaking back towards him and his own hand touch at the wing nut on the barrel and start to twist it free. He felt the metal cup come off...

It was happening easily. It was happening the way he had always—it was happening...

All the right things.

All the right things.

Everything was...

Just one inch ... just one...

He saw the smoke. He saw...

41

Just one inch...

The cup was off the barrel. He was putting it into the bamboo sheaf. Seconds. Seconds were ticking away.

It was all, all happening just the way...

The seconds were all used up. He saw the ambulanceman start to...

Moments, fractions, milliseconds...

*

In the Detectives' Room, O'Yee said in a gasp, 'Christ Almighty! What was that?'

*

It was gone. The ambulance sub-station was gone in a great gout of roaring, burning stark white flame that knocked people down in the street and smashed plate glass windows from one end of Cuttlefish Lane to the other.

Just one inch, just one inch, just one inch... The coolie was on his feet with the rifle in his hands. He felt the blast come racing up at him and he stood hard in it ferociously as it tore at him and tried to knock him down. It was a giant wind. He stood firm in it and drew his lips back over his teeth and grinned at it. He felt the rifle jump in his hands—he held on to it and yanked it back down again as the racing air tried to wrench it from his fingers.

The coolie had his cap on. He put his hand hard to the back of his head and pulled it down tight. He saw the ambulanceman and the traffic warden on the ground scrabbling to get up and he saw their silver buttons glint in the sun and then fade as someone ran past them—then glint again as the someone got clear.

He saw the ambulanceman's stupid face open its mouth and then close it again and he saw—

The coolie yelled at the top of his voice, 'Hey!!' and the ambulanceman looked up and saw him.

The coolie saw his mouth open. The coolie saw him see. The

coolie saw him.

The traffic warden was looking up. He was saying...

Just one single inch...

The coolie raised his rifle and fired.

He saw the bullet pass between them.

A single inch.

He saw the bullet miss by a single inch.

The coolie yelled out, 'Hey! Hey! Hey!'

He saw his enemy.

The coolie drew a bead on the ambulanceman as he tried to get up, and shot him cleanly through the knee.

*

Sands yelled into the phone, 'I'm telling you, the guns are from a fully operational Japanese Second World War arsenal! Complete! Intact! Untouched! And there's more! There's—' He yelled into the phone, 'Hullo, hullo! Is there anybody there?'

*

He shouldn't have shot to— He shouldn't have shot to—

He saw the ambulanceman writhing on the ground.

He shouldn't have shot to hit. He should have—

Just an inch.

He should have missed by an—

Something had happened. With the shot something had happened. The coolie's hands were shaking. The coolie said, 'Yes. Yes... Yes...'

The coolie said, confused, 'I—I—I—' He felt a surge, a great wave pass over him and the "I" was gone. The coolie said— The coolie said—

He touched the trigger. The ambulanceman jumped. The coolie said, '*Yes!*'

He saw the traffic warden try to get up and the coolie killed him with a single shot through the head. He saw a spray of blood and bone cover the man's shoulders and then the body was going down again, jerking and— The coolie screamed, 'Yes!' The ambulanceman looked up. Blood was coming from his leg and he looked up and then the traffic warden's body jerked as another bullet went in and the ambulanceman—

The coolie shrieked, '*YES!*' Flame and smoke were still coming from the scythed down sub-station. A burning tyre burst out from the hissing flames and rolled down the street.

The coolie saw the ambulanceman move.

The coolie said, 'Yes!' and killed him with a single shot.

The coolie shouted, 'Yes! Yes! Yes! *Yes!*'

People were running.

The coolie began shooting at them. He brought a man down by the side of his car, a middle aged Chinese, and then his wife, and then someone in the doorway of a shop, cowering. The bullets were flying off the roadway and smashing into window displays and exploding their contents out into the street. He saw a man try to scoop up a radio from the pavement as he ran and the coolie brought him down with a shot in the hip.

The ambulanceman was still moving. The coolie shot him again and then swung onto a running woman and sent her spinning with a bullet through the ankle.

He saw the traffic warden twitch. The bullet hit him dead centre in the chest and he thumped backwards onto a wall like a lump of meat. The echo of the explosion was coming back from the mountain and rumbling up and down the street.

The coolie heard screaming and the sounds of battle and felt the hot, burning air in his nostrils.

The coolie fired again, and the gun clicked open empty and he reloaded another magazine and went up and down the street with the sights shooting everything that moved.

The coolie said, 'Yes! Yes! *YES!!*'

At last. At long last. After all those years—

*

44

Sands shouted into the phone in a vain hope of raising someone, 'It's an entire Japanese arsenal from the Second World War! I'm trying to tell you, it's entirely possible he's some sort of bloody Japanese *hold-out*! A soldier! A—' He shouted, 'Is anyone there? Can anybody hear what I'm *saying*?'

*

His life had reached its consummation. Holding aloft his rifle in victory as the street burned, the coolie said, '*Yes*!! *YES*!!'

Beneath the faded Sergeant's cap of the Japanese Imperial All-Conquering Army his face was shining with glory.

He put his free hand to the back of his head to set the cap more squarely on his—

The coolie said, 'Yes! Yes! YES!'

The gun would go back into the bamboo sheaf and the cap into his pocket and he would put the coolie's veil back on and as he went back into invisibility in the city, no one, not a living soul would ever know ... would ever know ... *anything*!

The street was burning fiercely. He heard the screaming and saw the blood. He saw flags, flickerings, movements. In his mind he heard again bugles and the sound of men advancing and the joy of comradeship and the acts of fire and steel. It rose in him like a great storm, building up, pressing out, wanting to burst.

His moment had arrived.

The coolie yelled, '*YES*!!!'

At the top of his voice, the words echoing across the flat roof of the fishmarkets and down into the bloody, burning street, the coolie at last himself, shouted in Japanese, 'Yes!'

The coolie, the veins in his temple and neck throbbing with ecstacy, shouted, 'Banzai! *Banzai*! BAN—*ZAI*!!'

4

On the phone to the Detectives' Room the Commander's voice said incredulously, 'He was a what? And he yelled out what?'

His coat and shirt still smelled of smoke. Feiffer changed the receiver to his other hand, 'Banzai. It's Japanese. It means—'

'I know what it means! It means "Ten thousand years" and that about sums up how long it's been in this part of the world since anybody in his right mind's ever actually said it!' The Commander said irritably, 'It isn't enough that bloody Sands rings me up on the edge of hysteria telling me there's an entire Japanese arsenal hidden away for forty years in this bloody town, now you're telling me—what? That there's an eighty year old Japanese arsenal keeper going around shooting at people and discharging phosphorous grenades into empty ambulances?'

Feiffer said evenly, 'And killing people. I've just come back from the scene and apart from the two who were killed outright there are at least three others who aren't expected to live and one other who, if he does live, is going to be permanently paralysed from the waist down.'

'I'm not denying what this character did. What I'm denying is the rising feeling that he's some sort of Japanese hold-out sitting on his keg of bloody gunpowder just awaiting the resurrection of General bloody Tojo!' The Commander said reasonably, 'Harry, this isn't some sort of uninhabited Pacific island on the edge of nowhere full of high grass and hidden booby traps, this is one of the busiest, most densely populated cities in the world.' His reason faltered, 'Jesus Christ, all some mad bloody geriatric Nip would have to do to know the war was over was look up—any time of day or night—and see Japan Airlines coming in wing by friendly bloody wing with TWA, bloody British Air and bloody QANTAS! Or turn on a transistor radio and listen to Downtown Tokyo Radio playing American hard rock and humburger commercials!' The Commander said dismissively, 'No, it's ridiculous. And the fact that he seemed to be wearing some sort of Japanese kepi is just as ridiculous—in that case half of bloody Hell's Angels would be Adolf Hitler with rejuvenating pills.' The Commander said, 'No. Advice from on high. Final. You've got some sort of murderous maniac on your hands with access to Japanese guns from World War Two, but what you haven't got is any hold-out World War Two Japanese soldier! The end.'

'All right.'

The Commander seemed to hesitate. 'How could it be? How old would he be? Where would he have been all these years?'

Feiffer said tonelessly, 'How old are you?'

'I was about eighteen years old during the Second World War and whatever I might have done then or had done to me is over and forgotten! It was forty years ago—and for the last forty years I've been getting on with my life!' He said as a barely audible aside, thinking of Ballistic Experts ringing him up raving about Japanese arsenals, 'For the last thirty of them I've been here putting up with all this.' He became efficient again. 'From what I could make out from Sands' mixture of gunpowder and gabbling the shells your people picked up in the drains and the bullets he got from the walls are something rare. Is that how you understand it?'

'They're from guns made at the Nambu Rifle Manufacturing Company in the mid thirties. Evidently they're an early version of an assault rifle capable of semi and fully automatic fire issued to the Japanese Army—'

The Commander said tightly, 'Then he's got that wrong too. The Japanese Army didn't have assault rifles. They had Arisaka bolt action—'

'—on an experimental basis for use in Manchuria, but never adopted. The shell cases didn't have identifying headstamps because they were a consignment hand-built for the tests. After

Hong Kong fell in 1941 the rifles were brought here for reshipment back to Japan, but they were never despatched. According to Sands, the factory records list two hundred and twenty trial pieces consigned and almost half a million rounds together with accessories like grenade launchers, cups, blank cartridges for the grenades, bayonets, cleaning kits, spare parts—'

The Commander said, 'And whoever's found them has got the lot in mint condition, right? All nicely packed in grease and put away in waterproof banded boxes.'

'Evidently, yes. Sands suggests they were stored in an arsenal here which was probably sealed by bombing or landslip and they've been here undiscovered ever since.'

The Commander said warningly, 'But not with their little Japanese quartermaster though—left there alone and bloody friendless in the dust. Right?'

'If you say so, Neal.'

'I don't say so. Common sense says so.' The Commander said tightly, 'Listen to me, Harry. We've got good relations with the Japanese these days and they want to forget the bloody war even more than we do, and we don't want it all dredged up again with the popular press reprinting bloody atrocity stories that find their way into the nearest Datsun or Mitsui or bloody Mitsubishi office. The Japanese who run things these days aren't the same gang who ran things when they had a mad urge to take over the rest of the world and if you think you've seen the Chinese react wildly when they think they've lost face you just haven't seen anything until you've witnessed the Japanese version.' The Commander said carefully, slowly, 'I hate to sound like a politician, but it may come as a shock to a lot of people to know that if it wasn't for Japanese financial partnership and investment in this Colony we'd all be in a lot worse state and quite probably considering asking the Chinese Communists to send us food parcels to keep us all from starvation.' The Commander said finally, decisively, 'No. Whoever it is, it isn't a hold-out Japanese soldier, and anyone, anyone who suggests it is, especially within hearing of the gutter press, is going to find himself getting very Japanese indeed and

48

trying to find out where he can take a few quick hara-kiri lessons!'
The Commander said, 'I trust I make myself clear?'

'Yes.'

There was a pause. 'Harry, we don't want it all brought up
again, can you understand that? I don't know how much you
know about the history of Hong Kong under Japanese
occupation—' He asked, 'How old can you have been? Eight or
nine?'

Feiffer said quietly, 'I was evacuated to Australia. My father
was a cop in Shanghai. He was shot by a firing squad in 1940
during the Sino-Japanese War.'

'Then you know what I'm talking about!' The Commander said
quietly 'There were things that happened in those days...' His
voice trailed off. 'China was split. The Japanese were fighting here
for years before Pearl Harbor, before any of that. It wasn't just
split into the good guys and the bad guys—the Japanese invaders
and the poor suffering, defending Chinese masses: it was split into
the Japanese and the Communist Chinese and the Nationalist
Chinese and the Chinese–Japanese collaborators and the secret
societies and the Communist collaborators and the Nationalist
collaborators—it was split into bloody pieces. When I first came
here as a young Inspector just before the Korean War we were
still, still finding people in ditches with bullets in the back of their
necks and their so-called crimes engraved bone deep into them
with razors. The War Crimes Tribunals were still in force, even
the—' The Commander said earnestly, 'It was a disgusting, evil
few years and I don't want the families of anyone who was
involved—on either side—having to hear it all brought up again
and all the old hatreds resurrected.' The Commander said, 'I
want this down as a mad sniper who's taken on a police station
and an ambulance depot because he likes chalking stupid bloody
messages on fishmarket roofs, or a demented gun freak who likes
guns and using them on people, or a gang of kids with a pet
arsenal, or even the lead-up to the Third World War between the
Chinese and the bloody Russians, or even, if you like, the Kurds
and the bloody Persians, but I do not want it down, under any

circumstances, as a Second World War Japanese hold-out bloody soldier! *All right?*'

Feiffer paused for a moment.

'*All right?*'

The pause continued. Feiffer said evenly, 'Neal, at the moment, apart from a vague description of a figure on a roof top, all I've got to go on are the guns. I have to get in touch with someone and tell them they're Japanese even if only to find out where they were hidden.'

'I've no objection to that.' The Commander said with uncharacteristic obstinacy, 'If they were never used by the Japanese Army then they're not Japanese Army guns. Get in touch with whoever you like, provided he isn't Japanese.'

'I just don't see how anyone else would have found them. If they'd been turned over by an earth mover or in the course of land reclamation or—' Feiffer said reasonably, 'Neal, unless he had them buried in his back garden I don't see how any one man could have found them—' There was a silence from the other end of the line. Feiffer said carefully, 'I don't want to sound like a politician either, but with land in this Colony at a million dollars a square yard, an arsenal of the size you're talking about, presumably with living quarters for the staff, would have to be so big that—'

The Commander said tightly, 'No one has come back to claim them. The guns were found accidentally by a local.'

'There just isn't that much free land in Hong Kong. And if it was sited near the waterfront as it probably would have been and it was sealed by bombing—' Feiffer said, 'I just don't see how anyone could have dug their way in without someone hearing about it. Not *in*.'

'What the hell are you suggesting?'

'I'm not suggesting anything.'

'*What the hell are you suggesting?*' The Commander roared into the phone, 'My God, man, are you seriously suggesting that after forty years—*forty years*—someone in that arsenal has dug himself ... out? Are you—' The words would not come. The Commander said, 'My God, are you— Like ants coming out from a—'

The Commander said over and over, not giving an order, but resisting something, 'No! No! No! Harry, *no!*'

*

In the arsenal, the Bannin closed the steel door behind him and looked up at the hurricane lamp burning on the cement ceiling of the war room. The ceiling was white and powdery with dryness and there were dustwebs clinging to it, swaying faintly in the disturbed air from the burning lamp. The Bannin's eyes were full of tears and he wiped them with his gloved hand and stood silent for a moment, listening.

Through the thick concrete and rock of the walls of the room the sound of the sea a long way off rolled and thundered and shook dust loose from the last of the masonry adhering to the cement. He heard a crackle like small arms fire as somewhere in the tunnels rocks fell, and then a louder, deeper vibration that shook and trembled in the stale, urine-smelling air and then dissipated into echoes.

The Bannin looked down at his uniform and saw it was in tatters. He brushed at it with his hand and a little piece of rotted material broke loose from the weave and fluttered to the ground.

He looked back to the steel door and bit his lip to hold back the tears.

The other man in the room said gently, 'Bannin? (Watchman?)' and the Bannin swallowed and took something from his pocket and handed it to him.

It was a little metal Army issue cigarette box and the other man opened it carefully and looked at the lock of hair and fingernail parings it contained and then closed it again.

The other man in the room said quietly, 'Cuttlefish Lane, Bannin. There were people killed.'

'*Asi wa arauku tame ni arimasu.*'

The other man said gently in Cantonese, 'I don't understand.'

'One's legs are there in order that one may walk.' The Bannin said quietly in the holy place, reverting awkwardly to Cantonese,

'It was my Sergeant. He has fought his last battle and his end was glorious according to the code of Bushido. I assisted him at the last and he died without a murmur.' The Bannin said sadly, 'I have no way of returning his personal momentos to his family in Japan, but I have made arrangements with his enemies that his last battle be recorded.'

The other man said softly, 'Bannin, please. I'm a technician. This doesn't have to happen. I can do a set-up like the one in Yellowthread Street any time and your section—'

'My section are soldiers.' The Bannin said without anger, 'I don't expect you to understand this, but it is not something they want to do, or I want them to do, it is something they are all entitled to do.' He gave The Technician a thin smile, 'After forty years, it is the very *least*.' The Bannin said, 'He tried. The Sergeant. Before he committed seppuku, he told me he tried to reward your friendship—to assist you in your plans—he tried to miss *by one inch*, but, after all those years—' The Bannin held his gloved hands together like fists straining to explain something inexplicable to others, 'But the freedom, the great stirring in him as he—as he liberated the weapon—as the sword leapt from the scabbard—' He smiled again, 'I don't expect you to understand, as a Chinese.'

'Bannin—please—'

'No.' The Bannin said, 'We are all going to die. You must accept it. The entire section. It is our duty.' He heard the sea a long way off thundering against the solid rock on the other side of the war room wall, 'It is our glory. Like the sea, our inevitability.' He listened for a moment.

'Bannin, I have only just found you!' The Technician said, 'Please, won't you still help me?'

The Bannin listened.

The Bannin said after a moment, 'Yes.' He looked down at his uniform, his rags. The Bannin said with a strange, sad smile, 'The Sergeant was dressed in the clothing of a Chinese coolie when he fought his last battle, but he still wore—he still wore—' The Bannin said, 'I have made arrangements.' He looked back at the steel door anxiously, 'You know where the guns are.' He became stiffly correct. Major (Quartermaster) Juzo Takashima of the Japanese Imperial Army 38th Division in Hong Kong said formally, 'You will excuse me now. My command is not yet exhausted and after they and I have completed the formalities with our dead comrade, there are orders to be given.'

The far off force of the sea was shaking at the walls and roof of the underground chamber and The Bannin paused for a moment listening to it, the nodding, turned and opened the steel door and went through.

After a moment, there was the sound of a scratchy record coming from somewhere inside the room, being played on an old hand-wound player.

It was the Kimigayo: the Japanese national anthem, and about it, the rest of the command were silent, in mourning for one who had been lost to them.

The Technician said softly to himself in desperation, 'Please, do you have to keep on killing people?' His eyes fell on the closed steel door and he heard the music stop.

There was nothing to be done.

The Technician took down the hurricane lamp from the ceiling to go to the gun store and plunged the dry, ancient room back into darkness.

*

Up on the roof of the fishmarkets Sands collected the last of the expended shell cases and gazed down at the chalked message. It was in cursive, grass script and he could not read it.

He looked down at the cases in a plastic freezer bag in his hand. They were the same as the others.

Across the street he could see the firemen still spraying the ambulance sub-station with foam to make sure that the last of the phosphorous from the incendiary grenade was out and would not suddenly flare up again.

Over the last two nights, the expenditure of ammunition had

been approximately three hundred and ten rounds of blank, and on the third floor of the building in Yellowthread Street, counting both the rifle fire and the automatic gun, a minimum of four hundred live rounds.

There were eighteen empty cases in his freezer bag.

Three hundred and ten, plus four hundred, plus eighteen, plus one rifle-launched phosphorous grenade, plus an allowance for error, plus—

Not a spit in hell.

Starting with a base supply of two hundred and twenty guns and half a million rounds, they represented not even half a spit in hell.

Under his coveralls Sands wore a stubby stainless steel Detonics Mark VI .45 combat automatic in Condition One: cocked with the oversized safety ready to be flicked off as it came out of the leather.

He felt its weight under his armpit.

"... *The carrying of firearms by police, apart from their purely defensive function, is designed to give confidence in a situation where otherwise the officer might be reluctant to engage upon a course of action consistent with his duty...*"

Sands' duty was the open, exposed flat roof.

He glanced down into the street below where the ambulances had taken away the dead and the dying and found that his gun gave him no feeling of confidence at all.

There was a high building in direct line with the roof—over on Stamford Street—and something glinted momentarily on a sixth floor window and made him start before, at 3.05 p.m. in the afternoon, he realised with relief that it was only the sun.

*

It was there, faded with the sun. At the back of the fishmarkets, Auden said curiously, 'What is it?'

It was on the far side of the giant flat building, held by a length of tattered material with a knot. Auden said again, coming closer,

54

'What is it?' It was facing East, the last direction he would have expected the sniper to take if he had been escaping from the north side of the roof in a hurry.

It was a length of thick material, folded over like some sort of money belt or sash. It fluttered a little in the breeze from the sea.

Whatever it was, it seemed to have stitches in it in no apparent order, serving no apparent purpose.

Spencer said quietly, 'It's an *obi*, a Japanese ceremonial belt.' He touched at it gently and one of the coloured stitches in the material gave way and broke into ragged threads. Spencer said quietly, 'It's a thousand stitches obi given to Japanese warriors and suicide pilots for good luck.' He turned it over gently on the wall and the length of material fluttered briefly like a pennant.

Auden said quietly, 'Bill?' He saw the man squint at a line of faded characters written by hand along a seam of the stitches.

Spencer said, 'It's a name. I can't read it except for this one character here.' He indicated a single character evidently written a little later or with more pride than the rest, 'Sergeant.' Spencer said, 'And this bit here, I can make that out a little. It says 38th Division and these two characters here are the Japanese for Hong Kong.' He looked harder, 'And this, this line of characters is the way the Japanese do the date.' He began reading aloud, 'Sho-wa—' He said quietly, 'I can't make it out.' He said suddenly, 'Yes! 1942. Showa ... ju ... hachi...' Spencer said quietly, 'Nineteen hundred and forty two.' Something else fluttered in the breeze behind the obi and Spencer leant forward quickly and caught it before it fell to the ground.

Spencer said, 'And this too. 1942. The Japanese Imperial Army 38th Division in Hong Kong.' He read without expression, 'Sergeant Quartermaster—I think ... something...'

Auden said with sudden irritation, 'It's a bloody joke!' He saw Spencer look back to the faded characters on the obi again.

Spencer said, reading the obi, 'Sergeant Quartermaster—' Spencer said, 'Is it?'

'Of course it is! How the fuck can it be from 1942? It's something somebody's tricked up! You can get this stuff

55

anywhere. There's plenty of this stuff around. People collect it. If you want a bloody World War Two obi all you have to do is—'

Spencer said quietly, 'What about this?' He held the second object out and let Auden see it. It was a piece of card with the characters clear on it, written as if yesterday or kept carefully from a long time ago and protected against the light. Spencer said with sudden anger, 'And where the hell do you think he got this?'

He turned it over in front of Auden's face.

Auden said softly, 'Christ!'

It was a photograph of a man in Army uniform standing with his wife and child outside an army barracks and smiling as they glanced up at a sign in Japanese reading *Quartermasters' Training School, Hiroshima.*

Auden said, 'It's a fake, isn't it?'

Spencer said, 'No.'

Far off in the distance, you could see the domes and buildings of the city destined to be the first victim of the Atomic Age. Then, in 1942 or earlier, when the photograph had been taken and the man on the roof had put it in his pocket to keep all these years, that city had been completely, totally, and obviously ... intact.

Auden said again softly, 'Christ...'

He touched at his gun under his coat, but it seemed a very insignificant thing indeed, and he took his hand away and looked back to the fluttering obi and shivered.

*

There was a flash at the window again and Sands clenched his fists together and said, 'Damn it, it's the sun!'

There was nothing there.

He saw another shell case on the roof and, picking it up, glanced back again and ordered himself, 'Keep your mind on the job!'

3.28 p.m.

He just wanted to get back to his Police Armoury and close the door behind him.

The phone rang. It was him. At his desk O'Yee felt himself stiffen as the voice said evenly and unhurriedly in Cantonese, 'I have a divine mission to eradicate all the uniformed forces of colonial repression in the world and I have now made two beginnings.' O'Yee stayed silent. There was nothing more from the voice, but the line was still open.

Feiffer was outside in the charge room with the Uniformed Branch and there was no one else in the Detectives' Room but O'Yee.

'O'Yee said with no emotion in his voice, 'Anata wa nihongo wakarimas' ka?'

There was a silence.

The words meant, he thought, 'Do you speak Japanese?' The words were in Japanese.

O'Yee could hear the man breathing at the other end of the line. He could hear the breathing coming in gasps.

O'Yee said—

There was a single click as the caller suddenly hung up, and then, in the burring of the dial tone that went on and on in O'Yee's ear for a very long time, nothing.

*

On the ground below the obi there was yet another object. It moved as Auden stepped back and touched it with his shoe.

It was a single three quarter inch ball bearing, and, since there were no machines in the fishmarkets, just as there were no Japanese soldiers left in Asia, it also had no right to be there.

The ball bearing was brand new, with a fine sixteenth of an inch hole drilled all the way through it like the worm hole in an apple.

It had not been meant to be found. It had fallen out of someone's pocket and in the confusion either the sniper had not noticed it or it had rolled away and he had not been able to find it again.

Or perhaps he had not even cared.

The ball bearing was nickel plated.

Like the window in the sixth floor building across from Sands on the roof, it glittered brightly in the mid afternoon sun.

5

In the silent underground vaults of the Historical Archives Store under Icehouse Road, The Keeper Of Secrets looked at Feiffer for a very long time before answering. His office was bare, windowless and without even a picture or a sign of personality in sight. The Keeper Of Secrets said, 'I don't speak the language, but I read it,' turned his face and the glassene envelope encased obi away under a desk lamp and put on his glasses. He said, 'My name, for your records, is Mr Owlin.' He looked back with the glasses on his face and waited for the inevitable comment, then, when it failed to come, turned the obi over carefully in long scrupulously clean hands and read, 'Sergeant Quartermaster Seichiro Tanino, Japanese Imperial Army, Thirty Eighth Division in Hong Kong, the equivalent of nineteen hundred and forty two.' His face, in the soft light, looked Chinese. He turned back slightly and all the bone structure went and, except for the black hair, it was a European Nordic face. He took off his glasses and the bones changed again and became Korean. The Keeper Of Secrets said, 'It's a thousand stitches obi from the Second World War probably taken from a living man.'

Feiffer looked curious.

The Keeper Of Secrets said, as if it was simplicity itself, 'No blood.' He turned the transparent envelope over carefully. It made a crackling noise. 'And very little evidence of sweat, so it was washed regularly and removed from the owner while he was calm and not in battle.' There was a single thick file on his desk marked *Events At Leighton Hill, Feb–April, 1897—not to be opened without Written Authority* and The Keeper Of Secrets looked at it for a moment, then put the obi carefully down on his desk. The

Keeper Of Secrets asked without expectation of a reply, 'Can I ask where you got it?'

'At Cuttlefish Lane.'

The Keeper nodded. He glanced back behind him to a single locked door to the main records store.

Feiffer said, 'What were they used for?'

'As stomach warmers. And as good luck talismans. The wife or mother of the recipient stood on a street corner in Tokyo or Osaka or wherever her relative was billeted and asked passers-by to insert one single stitch into the material as a sign of good wishes and luck for her relative's forthcomig death. When she had a thousand the obi was presented to the soldier as a sign of his countrymen's hopes for him to die well in battle.' The Keeper of Secrets could not have been more than thirty five years old. He said with the authority of one who had been there at the time, 'This man was a soldier late in life or he was a regular soldier. If he had been inducted into the Forces at the time of the Sino–Japanese War or after Pearl Harbor he would have gone in as a private and the belt would have been presented to him then. In which case his previous rank would have been erased or crossed out when he became a Sergeant. The date 1942 was the date on which he was given the obi and the 38th division was the unit he was attached to at the time.' There was the faintest movement in the young-old man's face. The Keeper Of Secrets said, 'The thirty eighth division was the unit based in Hong Kong who cut down all the trees.'

'Pardon?'

The Keeper Of Secrets offered the obi back. There was the feeling of tenseness about the otherwise gentle move. The Keeper Of Secrets said, 'The thirty eighth division atacked Hong Kong from across the border on the morning of the eighth of December, 1941 and fought their way across Kowloon to Hong Kong until the General Officer Commanding, Major General Maltby, was finally forced to surrender on Christmas Day of the same year. And then Hong Kong was occupied until Liberation in August, 1945.' The Keeper Of Secrets said softly, 'During that period the

60

Thirty Eighth Division cut down every tree on Hong Kong for firewood, including cypresses and junipers and oaks planted by the first settlers a hundred years before.'

'I see.'

The Keeper Of Secrets said, 'The cypress and the juniper are symbols of longevity to the Chinese. As well as the commercial aspect, it was a political move to subjugate them,' The Keeper Of Secrets said, 'My family has been on the China Coast for five generations, first at Macao and then, when it was founded, here in Hong Kong. My family planted some of the trees.' He asked, 'Do you like trees, Mr Feiffer?'

'Very much.'

'All of the old trees were replaced after the war by quick growing varieties. I helped plan some of the plantings.' He looked down at the obi, 'But, like the philosophy that created your obi-wearing Sergeant all the old, solid, ancient things have gone.' He gave Feiffer a faint, sad smile and looked down at the floor of the windowless, air-conditioned room, 'I miss them. The old trees before the war.'

'You couldn't have even been born before the war.'

'No.' The Keeper Of Secrets said, 'But the records were.' He moved his hand back to the closed door behind him, 'All the records were. They were all here underground and they survived, all of them.' He looked up, 'This room and the rooms behind it will survive a nuclear explosion, so they will always be here.' The Keeper Of Secrets said, 'I can go in there and take out files and records and photographs and there never was a war. I can take out a map and a guide book and I can walk down all the streets and through all the villages where my family planted trees to last forever and I can even read their letters to nurserymen asking advice and their receipts for payment and their shipping invoices as each one of the oaks and the junipers and the elms and the larch trees came in. I can read how many inches each tree grew each year—'

The man's face was pale and bloodless. Feiffer said gently, 'Do you ever go out?'

'No. The world above me is not the one I—' He stopped. The Keeper Of Secrets said with a quick, nervous, embarrassed grin, 'Like some burrowing mole I could survive down here in the past forever, dreaming my own dreams and—'

'Do you have the records of where the Japanese military establishments were during the Occupation?'

'Some of them, yes.'

'The arsenals and the—'

The Keeper Of Secrets said, 'No.' He paused for a moment, 'My predecessor kept these records all during the Occupation and the Japanese didn't even know he was here. But he, unfortunately, because of it, was hardly in a position to file away military secrets.'

Feiffer said with alarm, 'Do you mean he was here undetected?'

The Keeper Of Secrets nodded.

'For four years?'

'And one day.'

'How did he live?'

The Keeper Of Secrets smiled.

'Is it possible to—'

'Certainly.' The Keeper of Secrets said with a secret, mad smile, 'This place is bomb proof, like all—' He leaned forward at his desk, 'Do you think that in Europe, for example, when they hid the Mona Lisa and the Rembrandts and all the important things of the world that they didn't make arrangements for the hiding to outlast the temporary aberration of *war*?' The Keeper Of Secrets said, 'In France there was a case where a group of soldiers were entombed in a block house for almost twenty years!'

Feiffer said barely comprehendingly, 'And when they came out?'

The Keeper Of Secrets said, 'They were all mad. Of course.'

Feiffer waited.

The Keeper Of Secrets said with triumph, 'But their philosophy was intact.' The Keeper Of Secrets said, 'And that, in the long run, in the movement of time, is all that matters.' The Keeper Of Secrets turned his face away from the light and stared hard at a blank wall and saw—God knew what. The Keeper Of Secrets said, 'The trees, they are the only transitory things of this world that I miss, but if I wait long enough, even they—'

Feiffer said evenly, 'The Thirty Eighth Division, what happened to them after the war?'

'Nothing.' The Keeper Of Secrets said, 'They were transferred to another posting in early 1943—to Guadalcanal. They were all killed.'

'All of them?'

'All of them.' The Keeper Of Secrets looked down at the obi in its little stapled envelope.

Feiffer felt a cold shiver up his back.

The Keeper Of Secrets fixed him with a fierce, strange look and thinking of the trees, said quietly, 'They were all cut down.' There was a faint, unidentifiable, other wordly look on The Keeper's face. The Keeper said after a moment, still smiling, 'Weren't they? Just like the trees. They were all—all of them—*felled*.'

Behind him, through that closed door, there must have been miles of corridors and shelving and acres of folders filled with papers and memories and photographs all straining to be free of the timeless order in which they were arranged and classified and fossilised, but as The Keeper Of Secrets kept smiling, from behind the door there was not even the faintest rustle to indicate their presence.

*

HONG KONG. FINAL MESSAGE.

The General Officer Commanding authorises me to state that the white flag will be hoisted and all British, Canadian and other military operations against the Japanese Army will cease forthwith. You will consider yourselves prisoners of war. Issue orders to all those concerned to cease fighting.

    For:

       GENERAL OFFICER COMMANDING, British Forces in China.

God Save The King!

Hong Kong, 25th: 12:1941.

*

The Keeper Of Secrets looked at him.

The obi was in Feiffer's hand.

There were one thousand stitches in it exactly, each lovingly placed there a lifetime ago.

Sergeant Quartermaster Seichiro Tanino, Japanese Imperial Army, Thirty Eighth Division in Hong Kong, 1942...

Feiffer saw The Keeper Of Secrets still looking at him silently, and, in the deep, air-conditioned room he put the object back carefully onto The Keeper's desk and, through the sealed, tagged, glassene evidence envelope, felt it cold and dry, like death.

*

The telephone number of the Japanese Embassy was 4–50153.

The only country left in the world, leaving aside Switzerland and Andorra, without a standing offensive army.

Anata wa nihongo wakarimas' ka?

It was the only Japanese O'Yee knew.

And it was probably wrong at that.

O'Yee looked at the replacement telephone on his desk and tried to think who he knew who spoke the language. And who he could trust.

The telephone number of the Japanese Embassy was 4–50153.

The Emergency Unit were moving sandbags in to cover the broken windows and laying out bullet proof vests on the floor around him and he found it hard to think.

*

He was committed. He had no choice. In the engine room of the moored police launch in Fisherman's Cove, The Technician worked in the failing afternoon light with his rifles. Through one

64

of the portholes by the twin diesels he could see the upstairs room of the double storied building where the Police were having their afternoon conference before changing shifts. There was no one around. It was the same theory as speeding in the exact five minutes between the change of shifts of traffic cops, and even the Constable at the open wire gates to the wharf area was inside changing into civilian clothes and thinking that he had earned a good day's pay for a very easy day's work.

He saw a movement on a disused wharf a hundred feet away and for an awful moment thought the cops knew he was there and were watching him through binoculars to catch him in the act.

The Technician crawled on his hands and knees to the porthole and shot the cuff of his mechanic's coveralls quickly to check his watch.

The shift was still changing and The Technician, short on time, squinted hard at the thick glass of the engine room porthole to try to make out who it was.

He knew him.

The man was wearing a fisherman's smock and a wide boat people rattan hat to cover his features, but The Technician knew who he was.

The Stores Corporal.

It was Corporal Sakutaro Ozawa. For a moment the wind caught his smock and The Technician saw his thousand stitches obi around his stomach.

The Technician said softly in Cantonese, 'No...!' and looked back to his set-up.

The Corporal had been carrying something long and dark under his arm, wrapped up to look like a length of wood under a medium mesh fisherman's net.

The Technician, hurrying, glanced back through the porthole and the man was gone.

*

5.59 p.m. By a disused warehouse facing the sea, the Corporal paused. There were ball bearings in his pocket, together with a few coins and bits and pieces of screwed up paper.

By the warehouse there was a public telephone booth for the use of fishermen and their families and, going to it, he stood looking down into the dark water at his own reflection.

The ball bearings were no longer of any interest to him.

Dropping them into the sea, one by one, he saw his reflection at first ripple then distort, then, in the disturbed water, pass from reality altogether.

He touched at the rifle hidden in the rolled up medium mesh net and smiled.

*

On the phone in the Detectives' Room O'Yee said, '*What?*' He changed into Cantonese, 'I can't understand you. *What?*'

The voice at the other end of the line was old, croaking, it seemed to be coming from a long way off. Somewhere in the background O'Yee could hear what sounded like a faint wind pulling at the voice and taking it away. There was a ship's siren, noises and sounds of time and distance and—

The voice said, '*Eigo o narau tame ni Eikoku no husu o kikimas—*' It made a harsh cackling noise.

He listens to English . . . in order to . . . learn English . . . O'Yee heard the word, '*but*'. O'Yee said desperately, 'I can't speak Japanese! I don't know what you mean! I know you speak Cantonese! I—'

It wasn't the same voice.

O'Yee said, 'Eigo wakarimasu ka?' Do you understand English? It wasn't right. It should have been—

Far off behind the voice he could hear the sound of the wind and—

O'Yee said, 'Tanino! Sergeant Seichiro Tanino. Are you—'

'Ie.'

He knew that word.

It meant, 'No.'

66

The voice said slowly, an old, old man's voice coming from a long way away, 'Ozawa. Sakutaro Ozawa.' There was a burst of numbers and technical words that could have been some sort of serial number and rank. The voice said something that sounded like, 'Bushido.' It said something that sounded like, 'Seppuku.'

O'Yee waited.

Outside, it was becoming night and the darkness was moving in through the holes in the wall over the grey sandbags like seeping gas at a parapet. There was no one else in the Station.

Behind the caller's breathing, he could hear a faint wind taking all the words away.

O'Yee said . . .

Night. Outside it was becoming dark, secret night.

O'Yee said—

There was a silence and then, to someone a long time ago, perhaps someone in a place long gone and a time never to be returned to, the caller said sadly in Japanese, 'Goodbye.'

The voice said softly and sadly, not to O'Yee, 'Sayonara . . . sayonara . . .'

It sounded for a moment as if he was crying.

O'Yee said—

Outside, it was dark, black, friendless night.

O'Yee yelled into the phone a moment before the line went dead, 'God damn it, *who are you? What do you want?*'

"I have a divine mission to eradicate all the uniformed forces of colonial repression and I have now—"

That? Why hadn't he said that?

The night was dark and full of terrors.

O'Yee said desperately in the empty Detectives' Room, surrounded by the sandbags and flak jackets and guns, 'My God, how many of them are there?'

*

The ship's name was the *Osaka Maru*. On its way out to sea it passed across his line of vision with all its running lights on and its

67

leaving port pennants fluttering in silhouette in the wind. He saw some of the crew leaning on the fan tail looking down into the foaming water.

It was going home.

There was nothing now to go home to.

He was crying a little.

Corporal Sakutaro Ozawa of the Japanese Imperial Army 38th Division in Hong Kong, high up on the roof of a disused warehouse facing the sea, slipped the photograph of his long dead parents safely inside his thousand stitches obi, rested his hand on the waiting Nambu M1935 Experimental Assault Rifle by his side, and settled down to a dreamless, final sleep.

There was a cheap, mass produced, Japanese Army issue watch on his wrist, held by a frayed and cracked black leather band.

At exactly 6.03 a.m., its mechanism all clogged and old, without warning, it suddenly stopped.

6

At the 5 a.m. Headquarters news briefing this morning a police spokesman reaffirmed that the weapons involved are .303 Lee Enfield rifles abandoned by units of the defending Canadian Army during the battle for Hong Kong in 1941.

The spokesman went on to strenuously deny reports given by eye-witnesses to this newspaper that the sniper wore the uniform of a Japanese Army officer and that the grenade which destroyed the ambulance sub-station in Cuttlefish Lane was of a type stored in Japanese arsenals during the Occupation.

He also refused to confirm that counter sniper units had been attached to regular police patrols and that there was increasing Emergency Unit activity on the streets.

The Spokesman said the police were treating the shootings as purely criminal incidents without political motive.

A spokesman from the Japanese Embassy said late last night that in the absence of an official approach from the Government his office could make no comment on the incidents.

A further news conference had been convened by police for this morning when more information is expected.

Following the death early this morning of one of the victims of the Cuttlefish Lane shootings the condition of the other victims in St Paul de Chartres' Hospital is said to be stable . . .

*

There was a ragged junk making its way back into harbour through the lightening purple dawn, its stern auxiliary motor popping and bubbling a wake that flowed against the side of Lew's police launch and set it bobbing slightly against its moorings and

Sergeant Lew, shivering a little in his coat, kicked his boots against a bollard on the wharf, thought of clean open seas and seagulls and looked away as a human turd surfaced in the phosphorescence and then sank again like a submarine. At the stern of the junk there was a wooden circle with a hole cut out of it set out over the wake—the Chinese junk fisherman's mod cons—and one of the fishermen using it. "Jaws" nothing. In Hong Kong harbour you ran a bigger risk of being crapped to death than eaten. A sampan passed a little behind the junk, well out of range, and there in the absence of a wooden seat there was a splash as someone threw over an entire plastic bag full of something.

Lew heard the bag seethe as it went straight down to the gutters of Atlantis and the Atlantean street sweepers, seeing it, made bubbling noises and went instantly out on strike.

Lew had been educated in an English speaking Catholic missionary school on Kowloon. Knowing he came from a long line of boat people one of the Brothers had set him to learning Masefield's 'I Must Go Down To The Sea Again' and Lew, watching as yet another turd surfaced said quietly to himself in English, 'Give me a tall ship and a star to steer her by . . .' There were no stars. Pre dawn, it was dark and overcast. And no tall ships. Just shit. Lew looked full at Constable Pan at the door to the engine room and said, irritated, 'Pan, if you haven't got the fucking wit to open a door I'll fucking find someone who has!'

At the varnished door to the engine room, Pan said back, 'It's locked.'

'That's why you've got the key.' Maybe, on balance, being a sea turd wasn't so bad. At least you had the place to yourself. Lew said, 'Take the key in your hand, place it carefully in the lock, give it a little turn while at the same time maintaining a steady pressure on the door handle . . .'

Pan said, 'I've done all that. It's locked. Someone's locked it from the inside.'

'The door leads to the engine room. Engine rooms are not locked from the inside because if they were and something terrible happened then the engineer inside—' Lew said, '—who is you—

might be stuck in there and he might drown.' Briefly it was a thought that did not lack appeal. Lew said with an effort of sweetness, 'Look, Constable, the night patrol is due in in three minutes and we're going to look a bit silly if we can't get our door open, aren't we? So try again, would you?' The coxswain was in the wheelhouse taking the night covers off the instruments and Lew hopped down onto the deck, glanced up at him, and seeing that at least everything was all right in there—that he hadn't forgotten to order a goddamned wheel or anything—went down to the engineer and took the key.

Pan said, 'I'm only new, Sergeant. When I trained we had the newer type of launch. It had a combination lock on the engine room door.' He was a big moon-faced ex fisherman, probably still counting his luck that he had a toilet that flushed and a helmet that protected him against those who didn't. Lew said with a shrug, 'O.K., as a matter of fact, this door does get stuck occasionally.' He put the key in and gave it a turn.

It turned.

Lew said, 'There. It must have been a sea water warp or something.'

He pulled at the door handle and nothing happened.

Constable Pan said, 'See?'

The junk passed off to starboard, going pop-pop-pop and then, yet again—the entire crew must have waited through the vast South China Sea for the exact moment they passed the Water Police moorings—plop-plop-plop. Lew said, 'What's that smell?'

Constable Pan said, 'It's the wind. It's blowing in the—'

'No.' Lew leaned forward, 'On the door.' He got up close and put his nose against the varnished timber and sniffed, 'It smells like acetone or—' He saw the coxswain and two of the deckhands lean out from the wheelhouse and smile at him and he roared, *'Which one of you bastards has put Super Glue on the engine room doors?'* He took hold of the handle and wrenched at it in a fury, *'If one of you bastards thinks this is funny you'll be thinking it from the other side of the Police Disciplinary Board carpet!'* Lew shouted, 'Are you out of your minds? The night patrol boat has got a Chief Superintendent on

71

it—it's Superintendent Allison—and when that man hears about this there won't be enough left of any of you to use for shrimp bait!' Lew said in a trembling mutter as he pulled hard at the door to free it, 'Holy Mother of—' He ordered Pan, 'You! Get around to the porthole and see what the hell's holding it. It better not be glue! It'd better be an oily rag stuck in the jamb—which is only two month's suspension—it had better not be glue, which is instant gladdamned *death*!' He saw Pan staring at him like a moron waiting to be told which foot to put forward first in order to walk. Lew ordered, 'Get around to the porthole and have a look in!' He saw the man start off in the darkness, 'And take a flashlight, you nincompoop!'

The door was stuck. He heard Pan tip toe around the edge of the boat with all the nautical grace of Moby Dick in his death throes and he called out, 'Well? Can you see anything?' It was Super Glue: Lew could smell it.

Pan called out, 'No. I can see the door where it says something about a divine mission and the usual ship's blessing, but I—'

Lew said, 'What?'

Pan said, 'But I can't make out anything else for the smoke.'

Lew said, 'The what?' He thought his ears must have— Lew said, 'The *what*?'

Pan said, 'Yes, I can. It says, "to eradicate all the uniformed forces of—"'

Lew's voice was a gasp. Lew said, 'Is this a *joke*?'

'No. No, it says—'

The night patrol launch was coming in. Lew heard it. Lew shouted to the coxswain, 'Get off! Get off the boat!' He saw Pan coming around, smiling at him and playing the flashlight on the ground to make patterns. Lew shouted at him, 'Get off! Get off the boat!' He saw the night boat coming in. All along the wharf there were police boats and auxiliary craft moored in a single unbroken line. Lew shouted, 'Clear the area. It's a set-up! Clear the area!' He saw the coxswain and the two deckhands start to come towards him, not sure of what they had heard and he took the first deckhand by the scruff of his neck and threw him overboard into the sea.

The coxswain heard him shout again, 'Set-up!' and as Lew went past him leapt a full twenty feet from the deck onto the wharf and began running.

Lew shouted, 'The moorings! Cast off the moorings!' as Pan and the other deckhand followed and made for cover.

The diesels were self starting. Lew pushed the two buttons and they roared into life. He heard someone shout, 'The moorings—' and he yelled back, 'Cast them off!' waited not a moment later and putting the engines into Full Ahead ripped the wharf to matchwood and put the vessel at top speed into the centre of the harbour.

He smelled smoke.

It came from under the door of the engine room. He saw it seeping up through the decking in the wheelhouse.

The night boat was coming in.

He saw them come about to hail him. Lew shouted—

It was no good. It was too far away.

There was an electronic loud hailer on the ceiling of the wheelhouse and Lew flicked it on and yelled out a single word in Cantonese that carried past the junks and the sampans to the night boat and rose above his roaring engines.

That word was *'Bomb!'*

*

On the roof of the disused warehouse facing the sea, Corporal Ozawa awoke.

He had been in a long, deep sleep. He touched at his thousand stitches obi and began to undo it.

Like a sudden dragon, he awoke.

*

Coming across the harbour from Lamma Island, Lew saw a ferry. It was full of people. The night boat had turned off and was pacing him, coming up a little astern as he put the bow of the boat out towards the open sea and kept the throttles forward. Something was burning through: he saw the black oily smoke coming up through the deckboards.

The engines were roaring, racing, without their water jackets filled glowing red hot and warping out of true, buckling, going wild.

He heard a click. It came up through the boards, then there was more of the smoke and then something hot and fast pushed up and made a whoomph sound under his boots and one of the smaller fuel tanks gave and spilled oil over the engine room floor. Lew could see it in his mind as the black oozy stuff flowed unstoppably towards the glowing engines.

Something inside the engine room was burning and making pinging sounds. They came as punctuation in the roaring of the engines. He could feel the boat glowing, going faster, becoming bright like a light bulb about to burst.

He heard it. He heard a solid, loud bang as something like a gunshot went off inside the hull. He knew something had gone, been fired, done something. He knew that whatever was happening had started to happen and he was—

Seconds.

Less than seconds. He got the wheelhouse door open and then ducked as it smashed back with the speed and all the glass went.

The boat was going for the open empty sea. He saw the night launch behind him in the wheelhouse mirror chasing him, its bows cutting twin white knives through the rolling sea.

Lew said at the top of his voice, forgetting all his Catholic education, 'T'ien Hou, Goddess of the Sea, protect me now!' and spinning the wheel hard to port to break the boat's back propelled himself out through the smashed door and into the foaming dark, enveloping sea.

*

He awoke. From a long, deep, dark sleep, he awoke and he was young again and the rifle was by his side.

Bushido.

The code of the warrior.

It was fast becoming dawn and he could see across the water and he had his rifle.

Corporal Ozawa stood up.

*

The boat was on fire. The engines stopped and it began drifting. In the water, Lew said over and over, 'Oh, God, oh God, oh, God . . .'

If he had been wrong . . .

The boat was drifting back, turning in circles, intact, its back solid and hard. It made a one hundred and eighty degree turn and he saw it and then, less than two hundred yards away, what he had done to the wharf and the moorings.

Lew said, 'Oh, God, oh God . . .' and wished that his sodden clothes would pull him down into the sea.

The boat was burning in great rolling billows of white and black smoke, floundering as it turned and then came about again and then, rudderless, turned again and began drifting back towards the shore.

Lew saw the night patrol boat cut its engines and come to a stop in the water: he felt the ripples wash over him and then abate and then stop altogether and he was floating in a still, Limbo sea as the night boat and Superintendent Allison came towards him with murder in his eyes.

He saw them all lined up on the after deck of the boat, one or two of them with boat hooks ready to pull him out and Lew, treading water, touched at his holstered gun and thought, 'That's ruined too. All my uniform and equipment, it's all ruined because of an oily rag in the—' He thought, 'No . . .' He touched his head and felt something warm on his temple and he thought with great, happy gratitude, 'I'm hurt. I must have banged my head so at least I've got a wound to show them.'

His boat was turning in slow circles, the smoke fading and whispering out into white puffs.

Lew thought, 'I believed that idiot Pan. It was all a joke and I believed him.' He touched at his head and could have wept that at least they had to be sympathetic to a wounded man. He saw Superintendent Allison's face and he was afraid to wave at the man to signal the pick up in case it showed he wasn't really hurt and—

The fire on the boat had gone out.

Lew said, broken hearted, 'Oh, no...' The boat was drifting back in the water, all the fires out, not a mark on her except the broken wheelhouse door he had smashed himself.

On what was left of the wharf Pan and the coxswain would be saying, 'Me? No, I didn't know anything about it. He just went crazy and threw me overboard and then he started running back and forth like a lunatic telling everyone to get off—'

Back to the goddamned junks and the aft shit seat. Lew said softly to himself, 'You've screwed it up. You've screwed it up...' The boat was drifting back to the shore, less than a hundred yards away from the wharf and he struck out for it as the night boat came to get him and a voice hailed, 'This way. Swim this way!' and Lew, crying, shook his head and made for his own craft to salvage it.

There was a puff of smoke from the engine room area.

The night boat started its engine and came about at dead slow to cut off his path.

They were all drifting back to the shore.

Lew said with salty tears running down his face, 'I'm sorry... I'm sorry...' He heard a faint pop from his drifting boat and as he struck out for it in a fury, Lew said with blood all over his face, 'No!' Not twice! Not again, you bastards! *Not twice!*' and then, in a sudden swelling of the timbers there was a great pressure inside his boat—he actually saw the plankings bulge—and then in a sudden, roaring, blasting, liberating boiling explosion the boat disappeared from the surface of the sea and sent him down into the

76

sea in a gout of boiling water and matchwood.

He felt a terrific whack in the shoulder as he sank and he thought—

He looked up from the darkness below the surface, sinking, and he thought for a moment that the entire sea was on fire.

*

The windows went. All the windows in Beach Road went and came crashing down in shards and splinters and entire sheets of plate glass into the street.

In the Detectives' Room, O'Yee said, 'Christ! It's happening again!' He saw Feiffer and Auden and Spencer go for their Armalites. Sandbags had collapsed from the shored up windows and the room was a flurry of papers and bits and pieces of wood and sand and material.

The explosion was rolling, echoing, never ending.

O'Yee said, 'Christ! It's happening again!' O'Yee said over and over, trying to find his Armalite, his flak jacket, anything, in the mess, *'Christ, it's happening again!'*

*

His eyes were bright and shining.

He awoke.

After forty years, the rifle was at his shoulder and it had living men in its sights and, after forty years, he awoke.

He pressed the trigger and it was like a great gust of clear clean revivifying air and, at last, again, he was himself.

*

On the night patrol boat, Superintendent Allison said, 'Jesus!' He saw the windows in his wheelhouse go and then something hard smash against it in a splash of blood and then reel back again and disappear from sight. Bullets were ripping the woodwork

77

around the wheelhouse to pieces. He saw a flash from the shore—the sounds were echoing out in the roaring reverberations from the falling pieces of Lew's boat—and for a moment he thought he saw Lew surface in a circle of blood and then go down again and he shouted to one of the deckhands, 'Take the wheel! Take the—' and then the man was down and kicking on the deck as a spout of blood ripped through him like a lance and cut him in two.

Bullets were flying off the metalwork. Allison saw a shower of sparks as a davit buckled and then something hard came down from the superstructure and scudded along the deck.

He saw the engineroom door open and a head come out. He actually saw Constable Ling in there open his mouth to say something and then look surprised as a bullet cut him through the throat and almost decapitated him.

On the ferry, a long way off, there was screaming: he heard the old engine thumping in the craft as the Captain issued an order the engineer had never heard before in his life and then a bullet hit the flare locker on the police boat and a cauldron of white and red and green boiling fire covered Allison and burned through his hair.

He was on fire. He saw something fly off the woodwork an inch from his hand and then the pyrotechnics burned into his face and he thought, 'Oh, my God, I've been disfigured and I—' and then something hard hit him in the centre of the stomach like a sledge hammer and he went over backwards and felt water on his back and the taste of salt.

Engines. He heard engines. He looked up from the water and all the fires on his face had gone out. There were sampans coming, and junks. He looked around for Lew and saw nothing.

Two of his men went down on the deck and then someone came out from below decks carrying something and a bullet took him in the chest and dropped him like a ninepin and Allison screamed out into the water, *'You're killing all my people!'* He saw Lew. He reached out for him. Something hard hit the water beside him and for a single mad moment he thought it might be a duck or a nightbird hunting for minnows.

78

The dawn was coming up. He saw a flash from a warehouse on the shore. The flashes were coming from there.

Crazy. Crazy. Allison, underwater, reached for his gun.

He saw Lew's hand, reaching out for him: a claw covered in blood and he grasped it and thought—

Something touched the side of his head: a great unstoppable metal weight, but so lightly that he thought he had not been touched at all, and with his hand still grasping Lew's, he floated still and dead in the water with only the faintest look of curious surprise on his face.

On the night boat they were all dead and it drifted for a little before the other boats arrived, then, slowly, holed and torn in secret places out of sight, it began to wallow like a raft, and washing the blood and tissue on its decks regularly and evenly out through the gunwales into the sea as if, sure of salvage, there was all the time left in the world.

*

Dawn. Corporal Sakutaro Ozawa of the Japanese Imperial Army 38th Division in Hong Kong saw, for the last time in his life, the glory of the rising sun in the east.

It gave him great joy and happiness and, at long last, at its closing, sliding the rifle back into the rolled-up net and beginning to move, he regretted his life not at all.

7

'Radio Hong Kong. News at Nine . . .'
All the news was bad.

*

On the phone the Commander's voice asked with concern, 'Did you know him? Allison?' He must have had the same batch of ghastly photographs on his desk that Feiffer had. One of them showed Allison floating with half his head blown away and globules of water on his cheeks that made him look as if a moment before the bullet hit he had been crying. The others, of the wreckage of his boat and the dead deckhands, showed . . .

'Yes, I knew him. As a matter of fact—' Feiffer turned the photograph on his desk face down but the image remained. Feiffer said, 'Look, Neal, I've been reading the statement Lew made in the ambulance and I get the distinct impression from what he says that the first bang he heard wasn't a fuel tank exploding at all, it was a blank cartridge being fired in the engine room. I've been in touch with Forensic on the scene by radio and they say they've located the engine room door and as well as having Super Glue on it it's got a bloody great ragged hole blown through it surrounded by powder burns.' Allison had had two children, one of them the same age as Feiffer's pre-school son. Feiffer said, 'I get the feeling that whoever set up the arrangement in Lew's boat wanted to give him time to get clear before it went up and that Allison's coming on the scene made him nothing more than just—'

'Than just what? A convenient target?'

'No.' Feiffer paused. 'For the person who set up the blank

cartridge and the explosives I don't think he was any sort of target at all.' The dead deckhands had been laid out in a row on the swamped launch for the photographers. Feiffer said, 'I think whoever set the charges could have quite easily have given them an instantaneous fuse set to ignite the moment the door was tried, and I think, even if he hadn't the wit or the equipment to do that, he could have shot every one of Lew's men off the deck like ninepins while the launch was still at the wharf. By the time the shooting actually did start Lew's people were about six miles away and still running.' Feiffer said cautiously, 'Neal, I hate to sound like Nero Wolfe sitting in his barricaded house in New York growing orchids and solving cases by remote control, but I think there are at least two different courses of action going on and at least one of them we don't understand at all.'

The Commander said with heavy irony, 'And one of those courses was Corporal Sakutaro Ozawa that well known geriatric Jap who, like his mate, Sergeant Seichiro Tanino, late of the Cuttlefish Lane fishmarkets, so conveniently left us his obi and family snaps for our delight and inspection. 'Right?' He waited for Feiffer to say, 'Yes.'

Feiffer said, 'Am I allowed to say yes?'

The Commander said, 'What is the other one?'

'The other one is whoever keeps ringing us up telling us what imperalist pigs we are. The other one is someone who either doesn't or won't realise that in the Colonial repression stakes the Japanese Imperial Army only ran a close second to Julius Caesar and Adolf Hitler combined.' Feiffer said quickly, thinking of Allison, 'The other one is the one who set up rifles across from us that in the course of firing Christ knows how many rounds didn't hit a single living human being, and the other one is the one who loads the first link of his machine gun belt with a blank so even bloody Auden has the time to realise he hasn't been killed and get down under the field of fire.' Feiffer said, 'And his mates, the Japanese soldiers—'

The Commander said, 'No.'

'The alleged Japanese soldiers—'

'Not even that, Harry.' The Commander said, 'So far so good.'

'What, the logic or the politics?'

The Commander said, 'Go on.'

Feiffer said, 'I think that someone's found a Japanese arsenal and he's decided to use it. I think all this bullshit about colonial repression is just a mask to cover whatever he's planning to use it for—'

The Commander said, 'Kids? Are you saying that kids found this dump and they—'

'No, I'm not saying it's kids. I'm saying that the arsenal came first and he sat down and decided how best he could use it and he came up with a primary idea and that the notion that the best way to go about achieving that idea was to convince us that he's some sort of Masked Anti Imperialist Avenger and that—'

The Commander said with gratitude, 'Anything that lets the Japanese angle out. Anything that—'

Feiffer said, 'And I think that he found something else in that Arsenal that—'

The Commander said warningly, 'What? A few old photographs and obis and—'

'No, some *one*!' Feiffer said desperately, 'What else have we got to go on? According to Christopher O'Yee—'

The Commander said, 'I can't ask the Japanese for the location of their secret arsenals during the Second World War (a) because I can't ask the Japanese anything, and (b)—'

'I know. And (b) because all the papers giving their locations were destroyed.'

'They were. Most of them were kept in Tokyo until the bombings and then they were moved for safety to Nagasaki. And those that weren't went with the 38th Division to Guadalcanal.' The thing about diplomacy was that there were always reasons to say no. The Commander said, 'And if the arsenal is still here some forty years later it must have been bombed so we wouldn't find it anyway even if we had the location. And with redevelopment in this Colony—'

Feiffer said, 'Neal, I think our non lethal kid or maniac or whatever he is is being followed around by whoever else lives or was found in that arsenal!'

'Not by a bloody Second World War hold-out Japanese soldier!'

'No.' Feiffer said, 'No, *by a whole bloody section of them*!' The picture of Allison would not go from his mind. Feiffer said, 'Neal, please, can't we get the Japanese Embassy in on this? Would it hurt so much?'

'Yes! It'd hurt so much!' The Commander said violently, 'I'm not the bloody ogre in this. I've got my orders. Politicians have given me my orders and the economic advisers have given me my orders and the bloody London government have given me my orders!' He paused for a moment in frustration, 'Just let them thank God that they, unlike me, don't have to go around this morning and tell Allison's wife and his children what those bloody orders have led to! And they can thank God that—'

Feiffer said quietly, 'I was best man at Allison's wedding. I've already told them.' He paused with his hand on the photographs, waiting.

There was a long silence, then the Commander said with a sigh, 'Harry, do you know anyone at the Japanese Embassy?'

'O'Yee does, yes!'

There was a long pause.

The Commander said, 'Then ring them.'

'Neal, no one official need know. All of it can be kept totally—'

The Commander said fiercely, 'I don't give a damn! Ring them. And that's an order!' There was a silence as if the Commander, for a moment, listened to hear a tap on his line.

The Commander said again, clearly, not caring who heard, 'Ring them! *Ring them*!'

*

On the phone Mickey Okuno at the Japanese Embassy said happily in English, 'Christopher, everything I have is yours: my wife, my hibachi, my holiday house in the clear fresh air beneath the chimneys of the Mitsui leather tanning factories, the shirt from my back—but if you're after a free ticket to the Tokyo-Nagoya baseball final this season you can forget it.' Okuno's accent, after a Master's in Political Science at Berkeley was as perfect as Berkeley could make it. Okuno said, 'Tell me what you want, oh honourable flatfoot, and it shall be yours.'

O'Yee said evenly, 'I want a Japanese interpreter with a knowledge of nineteen forties military slang and usage and the mentality that went with it.'

There was a silence, then Okuno said, just as evenly, 'Is that you, Christopher? For a moment I thought I had a crossed line and I was talking to a cop or something.'

O'Yee said coldly, 'This is a cop and I'm making a request for—'

There was a brief pause and then Okuno said, 'And this is the Information Officer at the Japanese Embassy, Hong Bay, in the British Crown Colony of Hong Kong and those fucking rifles, ass-hole, are English or Canadian or something and have got nothing to do with us!'

'Mickey—'

Nothing.

O'Yee said, 'Mickey, we're in a lot of trouble. We've lost—' He hesitated. 'We've lost five of our officers and half a dozen bloody civilians and I get this bastard ringing up in Japanese and—'

Okuno said, 'No, you don't. You don't get any bastard ringing up in Japanese and that's official, and if you do it isn't a Japanese bastard, it's just some bastard who speaks Japanese!' Okuno said, 'Forget it. The war's been over a long, long time and we're not like the Germans going around suffering guilt pangs about it, we just want to forget it!' Okuno said, 'You want someone who speaks a few words of Japanese nineteen forties slang? O.K. 'Tora! Tora! Tora!' How's that?'

'I'm not trying to resurrect the war.'

'Good! Because it's staying buried!' Okuno said, 'Detective Senior Inspector, if you've got an official request to make to this Embassy then you have your Government make it and my

84

Government will consider it and then my Government will inform your Government—'

'I need someone who can talk these bastards in!'

'Talk them in where?'

'In! Safe! Someone who can make them understand—'

'Who the hell is "them"?'

'The spokesmen. The two who ring up. The spokesmen for the rest of them! The—'

'The rest of what?' Okuno said in a gasp, 'God, they're true, aren't they? The rumours. There's a hold-out, isn't there? There's a World War Two hold-out Japanese soldier on this island from forty years ago and he—' He stopped. 'What do you mean, "the rest of them"? *How many are there?*'

'*We don't know.*'

Okuno said, 'You don't mean there's a platoon of them, do you? You don't mean there's a—'

O'Yee said, 'A private interpreter, that's all I'm asking. Just someone the Embassy can recommend. A Chinese, for Christ's sake—'

'Oh, great! What the hell do you think we Japanese go around learning Chinese and English for? A Japanese speaking Chinese who understands the military slang of the nineteen forties—' Okuno almost shrieked, 'Under what circumstances do you think he would have learned it?'

'No one's asking to bring up the actrocity stories all over again!'

There was a hard silence, then Okuno said in a brittle voice, 'Oh. Were they atrocities? Were they? According to our code, is that what they were?' His voice became tight, 'Sorry, did we commit atrocities? Sorry, haven't we become westernised fast enough for everyone? Sorry. The dirty cruel Nips have done it again.' The conversation was going all bad. Okuno said, 'Yeah. Right. Shit. Just like Berkeley. Atrocities. Right. Just hang on a second while I put in my buck teeth dentures and settle my pebble glasses and then I can say in my hissing tone of voice, "Ah, dirty White Race" while I stick a few bamboo slivers up your fingernails.' Okuno said, 'Find your own fucking interpreter! And when you do, make sure you tell him to remember to tell the hold-outs that on the orders of General Macarthur the Emperor isn't a god anymore, but just a nice old man who lives in his Palace studying marine biology—*all right?*'

O'Yee said quietly, 'I'll do that.'

'Good.' Okuno said. 'Do you intend to make an official request? If you do I'll log it.' His voice was formal, stiff. 'Well?'

O'Yee defeated, said softly, 'No.'

There was a silence then Okuno said, 'Don't mistake it, Christopher, never, never mistake it. You're like me: the product of two worlds, but, at base, I know exactly who I am.' Okuno said, 'I only sound like an American, but what I am is a Japanese. You, you look almost like a Chinese and you are—what?' Okuno asked, 'Do you know?'

'Right now, what I am is mud.' The Commander had been right. O'Yee saw Feiffer looking at him with concern on his face.

Okuno said in a strange, sad voice, 'O'Yee-san, hazimete o-me ni kakarimas' ...' (Mr O'Yee, I meet you for the first time.)

'I don't understand.'

Okuno said quietly in English a moment before he finally hung up, 'No, I know you don't. And the pity of it is that I'd never, never realised it until now.'

*

In the underground arsenal The Technician sat on a stone arms shelf facing The Bannin transferring blocks of explosive from their tattered khaki bags into hessian sacks. The explosive was dry and intact and he broke a little off like chocolate and smelled it. Behind the Major the steel door to the other room was shut. The Bannin had his head bowed in thought, touching at the top of one of his polished leather boots and worrying at the flap. The Technician said without looking up, 'Corporal Ozawa?'

The Bannin said in Cantonese, 'He's dead. Like Sergeant Tanino.' A short disembowelling sword was across his knees and he rested his gloved hands on its scabbard and drew a breath,

86

'They were both old men. At their respective moments they died like birds, without murmur, and their souls—' The Bannin said, 'We have all resolved to die in battle, those of us who are able, and the rest—'

The Technician, still looking at the explosives, said quietly, 'All right.'

The Major said sadly, "One Hundred Million Will Die Together." That was what the Emperor promised.'

'Yes.'

The Major said, '"The survivors will them engage in general battle."'

It was no use at all. The Technician said, 'Those people on the boat—'

The Bannin said, 'Enemies.' He brightened up, 'Corporal Ozawa's obi and his family pictures are by now on their way to his home and his family—'

The Technician said quietly, 'You promised to help me.' There was no emotion in his voice. He was merely probing. The Technician said, 'The divine mission to eradicate the uniformed—'

The Bannin made a hissing sound.

'I see.' The Technician clenched his mouth for a moment to hold back the anger and the tears. The Technician said with a sniff. 'It seemed all right to you when we talked about it. When we finally found each other—'

The Bannin said, 'Things have changed.' He looked down at the sword, 'All my people are old. All my—' He said quickly, 'Private Masuo Morishita will be next to go with you. He wants to be next. Ozawa was his friend and he wants to be next.'

'Nobody has to go! Nobody has to die! Nobody has to die!' The Technician said in sudden vehement anger, 'Nobody has to—'

'Everybody! And then when everybody but me has gone, then I will go.' The Bannin touched at the sword and then held it. 'And you, you have promised to assist me at the end so I can find a glorious soldier's death! You, you have promised me—'

'And what about your promises to me? What about the—'

87

'Children's talk!' The Bannin started to stand up, drawing the sword. The Bannin said, 'All this colonial—all this—we were the. colonists! We held Asia like a trembling butterfly, but we— Honourable death is not a course or a choice, it is a necessity!' The Bannin said, 'Private Morishita will be next and you will lead him to the place.' The Bannin pulled at the steel door and was gone for a moment before returning with a rolled up object in his hand. The Bannin said, 'Here! This is our banner. It will be burned so as not to fall into the hands of the enemy and then we will do as you ask and fulfil your little plan and at the same time, culminate our own!'

It was all no use. The Technician said, 'Bannin—'

It was all no use. Totally, utterly, no use at all.

The Technician said, 'All right.' He heard the sea start to thunder against the rocks, as at 9.40 a.m. the tide change began.

The Technician said again, 'All right. If that's what you want. You can rely on me.'

The Bannin nodded. 'You are a good Chinaman and you will be rewarded.'

Cain and Abel. It came back to The Technician from Bible Study class he had once attended in the English Middle School in Hanford Road. The Technician said in Japanese, 'Thank you very much, Major Takashima.'

The Technician looked hard at The Bannin's eyes, but somehow failed to find them. They were not looking at him and The Technician thought that if he was going to do anything it had to be done today, before the man made everything go wrong.

The Technician, resolved on a course of murder, touched at the explosive charges between his knees.

He looked hard at his brother's polished leather boots and only concerned himself now with the best means by which to do it.

*

In the intensive care unit of St Paul de Chartres' Hospital Lew said so softly that Spencer had to lean over his bed to hear him,

'Did he get everybody, Mr Spencer?'

Spencer glanced at Auden. Auden was standing near the end of the bed with something in his hand, shuffling awkwardly from foot to foot. The smell of antiseptic and post-operative vomit and sputum was very strong in the room.

Spencer said quietly, 'Yes, I'm afraid he did.'

'And Allison?' There was pain in Lew's eyes. The pupils seemed to be swimming through a mist that kept building up and then, as the man grimaced, receded and then built up again.

Spencer said, 'Yes.'

'They're all dead except me?'

Spencer said with a smile, 'You're not going to die. You've got a broken shoulder and a little bit of extra ventilation in your uniform, but you're going to be all right.'

Lew said with effort, 'I didn't see a thing. The smoke—'

'We know. Your crew have made statements and—'

Lew said, 'Stupid goddamned Pan. He said he couldn't read the words because of the smoke. He said—' The pain in his eyes welled up and he had to pause, 'I thought for a moment that I'd—' Lew said in a gasp, 'I want a medal for him. I don't care who I have to see or who I have to beg: Allison came over to save me and I want a medal for him.' He was on the edge of tears. He asked again, 'Is he dead? Are you sure he's—' He saw Auden's hand as the man brought it to his face to try to clear some of the smell from his nose. Lew said, 'Is that them?'

Auden brought his hand down quickly.

Lew said, 'In that bag you've got. Is that them? The bullets? Are they the—'

Auden said, 'Yes.' He lifted up the plastic bag.

Lew said in Chinese, 'So many? Did he use so many? To kill— everyone?'

Spencer said softly, 'You're O.K. now. It's just a broken shoulder. You were lucky.'

Lew said, 'Which one of those did they take out of me?' His grip was going and he was drifting away with the effects of the drugs. Lew said, 'I want it. I want the bullet. Which one of the bullets is mine? I want the bullet and I want it reloaded and I want a gun that'll fire it and then I want—' His eyes lost focus and he couldn't seem to remember what he was saying.

Auden said softly, 'Come on, Bill.'

Lew said vaguely, 'The bullet—'

Auden said, 'Sure. You've got my word on it. It's yours. Just as soon as we've finished with it—'

Lew said, 'I can't. I can't hate whoever did it. I can't keep thinking of him long enough to hate him. I just keep thinking of Allison and how I never liked him and how—'Lew said in a sudden blaze, 'I want that bullet!'

Spencer said quietly, 'Lew . . .' but the man was already asleep and Spencer, straightening up, looked at the package in Auden's hand.

There were only some of the bullets in the package. The rest were still in dead men laid out on steel trays in the Mortuary in body bags and they still had to be recovered.

Lew's bullet, at least, had come out of a living man.

If it had been a bullet at all.

In fact, it had been a single three quarter inch ball bearing with a hole drilled through it, and, because he thought it was something special and it made a pair with the one from Cuttlefish Lane, Auden had it not in the packet with the rest, but bagged, labelled and safe in his inside coat pocket.

He looked at Lew's face on the pillow and touched at the bulge the object made in his pocket with his hand.

*

In the charge room of the Station, Ah Pin the cleaner swept at a mound of white masonry from the ceiling and scooped it up in his cut open five gallon drum scooper. No less than eighty years old, he was bent over from a lifetime of sweeping and Feiffer could swear that he had one arm which was longer than the other from leaning forward to simultaneously sweep, scoop, then scoop again.

90

Ah Pin said abruptly in a clear Cantonese enunciation that surprised Feiffer, 'Not far from here, during the Occupation, there was the Murder Verandah.' He went on sweeping, not looking up. 'During the Occupation, the Japanese Secret Police used to tie spies they'd caught in chairs and sit them out on the verandah of a hotel and torture them as an example to others.' He looked up at the ceiling where the masonry had come from, and at the bullet hole that had brought it down, 'Important spies and saboteurs: people who picked up twigs off the ground for firewood and people who painted their coal white and used them as paving stones to store them secretly for the winter, and people who—' Ah Pin said abruptly, not looking at Feiffer or anything but the dust, 'On the waterfront, that was a Japanese gun. I've heard them before.'

Feiffer said quickly, 'Those particular sort of Japanese guns?'

'No, just Japanese guns.' Ah Pin said, 'I've heard them before.' He looked through to the Detectives' Room where O'Yee was on the phone talking in Cantonese to someone from the Tourist Office about someone who might speak wartime Japanese and no, he couldn't explain why he wanted to know, but was it possible, was it possible that they knew someone who—.

Ah Pin said quietly, 'The Fireworks Man speaks Japanese.' He was an interpreter at the Murder Verandah hotel for the Japanese.' He looked up. He was at least eighty. There was something in his face that made Feiffer pause. Ah Pin said, 'But in reality he was a member of the BAAG—the resistance.' Ah Pin said, 'In those days a lot of people learned to speak Japanese.'

Feiffer said, 'Do you? Do you speak Japanese?'

'No.' There was no expression in Ah Pin's voice. It could have been true or false, but it was never going to change. Ah Pin said philosophically, 'That's why he prospered after the war, why he got his fireworks licence. He trained in Japan—with his displays and his fireworks—and the Japanese brought him back here after the invasion to interpret for them.' He said again. 'He was a member of the resistance. After the war he was checked carefully and his good deeds outweighed his bad so he was allowed to live.' He gave Feiffer a cracked smile, 'We all got government jobs after the war or we got special consideration for licences and trading concessions when the British came back—everyone who was in the resistance and who wasn't a Communist. We were called the British Army Aid Group, the resistance. Good Chinamen. Good loyal subjects of the King.' He went on sweeping, 'Depending on what we did or what job we had.'

'Will he help?'

'I don't know,' Ah Pin said. 'He was never any more than an interpreter. At his trial he said he often lied to the Japanese about what people said so some of the spies they caught escaped, but—' Ah Pin said with no trace of irony, 'It was all a long, long time ago and now we are all in our assigned, trusted places depending on what sort of men we were then.'

Feiffer said, 'What were you?'

'Now, I am a sweeper of police stations.'

Feiffer said nothing.

'And The Fireworks Man who was a fireworks man before he was an interpreter is back to being a fireworks man again.' Ah Pin said quietly, 'He may help you. But nobody wants to remember.'

Feiffer had seen the man every day of his life for so many years he had lost count. He had always been old. Feiffer said, 'Ah Pin, is there anything I can do to get you back your old job?'

'No.' Ah Pin smiled at him, 'I have it. Before the war, I was also a sweeper of police stations.' Ah Pin said, 'Sixty one years and not once have I missed a day's work.'

Ah Pin said quietly, 'During the war I was an engraver. I left men's crimes engraved with a razor in their bodies.' He saw Feiffer's face and looked down at the broom, 'I was loyal and as you can see, I have been returned to my proper occupation in life.' Ah Pin said, 'I am well satisfied.'

Ah Pin said, 'Ask The Fireworks Man. He knew the war-time Japanese. Ask him.'

He went on sweeping.

Feiffer looked into the Detectives' Room.

He could see O'Yee looking upset about his friend at the Japanese Embassy, Mickey Okuno, but in that moment as Ah Pin went on sweeping, Feiffer could think of absolutely nothing to say to him to make it seem right.

*

11.03 a.m. As The Technician drove the stolen furniture van onto a deserted hill in a public park overlooking the harbour he leaned out of the cab and glanced up at the position of the sun.

He was early. He knew where Private Morishita would stand and he was early.

He was resolved.

The spot he had chosen was well away from the paths and the lunchtime crowds would come nowhere near him.

11.04 a.m.

The Technician waited.

He had his fuses and his paraphernalia in the cab alongside him and he knew exactly, when the time came, how they would act.

11.06 a.m. He leaned out of the cab again and looked at the position of the sun.

He waited.

8

Once at the drains, lucky. Twice...

Standing in dejection at the entrance to one of the gaping black holes on the seafront, Auden said quietly, 'That bastard on the roof shot me. He blew all my chances and he shot me with a blank.' He had the two ball bearings in packets in his hand and he clicked them together and took a mental blood-oath. Auden said, 'He blew it for me whoever he was. I was doing fine with the cases we found and then some bastard had to set up something on a roof and shoot me with a blank.' He clicked again, 'I was doing O.K. I was just starting to think like a senior officer and now all I can think of is getting hold of whoever did it and blowing his fucking head off.' Auden said, 'What have I got to redeem myself? Two fucking ball bearings.' He said in utter despondency to Spencer, 'I'll never get to make senior inspector, I'll just spend the rest of my life like Buster Keaton being shot over and over by blank cartridges while the entire Police Mess sit around laughing at me.' He reached the nadir, 'And then, after the Examining Board have finished I'll be going around saying "Yes, sir" even to you.'

There was a half dead minnow flopping around in the sand at Spencer's feet trying to get back to the water. Spencer gave it a gentle push and it made it. Spencer said, 'No, you're a good cop. We found the cartridges together. If it hadn't been for you I wouldn't have even gone in there.

Auden said, 'If it hadn't been for you yelling to everyone that it was only a blank I'd have looked even stupider by starting to do my dead act on the fucking roof.' Auden said reasonably, 'I thought I'd been shot. Anyone would.'

'Sure.'

94

'Well, *you* didn't! *You* knew it was a blank!' Auden said, 'What the hell have we got? Two ball bearings and that's it, one from Lew and the other one—the other one could have been dropped by anyone.'

'They've both got holes drilled through them.'

'For all I know every ball bearing on Earth has got a hole drilled in it!' Auden said evilly as, for some mad reason, the minnow flopped back to suffocate and he watched it gasp, 'I don't think I'll worry about the promotion. I think I'll just let all the clever buggers solve all the cases and then I'll just come in at the kill like some dumb fucking blunt instrument and beat people up!' Auden said, 'Maybe that's why I haven't been promoted before. Maybe I'm just too dumb.' He looked down at the dying minnow and couldn't bring himself to punish it by prolonging its life. (Spencer gave it a gentle nudge with his shoe and it went back into the water.) Auden said, 'According to Harry, there may be two courses of action happening at the same time: the bloody Jap snipers and the inoffensive little bugger who sets up blanks and safe fields of fire to—' He protested to the heavens, 'Why am I falling back on what Harry says? Why haven't I got any ideas of my own?'

'You have a lot of ideas.'

Auden said, 'Leaving aside putting a .357 through the gut of the guy who shot me with a blank, name one!'

Spencer said, 'Well, um—'

The fish came back to the sand. Auden stomped on it. Auden said, 'I'll put a hole through someone's little ball bearing—!' He looked down at the fish and saw it drill its way back to the surface. Spencer bent down and put it back in the sea. Auden said, 'Hey, if a ball bearing is solid nickel steel and it's meant to protect the moving parts of a steel machine from wearing out, how the fuck do you drill a hole in it? With more steel?'

Spencer felt embarrassed. Spencer said, 'With a diamond tipped drill.' The minnow was definitely looking on its last legs. Spencer said gently, 'I wish you wouldn't keep—'

Auden said, 'You don't drill a hole in a ball bearing! It's crazy.

What for? A ball bearing spins—it turns : It isn't a disc turning on an axis, it's a ball that runs round and round and—' Spencer put the minnow back into the water and it climbed out again. Auden said, 'Unless you—' He got one of the objects out of its plastic bag and tested its weight in his hand. Auden said, 'Unless you—'

Looking at the crushed fish, Spencer made a tutting sound.

Auden said, 'Look!' He scraped his fingernail across the nickel of the ball that had come out of Lew's shoulder and a tiny sliver of nickel flaked off and showed grey underneath. Auden said, 'This isn't a ball bearing at all! It's fucking lead nickeled over to look like a ball bearing! That's how they drilled the hole in it. It's only lead!' He got out the other one, 'They both are!' The minnow came up for air and he kicked sand on it.

Spencer said, 'Listen, leave the fish alone!'

Auden said, 'What?' He looked down at it and then at Spencer's face. Poor bastard. Spencer was just never going to make it to the higher reaches of his profession. Auden said, 'You stupid bastard, that isn't a fish, it's a crab without a shell. Don't keep putting it in the water. It lives underground.'

So did the man who had drilled out the lead ball bearing.

Auden said, 'Shit! I've got it!' Auden said, Queeg-like, 'Click, click, click . . . I've fuckingwell got it! *I even know what it is!*' He held the two balls lightly in his thumbs and fingertips, pinching them slightly by the nails and said, tapping them together, 'Yeah? A section of Japanese soldiers from World War Two, is it? Yeah? Is it?' He went click, click, click, Auden said, 'Yeah? Is it really?' Auden, the senior inspector, demanded, holding the balls up on invisible strings, 'Well? Quick! What is it?'

Spencer said, 'Newton's Cradle. It's part of Newton's Cradle. It's an executive *toy.*'

Auden said with the sweetest of grins, 'Isn't it though? Isn't it though?' He could have kissed himself, Auden said, 'Isn't that, just exactly, precisely, what it is?' Auden said in triumph, '*Yeah!*'

Spencer glanced down at the shell-less crab on the sand.

In fact, it was a minnow, but the odds too much against it, it decided instead to become a corpse and expired on the spot.

*

He had been careful. The furniture van had come from the rear of a shop specialising in the restoration of heavy antique furniture for rich Europeans on the Peak and The Technician, knowing what was inside, calculated the position of the sun and parked it carefully in just the right spot.

He had time to spare.

He thought of Private Morishita watching with his rifle and his rolled up flag and he contemplated his destruction.

The Technician felt a pang of sorrow for someone he had never had a chance to know, but it was nothing the someone would return so he put it from his mind.

The Technician said quietly, 'Bannin, you were never any brother of mine.'

Divine mission to eradicate all the uniformed forces of colonial repression in the world.

It had seemed such a good idea at the time.

The Japanese.

Maybe all the stories about them in the war were true.

No, he *knew* they were.

And, in the end, they were going to make him a very rich young man indeed.

*

In the Detectives' Room, O'Yee said to no one in particular, 'My grandfather lived to be eighty nine years old and the only reason he isn't with us still is that he couldn't stand the suspense of waiting for the end so he killed himself to spare himself the worry.'

11.47 a.m.

The telephone on his desk was silent.

He lit a cigarette and put the burnt match carefully into his ashtray so as not to dirty up Ah Pin's nice clean floor and, glancing at the photographs of the dead from the launch Feiffer had left on his desk before he went out, wished he had had his grandfather's foresight.

*

In his underground vaults The Keeper Of Secrets said softly to himself, 'Come on, Owlin, *how?* How? *How?*'

He was in the labyrinths. As far as he could see in the dimly lit corridors there were papers and books, runs of periodicals, letters, diaries, reports, White Papers, everything the Colony had ever known since—

In the heavy silence Owlin's voice said, 'Come on, how? *How?*'

How to find a buried Japanese arsenal on the waterfront using trees?

How, with only one side of the story did you find the other?'

How?

A buried arsenal.

Buried by what?

By bombing? None of the Japanese papers from that period were there and the Hong Kong Occupation news sheets would never have been allowed to print that the glorious Imperial Empire was at last under attack from the skies, that—

Nineteen hundred and forty two. By forty three the Thirty Eighth Division was gone to Guadalcanal where they were slaughtered.

Nineteen hundred and forty two.

Owlin went to a shelf packed with yellowing single sheet newspapers headed *Occupation Newspapers And Official Proclamations Issued To Hong Kong Residents 1941 to 45, File Only, Not To Be Removed. For Office Consultation Only.*

He leafed through the pages.

Sunday August the 25th, 1942, Wharf Cove, Hop Pei Cove, Reservoir Bay—

Blackout.

After that Sunday there had been a blackout imposed.

98

That Sunday the first American bombers had hit.

... Wharf Cove, Hop Pei Cove, Reservoir Bay...

Monday September the first, 1942:

The blackout was extended to Hong Bay East, the area surrounding Beach Road and...

RESTRICTED AREAS.

The Japanese Government in Hong Kong informs residents that certain reconstruction works will be carried out in the Wharf Cove and Reservoir Bay districts beginning Wednesday, September third and that any persons found in these restricted areas or in possession of military objects from these areas will be shot.

Long Live The Greater Asia Co-Prosperity Sphere!

(Signed) Area Officer, Engineers

Imperial Japanese Army in China.

The military objects were bits and pieces of American bombs, and what?

And bits and pieces of damaged underground arsenals.

Owlin said quietly, 'Well, well, well...'

All he needed was a bombing map.

He walked to another labyrinth, flicking overhead lamps on as he went until he came to a section marked, *AIR FORCE, U.S.*

He even had the flight briefings of some of the pilots who had led the raids.

He touched at the first diary on the shelf and, opening it at the first page, felt the paper and, knowing that once, once that page had been made from a living tree, felt for the first time in his life, a strange, revengeful pleasure.

*

On the phone Feiffer's voice said curiously, 'Christopher, are you sure the address you gave me for The Fireworks Man is correct?' He paused for a moment and it surprised O'Yee that there was absolutely no sound of the city behind his call, 'I mean, *our* Fireworks Man. You're sure you got the right address from the files?'

O'Yee said, 'Where are you?'

'Well, I'm out at Maltby Point which is a bit like saying I'm out at the Eddystone Lighthouse.' Feiffer said, 'I had to leave the car at the end of a pebble road and then I spent twenty minutes wandering along the perimeter of what I assumed was at the very least a nuclear missile base before I realised it was the fence of a fireworks factory.' Feiffer said, 'The address you gave me is Maltby Point. I assumed it was probably a row of shanty houses. There's a bloody great sign saying that anybody who attempts to pass a point here carrying matches, metal or explosive or inflammable substances is liable to about five hundred years under the Dangerous Substances Ordnance, not to mention High Treason, and I thought before I handed in my boy scouts' tinder box and gun I'd better find out who the hell I was handing it in to.' Feiffer said, 'I'm ringing from a phone box a little way from the main entrance that's so isolated that not even the vandals have found it.' Feiffer said, 'It's incredible. The place is huge. Apart from the wooden two storey office building there are rows of wooden factory buildings and wooden storage huts and—would you believe, wooden cranes? We have got the right man, haven't we? I seem to remember The Fireworks Man as that rather disreputable bugger in a singlet and shorts that Auden and Spencer dragged out with them when they went listening for gunshots. What's his actual address?'

O'Yee said, 'Maltby Point is his actual address. He owns the whole shebang. That disreputable bugger in singlet and shorts is worth a cool couple of million dollars in terms of land alone.'

Feiffer said, thinking of Okuno, 'How are you feeling?'

'Fine. How should I be feeling?'

'You should be feeling fine.' Feiffer asked, 'No more calls?'

'No.'

There was a pause and then Feiffer said, 'O.K. I'll hand in my six shooter and silver mounted Bill Durham tobacco pouch.'

O'Yee said, 'That's *Bull* Durham.'

'Oh.' Feiffer said, 'Well, you should know.'

'*Why* should I know?'

'You're the resident American, not me.' Feiffer said, 'You did know though, didn't you?'

'Look, I'm not feeling bad about Okuno. All right?' O'Yee said, 'Thanks anyway, but—'

Feiffer said, 'It never ceases to surprise me how you can wander down a street in Hong Kong avoiding people who look like ten cents and never know they're worth—'

O'Yee said with irritation, 'Well, that's the bloody Chinese for you, isn't it? They don't like advertising their wealth!' O'Yee said, 'Look, I appreciate what you're doing, but you don't have to ring up and tell me what a good guy I am because Okuno has got me thinking I'm a shit, because I don't think I'm a shit!' O'Yee said, 'I made a boo-boo and lost a friend, that's all. You know better than I do about the bloody Chinese and it hasn't surprised you one iota that the local tramp is the official money lender to Howard Hughes because you've been here longer than I have and in the first place you wouldn't have made the mistake of ringing up bloody Okuno anyway! You'd have had more sense!' O'Yee said with difficulty, 'My grandfather lived to be eighty nine years old and the only reason he isn't with us still is that—'

Feiffer said, 'His friends all got around and smothered him with misconceived concern. Right?'

O'Yee said, 'That's right!'

Feiffer said, 'Look, it was my fault. When the Commander said we could ring someone at the Embassy I automatically thought of your friend Okuno—'

O'Yee glanced at the clock. It was 12.06. Ah Pin was in the charge room, out of earshot. O'Yee said, 'Harry, what are you doing—worrying about me?'

There was no reply.

O'Yee said, 'Are you there?'

There was another silence and then Feiffer said with a clucking sound, '*Bull* Durham. I'll remember.'

O'Yee said quietly, 'I appreciate it.' 12.08. There was no one else in the Detectives' Room. O'Yee said in his best Texas drawl,

'Say, pard, thanks for droppin' by. It gits a mite lonesome out here on the prairie when there's nary a—'

Feiffer said, 'O.K., I'll take my Bull Durham and I'll wander over to the Marshal's office here and deposit my hog's leg.

'You haven't got a hog's leg! A hog's leg is a long barreled Single Action Army—' O'Yee said, 'Forget it.' He looked down at his desk and smiled. O'Yee said with a grin, 'You know, with you around, maybe my old grandad might have made it to ninety.'

12.08 p.m.

He lit a cigarette and looked around for the ashtray and found that somehow, secretly, to cheer him up, Ah Pin had slipped him the cleanest one in the place.

*

Outside *Technotrex Toys And Games* in Wyang Street, Auden said urgently to the ticking of Spencer's stopwatch, 'I can take it out, Bill.' He watched the silver balls clicking in the shop window next to a display of chess computers and nickel plated toy Blondins balancing on metal wires designed to soothe the executive mind and said again with emphasis, 'There's just enough time if I see the smoke to get to his set-up and take it out before it starts working. I know there is.'

The clicking balls, five of them, were suspended from a central pivot by what looked like fishing line. The idea was that you drew back one ball and let it go and, miraculously, on a principle discovered by Isaac Newton, the force was transferred through the other three and caused the fifth, the one at the far end, to click out like a pendulum. It was supposed to soothe the minds of frazzled executives. Auden said, 'What he has to do is draw back the last ball and set it with some sort of fuse or string and then burn it through to make a timing device, then when the ball hits, it transfers the whack through to the trigger of the set-up rifle and fires it.'

Spencer said, 'The rifle must be set upside down with the trigger guard taken off.' He watched the balls clicking with one

102

eye on the stop-watch. 'It's very reliable.'

Auden said, 'And then the principle is that the last ball clicking back again hits the next in line and transfers the force back to the first which flies out and then hits the one next to it and repeats the process.' He said, 'That's how he gets the gun to keep on shooting. The ball keeps going back and hitting the trigger every time until it—' He asked, 'What's the timing between hits?'

Spencer said with a wary shake of his head, 'Less than one and a quarter seconds. If they were using the technique down in the drains then it was taking longer.' The balls in the shop window display were the same size exactly as the ones in Auden's pocket. Spencer said, 'I don't think you should make too much of what timing the one in the window's got. There's the question of recoil when it's tied up to a gun and you don't even know how far out the first ball was pulled to start the pendulum effect.' Spencer said, 'We know how it's done. That's something anyway. Sooner or later—'

Auden said, 'Sooner or later he's going to use it again.' He looked earnestly at Spencer. 'I cane take it out, Bill. After the smoke there's a period of time before the fuse or whatever it is burns through and then there's a blank before the live rounds start so that gives me—what? Three plus say two plus say two seconds before the first round—that's all of nine or ten seconds.'

Spencer said with alarm, 'That's seven!'

Auden said, 'Christ, in seven seconds an Olympic runner could get—'

'You don't happen to be an Olympic runner.' Spencer said, 'If anything, I could run faster than you. I'm thinner—'

Auden said, 'Yeah, but you don't have the motivation to do it.'

'Of course I don't have the motivation to do it!' Spencer said, 'The Army Bomb Disposal people are the ones who have the motivation for this sort of thing, not us—they've got remote control gadgets that can dismantle a bomb without anyone being within fifty yards of the thing!'

Auden said, 'In eight seconds?'

'Seven!' Spencer said, 'It's bloody *seven*!'

103

'Look, if I know the first live round's coming next all I have to do once I get into the hut or shed or wherever it's been set up is just to get to one side and—'

Spencer said, 'And if by any chance it's been set up with instantaneously—' Spencer said, 'Can I remind you that after the set-up goes fizz, fizz, click, click, bang, bang, it then goes ka— BOOM? Can I remind you that—'

Auden, not hearing a word of it, had his gaze fixed firmly on the swinging balls, Auden said, 'Well, what do you think?'

'I've just told you what I think! I think it's crazy!'

Auden said, 'I can do it. I know I can. I'm quick. I've got fast reactions.'

Spencer said in a mutter, 'You'll need them.'

Auden watched the swinging balls. Spencer's watch going tick, tick, tick, tick, echoed the click, click, click, click in his brain.

Auden said, 'And then we'll have all the evidence we'll need: the entire set-up, fingerprints, everything. Leave the Jap thing to the political experts and we'll just come in with all the hard evidence and dump it on their desks and come out whiter than white covered in bloody braid.'

Spencer said, '*We*? Where do I come in when you're doing your imitation of a hazy blur?' Spencer said seriously, 'No, Phil, don't even consider it.'

Auden said, still watching the balls and mesmerized by the steady clicking and ticking, 'No, I'm not considering it, I've decided.' Auden said, 'They get me once on the blank trick, but not twice.'

'What if that's the way they're thinking too and the first round isn't a blank?'

Auden said, 'No, don't worry.' He turned and crossed the road to go to the car, almost being knocked down twice, and, still clicking and ticking and dreaming dreams of glory said to Spencer's alarmed face, 'I'm really light on my feet. I can have the door to a shack down with my shoulder in about half a second flat.' He was smiling and nodding to himself and as he took off straight into the stream of traffic without an indicator light he missed a taxi by an inch and went decisively down towards Yellowthread Street to the stalls to put himself ready to await Starter's Orders.

*

All the names had been changed. The American pilots had been using the names of features on the island used before the Occupation and then the names had been changed by the Japanese during that Occupation and then, after the Occupation, in order to wipe out old memories and commemorate new ones, the toponomists—the namers of streets and features—had changed them again.

And they were only the names in English.

In Chinese all the names of all the streets and all the features and all the landmarks were different and always had been.

And, during the Occupation, the Japanese had changed them too, and then, after the Occupation, the Chinese again, had changed them back, and then—

In the vaults Owlin looked at a bewildering array of maps and briefings and government reports and tapped on his desk with his fingernail.

12.19 p.m.

Somewhere, on one of those maps or in one of those reports or mentioned in one of those briefings, the location of the arsenal awaited him.

As he always did, he set to work from the beginning and began doing the job minutely and slowly, a piece of evidence at a time.

Occasionally, he met a temporary dead end in his researches, but it bothered him not at all and, in the interests of accuracy, like any true scholar, he merely went back to the beginning and, undeterred and unhurried, began again.

*

There was no equivocation. In his picture windowed office

105

overlooking the harbour at Maltby Point The Fireworks Man said, 'No.' His face was set like cement. There was a sign on a door leading from the wooden office to the main factory complexes reading in both English and Chinese, *Absolutely No Unauthorised Persons Past This Point* and the sentiments and finality of the sign were mirrored exactly on The Fireworks Man's face.

The Fireworks Man, sitting at his surprisingly large mahogany desk in his well cut suit and expensive Thai silk tie, said at the helm of his surprisingly large enterprise, 'No. Not again. Not a word of the language. Never again. No. Not for anything anyone can offer me. *No!*'

*

He saw him.

Private Morishita.

He was dressed as a delivery coolie. Carrying a rolled up bolt of cloth he moved across the park to take up his position behind an old World War Two pillbox preserved and sealed in the park as a monument.

The Technician smiled.

The Technician got back into the cab of the van and moved it a few feet as if he was worried that the wheels sat on less than solid ground, and then, getting out again, satisfied, looked at the sun, entered the back of the van carefully, and unhurriedly completed his labours.

9

The Fireworks Man looked at the walls of his office and out through the wooden framed picture window across the compound to the wooden firework assembly huts. Everything in the place was either wood or cement. Feiffer noticed that all the pens and paperclips and even the scissors on his desk were either brass or bamboo—nothing that might cause a spark. The Fireworks Man touched at his own lined face—he wore a single jade ring—and said again, 'No.' He had a strange look on his face, midway between sadness and a smile. 'I'm seventy one years old—you're telling me these people are left-overs from the Occupation?' He said with force, 'I'm a left-over from the Occupation. Not only do these people, according to you, shoot, they *run*!' The Fireworks Man said with heavy irony, 'What have they done? Missed all the stresses of modern life and all the dangers of eating the wrong food by living in their caves for forty years?' He paused for a moment, 'And why are they running and shooting now? Why not ten years ago? Why not twenty?' The Fireworks Man said with rising age-wisdom anger, 'Why not *thirty*?' He looked hard at Feiffer and saw a man in his early forties whose eyes had not even begun to dull with the true comprehension of life, 'Have you any idea how long forty years is? Does it mean anything to you? It's your entire *lifetime*.' The Fireworks Man said slowly, looking down at his ring and twisting it, 'The other night on television—totally by accident, at the home of a business acquaintance—I saw a film about the Second World War.' He paused and his eyes came back to Feiffer, 'In the film which was made recently all the people had a modern cut to their clothes and their haircuts were all modern, and the attitudes they all had were cynical and up-to-date and—'

The Fireworks Man said, 'But it wasn't like that, the reality. The reality is that it was forty years ago. The reality was— The reality was that, now, now—in modern terms—it was all old-fashioned!' He saw Feiffer's face and thought he was simply not getting through to him. The Fireworks Man said, 'Don't you understand? It wasn't just another time—it was another *world*!'

Feiffer said nothing. He watched as The Fireworks Man's gaze strayed out the window again.

The Fireworks Man said quietly, 'We wouldn't do it again. Not like that. Not for the things we thought were important then, not—we wouldn't do it like that again because "we"— everybody—us, the Chinese, me, the Japanese—we're all old men!' The Fireworks Man said, 'No, I won't talk to whoever it is speaks Japanese. Use an official interpreter.'

Feiffer said quietly, 'An official interpreter, like your war film, could only talk in the modern idiom. We want someone who was familiar with the idioms of the time as well as the military—'

The Fireworks Man said, 'Someone has told you about the Murder Verandah, haven't they?'

Feiffer said, 'They told me you pretended to help the Japanese while at the same time working for the British Army Aid Group: for the resistance.'

The Fireworks Man said with a trace of irony, 'Did they? Is that what they told you? Who was that? Someone who was there? Or someone who just—'

Feiffer said, 'Someone who was there.'

'Another old man.'

'Yes.' Feiffer said quietly, 'You've helped us in the past. The other night you helped my two officers on the beach with the gunshots—'

The Fireworks Man said easily, 'That was for my licence. Every year my fireworks licence has to be renewed and I need a good character from the police to get it.' He nodded to himself, 'I'm a businessman.' The Fireworks Man said, 'I began my career in Japan. It was where I learned my trade. Before the war. I export seventy percent of my products to the Japanese.'

'No one has to know.'

'Of course people have to know! If these men are what you claim them to be who is going to stand up in Court next to them and interpret?'

Feiffer said, 'An official police interpreter.'

'You just said—'

'When we get them it doesn't matter who talks to them or whether the cut of their clothes is modern or old fashioned. Before that—'

The Fireworks Man said, 'No.' He shook his head. The Fireworks Man said, 'I've forgotten. It's the truth. I've forgotten the language.'

'Then how do you export to Japan? Do you let one of your juniors do it?' There had been no sign of any other office of comparable size in the ground floor corridor leading to The Fireworks Man's office. Feiffer said, 'This is your own business. If you built up any contracts in Japan before the war the last thing you'd do is insult them by passing them on to a junior—'

The Fireworks Man said, 'Very well, you know about the Chinese business mind!'

Feiffer said, 'And you know the Japanese military one.'

'Stop cajoling me!' The Fireworks Man said, 'Are you asking me or telling me? This business only exists because I have a licence to manufacture explosive substances. All the police have to do is—'

Feiffer said, 'I'm asking you.'

'*You have no idea what those times were like here in Hong Kong!*'

'No.' Feiffer said quietly, 'That's why I'm asking you.'

The Fireworks Man put his hand to his face.

'I understand that you—'

'You understand nothing!' The Fireworks Man said, 'To hear it all again—to see them come out of the ground like resurrected corpses—to bring it all back...' The veins in his neck were standing out. He looked like a very old man. The Fireworks Man said sarcastically, 'Maybe they can still shoot and run—after all, they were better men than us. That was what they always told us.

109

Maybe the great Japanese code of Bushido had a built-in longevity that we poor ordinary men—' The Fireworks Man said, 'I was married to a Japanese girl before the war, did your informant who was there tell you that?'

Feiffer said, 'No. My informant only—'

'Oh, your informant knew all right. Who was he? One of the BAAG men? One of the good loyal Chinese who my masters tortured on the verandah? Someone who helped try me after the war? Illegally!' He said suddenly, 'Yes, I was tried! Not by a War Crimes Commission, but by the Chinese vigilantes! By the righteous representatives of the people! Did you know they had executioners who—even after they'd killed you—stood over your body and cut your crimes into your body with a razor? Did you know that?' The Fireworks Man pulled the sleeves of his shirt up melodramatically. 'But do you see any scars on me?' He leaned forward and dragged at the collar of his open-necked shirt, 'Do you see any healed bullet wounds in my neck?'

'No one suggested you—'

'*Didn't they? Didn't they?*' The Fireworks Man shouted, 'Of course they did!' They just didn't prove it, that's all! They proved that I spoke Japanese and they proved that in order to keep my business intact—to keep my land out of the hands of the Japanese—to curry their favour—I interpreted for them! They proved that! And they proved I had a Japanese wife who had relatives in the Occupying Army! They proved that too! They proved that sometimes I lied to the Japanese about what some of the Chinese spies and saboteurs they caught said to me—they proved I helped—they proved I helped the Chinese more than I helped the Japanese! Or did they?' His breathing was coming in fast, hot gasps. The Fireworks Man said in a sly, provocative voice, 'Or did they merely prove, did they simply prove that I made sure a few captured spies were still alive at the end of the war to say that I was on their side and that the greater proportion—the ones who would have said I helped the Japanese more—had all been killed off and were not in a position to prove anything?' The Fireworks Man said, 'The Resistance, when they tried me in their

110

little cellar on Wyang Road—all standing around with their looks of hatred and their captured officers' pistols and their razors—all they ever proved about me was that there was nothing to prove!' The Fireworks Man said quietly, 'But they killed my Japanese wife.' He paused, 'The moment the news came through that the atomic bombs had fallen and that the Emperor had issued his Imperial Rescript telling the Japanese to lay down their arms, they killed her all right.' In the wooden, uninflammable room, it was as if The Fireworks Man looked around on his desk for a cigarette. The Fireworks Man said, 'Yes. She was easy. No doubt about her. She was Japanese. So they killed her.'

Feiffer said softly, 'I'm sorry.' People had been killed too in Cuttlefish Lane and in the harbour and on the half completed building across from the Station. Feiffer said, 'I have to ask.'

The Fireworks Man said softly, 'They asked me what she was like and I said, "She's a Jap" and that satisfied them. At the time, that was enough.' The Fireworks Man said, 'I married again, after the war. This time, a Chinese woman, and I have a son. A Chinese son.' He shrugged. 'So, after the war, that was all right.' He said with a bitter smile, 'My Chinese son, when I am dead, will get none of this.' He looked out at the compound, 'When I feel near death, everything I have here will be sold and all the profits given to charity for my soul and the soul of—of others—and nothing, nothing of what all this cost me will be left.' He said with heavy sarcasm, 'And then they can make an heroic film about the brave battles of Hong Kong and they can give me a younger face and a modern suit and with-it haircut and they can concentrate on making all the bodies of the too-young actors look attractive and they can forget the ugliness of the soul.' He demanded, '*Can't they?*'

Feiffer waited.

The man's eyes were dim and full of memories.

'I wasn't attached to the Army units, I was with the Kempeitai.' He smiled at the window and shrugged. He wiped at his eyes. 'You know, the Japanese Secret Police—the Gestapo.' His eyes stayed staring at the glass. 'On that verandah they tortured over fifteen hundred people and then the ones they

111

decided were spies—which was most of them—they shot.' The Fireworks Man closed his eyes. 'Several of the spies and saboteurs were people who had forgotten to salute a Japanese flag as they walked past it, which was a capital offence.' The Fireworks Man said, 'In one or two cases I got them set free by saying they were simpleminded and that what they said—even in Cantonese—didn't make sense.' He swallowed. 'And I got one or two of the resistance people off—one or two of the important ones, some of the executioners—by saying that they were part of my own little spy ring and that, if the Japanese let them off then they'd lead them to bigger fish.'

Feiffer said nothing.

The Fireworks Man, a long way away, said, 'Shooting is a very quick and clean method of killing. Do you find that?'

'No, not particularly.'

'A little cleaner and quicker, however, than sending men to their deaths by stealth and wrong information against them.' The Fireworks Man said quickly, 'Oh, they supplied the names—the Resistance—they had a list of people who could be eliminated in place of their own men. The only proviso was that I had to make sure the Japanese thought they would resist them to the death so they'd be killed outright and, rather than break in on them to capture them, they would come in shooting.' The Fireworks Man said, 'Which didn't matter anyway because the resistance had already killed them with Japanese weapons and wired their houses with grenades to make sure.' The Fireworks Man said, 'This man who told you about me, I know who he is. I've seen him in the Station. Did he tell you what he did during the war?'

Feiffer nodded.

The Fireworks Man said quietly, 'He is serving his penance too.' The Fireworks Man said reflectively, 'Ah Pin. The "Ah" as you know, simply denotes that he is a servant, a labourer for someone or something.' He paused, 'That was all he ever was.' The Fireworks Man twisted his jade ring, 'But he still wonders, I know he still wonders. I've seen him lately, each of us in our respective ranks, with our respective prosperity, and I know he still wonders about me...'

Feiffer said quietly, 'About whose side you were really on?'

The Fireworks Man looked on the verge of tears. 'Yes.'

'No one is still after you.'

'Maybe I am still after them.'

'Are you?'

The Fireworks Man said with a smile, 'No, anything that happened now would be murder. Then, on the other hand, it was glory.' He looked hard at Feiffer with a strange, hard expression on his face. The Fireworks Man said, 'Wasn't it?' He smiled. 'Yes. It was glory. Of course it was. I saw it all on a film on television, just the way it was. It was glory.' He looked at Feiffer with a strange, pitying look, 'The film was full of young men doing young men's things and it was made, my friend who follows these films tells me, by young men.' He asked, 'How can it not be true? Young men never lie.' He waved his hand at the picture window, 'Whatever I say or do, you will grant me the licence because you are a young man. All this is true. Surely.'

Feiffer said firmly, 'This has nothing to do with the licence and provided you haven't contravened any safety regulations the licence will be granted.'

The Fireworks Man said, 'Sure. Of course I believe you. I believe everybody: the Japanese, the Resistance—'

Feiffer said irritably, 'During the war, whose side *were* you on?'

The Fireworks Man said, 'I will speak Japanese to your hearty cave dwellers. I will tell them to come in in the idiom of the time.'

Feiffer said, 'I have my own reasons for wanting to know!'

'Why? Did you lose someone too? A father perhaps? An uncle? Someone who—' The Fireworks Man said between clenched teeth, 'Wonder! Think about it and watch your television films and read your books and think your own thoughts and—at the end of it—maybe when you are as old as me—*wonder. Wonder about it!*'

Far below, in the old cellars and air raid shelters beneath the fireworks factory at the end of Maltby Point they were testing some of the new run of heavy display fireworks.

113

The explosions in the contained, safe rooms, rocked and reverberated against the thick rock of the point, but, insulated from them in the fireproof, silent room, neither The Fireworks Man nor Feiffer heard them and they went on, unnoticed, until the test pieces were consumed and became extinct.

*

The pill box in the public park was a memorial to the men of the Royal Rifles of Canada and the Winnipeg Grenadiers who had fought during the seventeen day defence of the Colony in an heroic attempt to stave off inevitable defeat.

So the little brass tablet on the sealed structure read.

In the languages of the country, French and English, it commemorated the thousand or so of those men who had died during the defence or later from their wounds.

The pill box was pock marked with bullet and shrapnel holes and around the meshed-off gun slits, burned a deep brown colour where perhaps once, or perhaps at the last, it had been seared by a flame thrower or a phosphorous grenade.

With its Roman characters, the tablet meant nothing to Private Morishita and, glancing down at the rear of the furniture van as The Technician finished there and nodded to himself, he took off his thousand stitches obi and tied the frayed tapes carefully and reverently to a jagged piece of masonry and knelt down in the direction of the Imperial Palace in far away Tokyo to make an act of dedication.

The Rising Sun flag of his Quartermaster Unit was folded on the ground beside him, signed with many names, and he touched at it and then the rifle beneath it and spoke an ancient prayer for the last time.

2.04 p.m.

The sun was behind him, over his shoulder and, as The Technician had intended he would, he had a clear unimpeded view of the back of the furniture van and the ground behind it.

The uniformed forces of colonial repression.

114

Morishita smiled to himself.

2.06 p.m.

All he had to do was wait.

*

In Icehouse Road, Feiffer pulled his car over to—amazingly—an empty parking spot near the entrance to the Public Records Office and thought for a moment of going in to ask Owlin—

What?

About the Occupation? The Japanese? Arsenals?

About his own father?

The only photograph he had of his father showed a tall, fair haired man standing in his old fashioned Shanghai Municipal Police uniform somewhere on the Bund with ships and sampans and tenders in the background.

In the picture, it seemed to be raining.

After the war Feiffer had gone back to Shanghai with his mother from Australia and his uncles there—

His uncles there had never told him anything.

It was said that beneath the streets of London, if you dug deep enough, first you would come upon signs of the medieval city and then, even deeper, the Roman, and then, if you kept on digging, going deeper and deeper, you might find . . .

The streets of Hong Kong, like the buildings, all looked new and modern, clean and up-to-date and sure of themselves, and as if they hid—

Exactly nothing.

2.13 p.m.

After whatever happened next, The Fireworks Man said he would come to await the phone call.

After whatever happened next.

There were people everywhere in the city and the streets were moving like serpents, imperceptibly changing and twisting and coiling, swallowing them up.

Out of a clear blue sky . . .

Feiffer felt cold.

He started the engine of the car a moment before someone behind him honked for him to either get out of the car or get the car out of there and, still thinking of an old, old photograph and old, old streets, drove directly to the Station to wait.

Tick, tick, tick, tick, tick, tick, tick . . . eight seconds. At his desk in the Detectives' Room Auden pressed the lever on the stopwatch down hard and said to Spencer with a fierce nod, 'Eight seconds.'

Spencer was standing at a pile of sandbags looking out through the hole in the wall at the streets. Spencer said without turning around, 'It's—'

'I know. I know. Seven.' Auden said, 'I'll try again.' He saw O'Yee looking at him and grinned.

Spencer said, still without turning, 'It has to be less than seven. Seven is from first warning to finish line. Seven is the absolute—'

Auden snapped the stopwatch in his hand to reset the timing. O'Yee was still looking at him. Auden said, 'I don't know how far I have to run, do I? For all I know I could be right on top of it from the moment I start!'

O'Yee asked mildly, 'On top of what?'

Spencer said, 'Seven isn't a measurement of distance, it's the time you get from the first reliable warning to the end.' He turned around, 'You should be already there when you start thinking in terms of seven seconds!'

O'Yee said, 'Already where?'

'Well, I've got to assume that!' Auden said, 'How the hell can I tell where I'll be when I've got seven seconds if I don't know where I'm starting from?'

O'Yee said, 'Starting to do what?'

Spencer said with a curious look on his face, 'Forget it, Phil. There are just too many imponderables.'

Tick, tick, tick, tick, tick . . .

O'Yee said, *'What's he doing?'*

Spencer said with a sigh, 'Running.' He looked at Auden sitting at his desk with his eyes closed and a look of strain on his face, 'He's bloodywell *running*, isn't he?'

116

O'Yee said, 'Is he?'

Auden stopped the watch. 'Seven exactly.' He looked at O'Yee. O'Yee looked back. Auden winked at him and said with a nod, 'I'm off cigarettes for the rest of the day. They slow you down.'

Spencer came forward. He still looked cross, like a Mary Poppins nanny tired of explaining that umbrellas went up, not down. Spencer said a word at a time as if to a moronic child, 'You haven't got seven seconds! You don't know how long you've got whatever you do! For all you know you could start the seven seconds when you're still eight seconds away from it and then you've got minus one second and you haven't got anything!'

Auden said, 'It'll work,'

O'Yee said, 'What will?' He waited for an explanation, but none came. O'Yee said mildly, 'Excuse me for asking—'

The phone on Feiffer's desk rang and all three of them went for it at once, but it was only someone ringing up to report an act of gross indecency in a public park off Beach Road and O'Yee gave him the number of Vice and told him to get them to pass the message on to one of their patrols.

2.15 p.m. exactly.

Tick, tick, tick, tick, tick, tick . . .

The voice reporting the indecency had sounded muffled, as if it was someone trying to disguise his identity with a handkerchief over the mouthpiece. It was the usual thing with Vice jobs.

Tick, tick, tick, tick, tick . . . Auden said in triumph, 'Six seconds!'

Maybe it was some sort of new English game, like unemployment.

O'Yee said quietly to himself, 'I don't know . . .'

Tick, tick, tick, tick, tick, tick, tick . . .

He wondered why Spencer seemed to look so worried about it.

*

In the labyrinth of archives, The Keeper of Secrets, Owlin, moved to a shelf marked *Pacific War, Underground Bunkers Used By*

Japanese In.

One of the bunkers found on the island of Iwo Jima during the fighting had been no less than fifteen hundred feet long, cut thirty feet deep in the ground, and the American Marines who had entered it had discovered no less than seventeen concealed entrances and exits in the crazy subterranean jigsaw of the place.

The bunker had held three hundred men and enough food and supplies for them to hold out, if necessary, for up to three and a half months.

On the evidence, the Hong Bay arsenal held a single Quartermaster's section, and the size of a complex on an island the size of Iwo Jima compared to that the Japanese might have built in a garrison the size of Hong Kong...

Owlin did his sums.

It was unsummable.

It had to be huge: a complex for something the size of Hong Kong, against the unthinkable event of invasion by—

God, it had to be *enormous*.

It had to be at least—

It had to be...

On Iwo Jima parts of the complex had been destroyed by bombing and naval gunfire and become sealed off. Parts of it were so massive that at first the Marines, fighting for their lives gallery by gallery had thought there was not one, but a dozen, complexes, all—

Not one, but a dozen...

But it had only been one, and—

And, on wartime Iwo Jima—

And—

Owlin said in a fury at his own blind stupidity, 'You stupid *fool!*'

—And in peacetime Hong Kong, years ago, it had to have *already* been found!

*

They came. The Technician had made his call and they came.

118

The first of many. In plain clothes, they came.

One of them was a young Chinese woman. Morishita saw her clearly as she got out of the car and glanced around the park.

There was a man with her, still in the car—a European—and she was nodding at the van and asking him to do something about it.

He saw the man nod, then lean forward in the car to take up the radio telephone to ask Despatch for further information while the woman waited.

The man and the woman were in plain clothes.

Morishita waited for the uniforms.

The sun was directly behind him.

Even if they looked straight at him, they would see nothing.

2.35 p.m.

Appositely, it all hinged on the sun that was commemorated on the folded up flag that lay by his waiting rifle.

Concealed by the sealed-up pillbox, Morishita waited.

10

At the van Detective Inspector Winter touched at the flat Walther PPK concealed under his flowered shirt and said soundlessly to Woman Police Constable Minnie Oh, 'O.K.' He nodded, 'Open it.' He saw Minnie's long fingers close around the handle on the cab door and gently pull it down to free the lock. She wore flat shoes and slacks: Winter saw the muscles in her thighs tighten as she had to stretch to reach the handle and he sighed inwardly.

The door came open without a sound and he looked in.

Nothing.

There were a few candy papers and a street map of Hong Kong on the offside seat and the usual collection of dust, grime and bits and pieces of assorted truck driver effluvia on the driver's seat. The key was still in the ignition.

Minnie glanced back into the park. The sun was in her eyes and she could just make out a war time pillbox a hundred yards away and, behind it, a stand of trees.

Winter sniffed.

There was the faintest smell of something old in the cab, but whatever it was it wasn't something he recognised.

He sniffed again and the odour of it bit at his nostrils: something sharp and a little sour, like old canvas that had got wet mixed in with something more pungent—a smell of vinegar or some sort of acid.

Truck driver's effluvia. Winter nodded and Minnie closed the door a little without a sound.

There was no sound from inside the back of the furniture van and he crouched down—tried hard not to think of Minnie's legs under the grey slacks—and looked along the bottom of the truck's chassis to the rear wheels.

The wheels were still and if there was a brothel in full blast inside the back of the truck then they were being remarkably non-bouncy about it.

Minnie put her ear to the side of the truck.

Winter looked at her thighs as they tightened.

Minnie mouthed. 'Nothing.' She looked slightly annoyed and touched Winter on the shoulder to shepherd him a few feet back from the truck to where they could whisper. Minnie said softly in English, 'It's a hoax.' The side of the truck had a small discreet legend in English and Chinese painted in the typography Chinese merchants imagined small discreet legends should be painted in: a sort of elegant Georgian lettering that the Georgians, most of them barely literate, would have found almost impossible to read.

The sign read *Quality Furniture Restorations* and gave a phone number. Minnie said softly, still looking around, 'I've heard of this firm. They repair furniture for the rich taipans up on the Peak.'

Winter nodded. The smell was still in his nose. He was Dutch by parenthood and the smell reminded him of something he had smelled when his parents had been posted in Java. (Or more particularly, when his parents had been expelled from Java when the Javanese had decided they wanted it back.) He associated the smell with his father. His father had been a Colonel in the Dutch Marines—maybe it was just the smell of the canvas from the tents out in the jungle or . . .

Winter said softly, 'What's that smell? Does it remind you of anything?'

'What smell?'

Winter said, 'I'm not sure.' He looked at the back of the truck, 'What do you think? Do you want to call Stolen Cars and have them run it or shall we turn it over ourselves?'

Minnie looked at the wheels. Those shock absorbers were not absorbing any shocks. Minnie said, shrugging, 'I suppose it could be a gambling set-up and whoever telephoned was a big loser . . .' She seemed unconvinced. She shrugged again, 'We may as well have the arrest if there is one.'

What the hell was that smell? Even ten feet from the closed cab Winter imagined he could still smell it. He couldn't. He had it somewhere in his memory and it kept niggling at him and coming back as if it was real. Winter said, 'There's no probable cause. We can't even open the back of it without leaving ourselves liable to—' He looked at the legend on the side of the van, 'I'm not having someone say we got our dirty pawmarks all over their Louis Quinze commode.'

Minnie said, 'Their Louis what?'

Winter said with a smile, 'Or Tang pot or something.' What was that smell? Winter said, 'I'll give it the old "We know you're in there, Murphy" routine, but if that doesn't draw any reaction—'

Why were they whispering? Minnie said uncomfortably, 'Why are we whispering? There's obviously nothing in there. Just give it a kick and if there's nothing we call the Uniformed Branch and be rid of it.' She looked at her wristwatch, 'We've got to be in Court at 3.30.' The shock absorbers were still. The van simply sat there. It was obviously empty. Minnie said, 'It's all this business with the sniper. Everyone's going around being careful. Let's just turn it over and be done with it.'

Winter paused. He sniffed.

Minnie said, 'Will we?'

Whatever it was ... Winter said, 'Yeah, let's do it.' He was still whispering. He listened and heard a slight rustling in the trees a long way off. Across the park he could hear the sea against rock.

He could still smell that odour in his nose.

Minnie said, 'We'll do it now, will we?' She was still whispering.

Winter said, hesitating, 'Sure.' He stayed where he was.

In Java once he had ... He stopped again. A group of his father's Marines had been sitting around in a jungle clearing doing something with knives and canvas bags. Eating? No. Opening something? It was all a long time ago and he had only been a child ...

122

He tried to think.

He tried to get it straight in his mind...

He had gone down a little path out of the base and there were half a dozen of his father's Marines squatting around getting something ready for a—

That was it. *Getting something ready.*

The old, "Come out Murphy, we know you're in there" trick.

The truck was still, unmoving, anchored to the grass, becalmed.

Minnie said with a frown, 'David?'

Something he should have been a long way away from. They were doing something he should have been...

Winter said abruptly, 'All right.' Whatever it was, it was gone now.

Minnie said softly, 'Good.'

Still frowning slightly, she stood back a little as Winter flipped the restraining strap off his shoulder holster and went around to the back of the truck to do a little standard stentorian Murphy-flushing.

*

In the Detectives' Room, Feiffer said, 'He'll come. Once. He'll listen to him once and if he's a Japanese soldier...' He looked at Auden and Spencer. 'The Fireworks Man. He speaks Japanese.'

O'Yee was silent.

Feiffer said, 'After that, provided we issue him his good character for his Fireworks Renewal I don't think he'll ever help us again.' Feiffer said, looking a little embarrassed, 'Not our day, Christopher, is it?'

O'Yee said, 'No.'

Feiffer said, 'No.' He went into the charge room to smoke a cigarette and, standing there as O'Yee came after him with the recleaned clean ashtray, for a moment, seemed a very long way away indeed.

In the forty years since the end of the war the Public Works Department must have closed up more holes and tunnels in Hong Bay than the entire world's population of ants.

In the Archives Owlin came to yet another list of sealed-off, made-safe or cemented up tunnels, air raid shelters, bomb craters and assorted holes in the ground and said softly to himself, 'Damn it...'

If there was only one gigantic catacomb like Iwo Jima, then all the little holes led, like a honeycomb, to a central core.

If the gigantic single catacomb *was* a gigantic single catacomb and if, like Iwo Jima...

He had a map laid out on a table in front of him, held down by the yellowing pages of survey and construction gang reports and he began drawing little marks where they had sealed off each hole or repaired each cavity or made safe each abyss and hoped that sooner or later, just like a jigsaw, they might make one central picture.

'*Southern side of Great Shanghai Road, Hong Bay: Entrance to Japanese storeroom, impassable after ten feet due to bomb damage. Filled with cement and resurfaced for road works, Feb 5th, 1947.*'

Owlin ticked it off and made a little cross.

He looked at the map.

All the marks he had made were crosses. They stretched erratically almost the entire length of the old shoreline like some part of spreading, growing graveyard, some sort of giant unstoppable necropolis.

The centre. He needed the centre.

'*South-east Beach Road, Hong Bay: March 8th, 1947...*'

Owlin made another cross.

*

His fist froze on the rear door of the truck.

In the jungle clearing the Sergeant came over to him and gently

124

shepherded him away, glancing back at the men squatting on the ground with their canvas bags doing . . .

He could still smell the smell, the smell of canvas and damp and the smell of the stuff they were using that was seeping a little in the heat and giving off . . .

Winter said without looking away from the doors, 'Minnie, I don't think we should touch anything.' He looked at his fist an inch away from the doors and brought it down slowly, 'I think we should—'

The stuff the Marines had been using was TNT. He had smelled it.

Winter said, 'Minnie, I think we—' His mouth was dry. He swallowed.

The next morning he had seen the photographs on his father's desk of what they had set it up for. His father, grinning at the Sergeant, had seemed very pleased about it.

Winter said in a dry voice, 'Minnie, I'm not absolutely sure, but—'

The charge had decapitated the infiltrator. His head was in pieces on the ground near what was left of the tripwire and the—

Winter said in a croak, 'I don't want to make fools of either of us, but I think we should get on the radio and—' He turned his head slowly to look at her, but she was not listening.

Staring at him, she seemed rooted to the ground. She seemed to be trying to get her breath.

Minnie said in the same strange voice as his own, 'David . . .' She nodded at something written in chalk above the rear numberplate of the truck.

Divine mission to eradicate . . . It was written in small, joined up characters and Winter had to strain to make it out.

2.46 p.m.

The sun, moving west, was directly behind Morishita's right shoulder. It was in a clear blue sky and, in the absence of cloud, at its clearest and brightest as he took a preliminary sighting on the rear of the truck and worked the cocking handle to slip the first round in the magazine into the breech of his rifle.

125

He did it slowly and quietly and as Minnie and Winter began walking quietly and carefully across the grass to the car, their hands touching like lovers', there was only a single, muffled—
...*click*.

*

In the war room, The Technician looked at the closed steel door in front of him. The door was two inches thick, bombproof, grey and, to the touch, cold and unyielding.

He raised his hurricane lamp to it and it seemed suddenly to glow with warmth.

The Technician said quietly to the door in Cantonese, 'Damn you ... damn all of you ...'

The war room was the centre of a honeycomb of passages, all leading off in different directions.

The Technician closed his eyes and heard the hissing of the lamp as it glowed at the door and gave it life.

The Technician said quietly, 'Damn every last one of you ...'

Private Masuo Morishita, Quartermaster's Section, 38th Division, Japanese Imperial Army in Hong Kong.

The Technician shouted at the top of his voice in the empty, echoing room, '*Damn you all!*'

Divine mission to eradicate all the uniformed forces of colonial imperialism ...

Just given half a chance, it could have worked.

The Technician said softly, 'Juzo ...' but his brother, the Major, was no longer there and there was nothing but silence in the stone room.

The 38th Division of the Japanese Imperial Army in Hong Kong ...

In the war room he thought he heard a noise in one of the passages behind him and he raised the lantern quickly to see what it was.

It was nothing.

He looked at the steel door.

126

He was alone.

In his pocket he had two cartridge cases from the gun Morishita had taken with him to the park and he took them out, considered them for a moment, and then threw them away into the corner of the room.

2.51 p.m.

In the hissing of the lamp, unafraid, he took one of the passages and, moving quickly through it, made for the surface.

*

On the radio Despatch said without urgency, 'Yes, Car Victor Four?'

Winter saw Minnie's long fingers on the car door beside him. She was standing, watching. He saw her mouth tighten.

Despatch said again, 'Yes, Car Victor Four, go ahead, please.'

They were both right out in the open.

He saw Minnie look at him and force a smile.

Nothing but park and an old war memorial and a stand of trees, and between them and the truck, nothing.

Winter, swallowing, said as calmly as he could manage, 'Instructions, please, Despatch. We believe we have an emergency situation developing...'

Between them and the truck there was only their car: potential red hot tearing shrapnel, and the windscreen, a square yard—maybe more—of blasting, slicing, searing glass.

Winter said as calmly as he could manage—

The truck was just sitting there, unmoving, waiting—

Winter said in a sudden snarl, 'Despatch! God damn it! Acknowledge!'

*

If they wanted it, it was theirs, but they couldn't have anyone else—anyone—for at least an hour, maybe more. It was unbelievable. On the phone in the Detectives' Room, Feiffer said, aghast, 'Are you serious? You want me to take my people out into an open expanse that hasn't even been searched, into a situation you know is potentially lethal, and you say I can't have anyone to back me up for—' He couldn't credit what he was hearing, '*For how long?*'

The Commander's voice was tight, breathless. 'They have to change, Harry. They have to change into civilian clothes and then they have to get transport for their equipment and—'

'The damned bomb squad aren't in uniform! They wear coveralls and helmets and—' Feiffer said, 'Uniforms. Right?'

'Right.' The Commander said, 'And the Emergency Unit in their Land Rovers and their flashing lights and their bloody sub machine guns and—'

'*All right!*' Feiffer glanced at O'Yee watching him, 'What about securing the road? The park stretches along Beach Road and down into—' The Commander knew all that. Feiffer said reasonably, 'At least they could secure the street and keep the park bottled up.'

'They are. I've got all the uniformed men I can spare from North Point going over to do that, but if it is a set-up—'

'According to what you told me, Winter thinks the van's been stored there for later use. According to you he says the keys are still in the ignition!'

The Commander said, 'And the first two attacks were directly opposite a police station.'

'There's no evidence the attacks were directed solely at people in uniform. We weren't in uniform when he had a go at us and half the people in Cuttlefish Lane he dropped were about as uniformed as—'

The Commander said, 'I can't take the chance. It may be exactly what whoever's behind it wants. The calls say "the uniformed forces of colonial repression"—'

'The calls are bullshit!'

'All right, then it's your damned Japanese! In either event, it's aimed at bloody symbols and as far as I'm concerned, before anyone goes out and makes himself a target he's going to divest himself of every one of his bloody little shiny symbols and go out there looking like Elmer Cluck the well-known amateur lepidopterist!' The Commander said suddenly quietly, 'Harry, these people are bloody suicidal. It's well known. Documented. For all I know, I could run a line of bloody EU men and Bomb Squad right across the park and these bastards wouldn't give a damn about mowing them down like bloody hay! Because they don't give a shit what happens to them next!'

'What bloody people? You've been drumming it into me that this Japanese business is just a smokescreen for some sort of gun-happy psychotic!' Feiffer demanded, 'What bloody people?'

'The people who left the van there.' The Commander said reasonably, 'I agree with you. I agree that they wouldn't have left the van in the park with the keys still in it unless they intended to move it somewhere else, and I also agree with you that if the keys are in it they're not far away, but I also agree with my bloody self that it isn't a Japanese kamikaze force, but I have to take the reasonable way out and not put anyone at risk I don't have to put at risk!' The Commander said earnestly, 'No one will blame you if you don't touch it, but it's our only chance to get one of these set-ups intact and find out for once and for all who's behind it— Japanese or other.'

'Can you give me a helicopter overfly to at least survey the possible fields of fire?'

'*No!*' The Commander said, 'How low would he have to be? We don't happen to have our own Hong Kong Police satellite a hundred and fifty miles up in bloody space, we've got a few traffic choppers marked all over COP—SHOOT ME and to spot a sniper they virtually have to get down to tree top level and— you're the only plain clothes unit I've got in the area familiar with the situation. I'm not asking you to disarm the thing, I'm only asking you to—'

Feiffer said, 'To do what?'

'To bloody well go out there and get Winter and WPC Oh in if nothing else!' He said suddenly. 'They haven't shot at *them*, have they?'

That's because they may be waiting for *us*!' Feiffer said, 'Neal, I've got my own people to think of. I can't just—Look, I'll go myself. How's that? I'll go and relieve Winter—that's all you want anyway, isn't it? If they're not going to shoot two plain clothes officers they're certainly not going to shoot one. Get on the radio and they can leave just as I arrive.'

'No. The area has to be secure. I can't have civilians wandering onto—'

'I fail to see how the hell the area is secure in the first place since there are only two of them—' It was hopeless. Feiffer said, 'Bullet proof vests and aprons, can we at least—' He saw the vests and aprons on the floor. About the only thing they didn't have on them to identify them as police property was a large target pinned over the heart area and a few sighting gauges so the sniper could get his aim right before he left the aprons and vests completely alone and went straight for the head. Feiffer said, 'All right. One hour. We'll hold the area—if we can—for one hour and then, by God, the Royal bloody Emergency Unit Ballet had better have changed out of their working clothes into their bloody tu-tus or the only emergency they'll be handling for the next six months will be *me*! What sort of weapons do Winter and Oh have? I assume since we're trying to look like anything but cops we can't take our Armalites so what sort of firepower can Winter and Oh provide us with on the spot?'

'Winter's got a sidearm, I suppose.'

'Vice Squad's sidearms are little Walther PPKs! I meant, in the car?'

'I don't know.' The Commander must have had a print out in front of him. He said after a moment, 'Yeah, you're right, a Walther is standard issue ... and in the car nothing, not even a shotgun.' He paused for a moment, 'WPC Oh has got a—'

O'Yee said quietly in the background, 'A twenty two calibre derringer. I've seen it.'

The Commander said, 'Harry, Winter and the Oh girl have been there now for—' He paused, 'For too long. And they're close to it, trying to keep it under surveillance and they're—' The

Commander said quietly, 'Harry, Winter sounds very frightened indeed.'

Feiffer said, 'So am I. That makes it a clean sweep for everyone, doesn't it?'

'*Godammit, I've telephoned my wife to bring my civilian clothes from home but it's going to take an hour with the fucking traffic!*' The Commander demanded, 'What can I tell you? Reinforcements will be there, I promise you! I know you're worried about your people, but I assure you that reinforcements will be there!'

Feiffer glanced around the room. He saw Auden touch at the big Colt Python under his arm and heft it as if he was testing its weight. Spencer had a stopwatch in his hand, turning it over and over. He saw Feiffer looking at it and put it carefully on his desk then looked surreptitiously at Auden.

The Commander said, 'I don't want any heroics, Harry. I just want you to hold the area until reinforcements arrive.' Put reasonably, it sounded more reasonable. The Commander said, 'The van isn't live. According to Stolen Cars it was only taken a few hours ago. No one's heard a sound from it or seen smoke or—' He said, 'It's safe! The whole area's safe!'

'All right!' Feiffer said, 'All right, so it isn't a Japanese suicide mission, O.K.?'

There was a silence, then the Commander said with difficulty, 'I'm in Despatch. I can actually hear Winter on the radio—' He hesitated. 'He's doing all right, but he—'

The Python was too heavy. For some reason, Feiffer saw Auden swap it with Spencer for Spencer's airweight Detective Special. He saw Spencer, looking less than happy, glance at the big gun for a moment and then put it into his waistband. The stopwatch was still on the desk. Spencer touched at it and then slid it quickly out of sight into his drawer. O'Yee had one of the bullet proof aprons in his hand. He looked at it for a moment and then stacked it on a sandbag.

2.58 p.m.

The Commander said, 'An hour. I promise you, *one hour!*'

2.59 p.m.

Through the minutes, the van, and whatever else was in the park, waited solely and exclusively for—

3.00 p.m. and thirty seconds.

For whatever it was waiting for.

*

The crosses stopped. By 1955 the war had been over ten years and the novelty or the satisfaction had worn off and the Public Works Department hardly thought fit to mention less than an accidentally exhumed mass grave.

In the archives, Owlin, staring at the incomplete map—the crosses without pattern—said to the final secret hidden beneath the lines of streets and grids and contours, 'You bastard, where are you!' He looked hard at the map and the collated pile of useless reports, 'You rotten bastard, *where the hell are you?*'

Where else? Where else could he find anything?

The thousand stitches obi. Was there anything on it that might—?

Anything?

Feiffer had left it with him in his office for study and Owlin, staring at the maps, rubbed at his glasses with his handkerchief and, before going back to his office to look at it, racked his brains for everything he knew about them and wondered if there was anything about it he might have missed.

*

He was in the heart of the system: the centre hub of all the tunnels. The Technician touched at his throat and felt the warm dry air catch at him and make him want to cough.

He had stopped sweating. Under his shirt his chest seemed to be covered in a fine, white, dry dust.

He saw something glint in one of the side rooms of the main tunnel and he raised his lantern and saw the eyes watching him.

It was one of the Major's section—a Private, his rifle across his

132

knees—but the Technician didn't recognise him and, still touching at his throat and chest, passed on.

*

Morishita touched at the rolled up flag and raised his head a fraction above the pillbox to see the man and the girl by the car.

They were standing there together, unafraid, waiting, doing their duty.

Morishita nodded.

In his own way, he admired them.

He touched at the flag.

He knew about duty.

Far off, the engines getting louder as they approached, he heard the cars coming.

He touched at the flag.

11

Out in the open, perspiration was standing out on Auden's forehead. He was behind one of the two parked cars, the real or imagined protection of the engine block between him and the furniture van. Auden's fingers were drumming on the roof of the car. They went thumpety-thumpety-thump, thump, thump...

Auden said, 'Harry, the shots have got to come out of the back of the van, right?' He looked over at Feiffer on the other side of Spencer and Winter and got no reply, 'Right? But there isn't anything to shoot at in that direction so it isn't set up to shoot.' Next to him, Minnie Oh looked at him curiously and Auden dismissed her with a thumpety-thump on the roof, 'So even if—'

The van moved. There was a wind coming in from the sea with the tide change and the van moved a fraction. Winter said to Feiffer, 'Sir—'

'It's the wind.' Feiffer said with his eyes still on the van, 'Was the handbrake on when you looked inside?'

Winter said, 'Yes.' He looked to Minnie for confirmation and she nodded, 'And it was in first gear with the keys still in the ignition.'

Auden said, '—so even if there's a charge set up to blow the back doors open so they can shoot it probably isn't even armed yet—or if it is it's probably just a few ounces—'

Winter said with alarm, 'It's TNT. I smelled it. It only *takes* a few ounces!'

'Then a few bloody grammes then! In any event, it won't be enough to do any real damage because if it did it'll put the rifles in there off their aim so even if I got the doors open and the charge went off—'

Feiffer said, 'Phil, for the fourth and last time: we'll wait.'

'Harry, I could do it!' Auden said to Spencer, 'Tell him: I could, couldn't I?'

Spencer said, 'No.'

'What do you mean, no? You timed me. I've got at least three seconds to spare on the twelve seconds you said it'd—'

Spencer said, 'Seven seconds! Seven! Not twelve, not ten, not even eight, but *seven!*'

Winter ran his tongue across his lips. Auden's voice was a series of words and sounds but they were not forming themselves together in his mind into any meaning. Feiffer touched him on the shoulder, 'Have you done a walk around or have you stayed here with the van?'

Minnie said, 'We stayed with the van.'

Something moved. Auden said, 'Is that smoke?'

It was a leaf. Feiffer said quietly, 'Fine. You did the right thing. I want you to keep staying here and at the faintest sign of activity I want everyone down behind the car engine blocks. Then, if the shooting starts, I want everyone out of here.' He saw Auden about to open his mouth, 'It's a leaf.' Feiffer said, 'Phil, you're in charge of the retreat. At the first sign of anything you're to secure all the personnel here and evacuate them to a safe distance that-a-way.' He jerked his thumb vaguely in the direction of China, 'Understood? You're the senior man here and I'm relying on you to—'

Auden said reasonably, 'Harry, I can take it. I know how the guns work and I can disarm them.' He asked suddenly, 'Why am I in charge? I'm not the class bloody cut-up the teacher puts in charge to make sure he's got a responsible job! Where the hell are *you* going to be?'

Feiffer said, 'I'm going to take a walk around the perimeter of the park.'

'*And what if there's a bloody sniper?*'

'Then he'll shoot at me, won't he?' So far, if there was one, he hadn't shot at anyone. Feiffer looked at his watch. The changing-room brigade were still at least forty minutes away from arriving.

135

Feiffer said, 'I just want to make sure the area's secure before we—'

Auden said, 'It moved! The van moved!'

Winter said, 'It's the wind.'

Auden snapped, 'How the hell do you know it's full of TNT anyway? What are you—the big local TNT expert?'

'I've smelled it before.' Winter said, 'Have you?'

'Of course I've smelled bloody TNT before!' Auden tried to think where. Auden said to Feiffer, 'At least take Minnie with you. It'll look more natural if you've got a girl with you.' He looked at Feiffer's face and said with a beaten, 'All right, all right, I'll do what I'm told.'

Winter said in an undertone, 'At least I don't go around getting shot dead by blank rounds...'

Auden said, 'What did you say?'

Feiffer said, '*Auden!*'

Auden said, 'All right! All right!' He saw Feiffer draw a breath and step out from behind the car to start walking. Auden said, 'If anyone should do that, it should be—' He saw Spencer looking at him with that disapproving look of his. It was the same look the Examining Board gave him every year before they turned him down for promotion yet again. Auden said, 'Seven seconds, right? I remember. O.K? Seven seconds. Not eight or even seven and a half, but seven—right?'

Spencer said, 'Right.'

Minnie said quietly to Feiffer, 'Harry...?' She moved a step forward.

Feiffer stopped and turned around. He saw her face. One tiny .22 derringer hidden somewhere in her handbag. Feiffer said, 'Stay here.' He smiled, 'If you come too I'd never be able to keep my mind on the job.'

Minnie said quietly, 'Is it true about the Japanese soldiers?'

The van was moving slightly in the wind, rocking on its shock absorbers as the breeze pushed under the chassis and billowed against it like a lifting surface of an aeroplane. There was the faintest rustling from the stand of trees behind the sealed off

136

pillbox and the noise of the sea as it changed tidally and washed against rocks and sand.

Feiffer said, 'Yes, it's true.' They had to get to the set-up this time before it went off and turned into vapour. Feiffer said with a wink, 'Don't worry, this time we've got the element of surprise and it'll be our game.'

He looked again at his watch and, heading for the perimeter of the park where a railing separated it from the rocks and cliffs leading down to the sea, at 3.23 p.m. with the sun behind the van in his eyes making him blind, began walking.

*

Sergeant Quartermaster Seichiro Tanino, 38th Division, Japanese All Conquering Imperial Army in China, killer of ambulance stations.

At his desk in his main office Owlin took off his glasses and looked down at the spread out material in the protective glassene envelope on his desk.

Sergeant Seichiro Tanino ... nineteen hundred and forty two ... In the temperate air-conditioned room, Owlin bent down and sniffed the envelope and looked puzzled.

Sergeant Seichiro—a thousand stitches obi. The work of a wife or a mother or a sister or a friend who had made the long sash like object with care and then stood on a street corner or in a market square or a railway station somewhere in Hiroshima day after day until each of one thousand people had listened to her pleas and each, carefully, with expressions of luck and best wishes for her son or brother's health and glorious death in battle, inserted a single crude stitch in the fabric and then passed on their way.

A thousand, like-minded, unyielding people to whom the notion of defeat was unthinkable.

In the days when the Emperor had been a god. In the days before General MacArthur, that unmaker of gods, had decided, by simple decree ...

Owlin bent down and sniffed at the envelope and still looked

137

puzzled.

The envelope was labelled EVIDENCE—DO NOT OPEN and he took the label in his hand and tapped it against his thumbtip thoughtfully.

Sergeant Seichiro Tanino...

*

In the archives, there was nothing.

It was slightly moist in the office, suitable for people rather than paper, and there were a few drops of moisture condensing on the inside of the envelope and blurring slightly at the strange, ancient, totemic object inside.

The smell, somehow, reminded him of trees.

There were two staples holding the long transparent envelope shut and as Owlin flicked absently at one of them with his thumbnail, it came away and a section of the lip of the envelope fell open.

*

Behind the pillbox, Morishita said quietly, 'I am prepared.' He saw the tall man near the railing walking slowly and casually, looking around, his hand resting loosely against the open flap of his coat where his holstered gun was. The man was a long way off, walking the edge of the park, looking first ahead and then back into the park and then, casually, over the railing down to the cliffs and the sea. The man wore no uniform, but he was, nevertheless, the enemy.

The others would come.

In the slight wind coming across the park, Morishita could see the van rocking a little. He thought of what was inside. Morishita said softly to all the people who had sent their wishes to him in the stitches of his obi, 'I am prepared to do you honour.'

The girl was still there behind the cars parked fifty yards from the van, still looking worried.

He wondered why the uniformed people were taking so long.

He thought of The Technician.

He trusted him.

He said softly, aloud, 'No.' It was no mistake. He trusted him.

Private Morishita, still watching Feiffer, said with self encouraging determination, 'I will achieve success and I am fully prepared to die here in this place to achieve it.'

He touched at his flag and found either it or his hand was moist with what felt like perspiration.

*

Into the Valley of Death... On the phone in the Detectives' Room O'Yee demanded, 'What do you mean, "another three quarters of an hour"? You said one hour! That's an hour from the time of the call to the time the goddamned Cavalry arrives on the scene with their shiny little bugles blowing! The call came through to us at least forty minutes ago and you must have had it even earlier than that! What do you mean, another—'

'O'Yee!' The Commander said in a snarl, 'You're forgetting who the hell you're talking to!'

'I'm forgetting nothing! I'm sitting here watching the clock go around and I've got plenty of time to remember just about everything starting from the Book of goddamned Genesis to the last thirty episodes of goddamned Perry Mason!' O'Yee said, 'Three of my friends are out there waiting for you to get the proper equipment to them before some mad bastard starts shooting at them—and what do you mean by telling me that—' O'Yee said suddenly tightly, 'What the hell's going on? Have you told the Emergency Unit about the Japanese sniper or not?'

There was a pause.

O'Yee said, 'All right, then the goddamned South American sniper or the goddamned Lesotho-land sniper or the goddamned—*Have you told anybody that there's a*—' O'Yee said abruptly, 'You haven't! It's orders from on top, isn't it? There isn't any sniper, is there? The idea is that if you leave it long

139

enough—'

The Commander said, 'There isn't any Japanese hold-out sniper!'

'You hope!'

'I'm not discussing it with you!'

'You are! You are discussing it with me!' O'Yee said, 'Or fucking else!'

The Commander said, 'What did you say?'

O'Yee said quietly, 'I said, You lying bastard, you had better not have taken your orders from on high and sent my friends out there in the hope that if there's a bloody Jap sniper they'll clean him out for you before anyone finds out—'

'Are you threatening me, O'Yee?'

'They didn't even take a goddamned rifle!'

'You had better not be threatening me, Detective Senior Inspector.' The Commander said, 'I had better not have heard what I just heard.'

O'Yee said, 'Yes, you had. You had better have heard it— otherwise, if anything happens and I come looking for you—'

'That's enough!' The Commander said suddenly desperately, 'Damn it, it isn't *me*! What the hell do you think? That it's *my* idea?'

'The goddamned Emergency Unit and all the rest of them have their civilian clothes with them at their bases! They could have been changed in about—'

There was a silence.

'They could have changed in about—'

'Don't you think Feiffer knows that?' The Commander said, 'Don't you think I know that? Don't you think—'

'Bloody goddamned Japs! Bloody goddamned sensitive, two-faced goddamned *Japs*!' O'Yee shouted, thinking of Okuno, 'Who the hell won the fucking war anyway? *Them?*'

'Christopher, I'm standing here in bloody civilian clothes ready to go. I've got my orders too!' The Commander said, 'Christ, don't you think I want to go too? Don't you think—'

O'Yee said in a snarl, 'Twenty minutes! Whistle blowing time is in exactly twenty minutes! In exactly twenty fucking minutes I'm going around there with enough firepower to bring down the whole of Tokyo and the fucking Japanese Second World War Imperial Army and the Pearl Harbor attack force combined! In twenty minutes exactly—'

'Good, then you can meet me there!' The Commander said, 'I've given them fifteen! In fifteen, bloody career or no bloody career—'

The clock on the wall went *click*.

3.41 p.m.

O'Yee said softly, 'Christ, Christ...' He tried to keep the phone firmly in his hand, but his hands were covered in sweat and the instrument kept slipping from his grasp.

3.42 p.m.

His stomach was turning over.

O'Yee said softly into the phone, over and over, 'Christ ... oh Christ...!'

*

At the parked cars, Auden said quietly to Spencer, 'Bill, if that truck starts to go...' He looked at Spencer's face, 'If it starts to go...'

Feiffer was a long way off along the railing of the park. He was starting to turn inwards towards the truck from the far corner of the point.

Auden said, 'Bill...'

'All right.' Spencer nodded.

'I can take it.'

Spencer ran his tongue across his lips and touched at the big magnum in his waistband.

Winter said softly, 'I did smell TNT. I know the smell. I—' He looked at Feiffer, the only figure in a still, silent landscape, 'I saw someone killed by it once when I was a child.' He looked at Minnie.

Minnie said softly to Auden, 'I don't need anyone to tell me

141

which way to run.' She touched at her handbag, 'All I've got is a little—'

Spencer said quietly, 'There's an Ingram M-10 sub machine gun in the back of the car, under the rear seat.' He looked quickly at Auden, 'I put it in there while Harry was—' Spencer said, 'If there is a sniper.'

Auden said to Winter and Minnie, 'I can take the van. I know how it works. I can take it.' He looked across at Feiffer, walking slowly like a man thinking of something that had happened a long time ago. Auden said, 'The Japanese shot his old man in Shanghai, did you know that? Christopher O'Yee told me.' Auden said, '*I can take that van.*'

Feiffer stopped. He bent down and seemed to pick up a piece of grass and look at it for a moment.

Auden said, 'They're not coming, you know that. They're not coming until they know for sure that there won't be an international incident about it.' He looked hard at Spencer, 'Bill, you've timed me. You know I can do it.'

'Yes.'

Auden said, 'Minnie? The Ingram?'

Minnie said, 'I know how to shoot one.'

'Winter?'

'Yes.'

3.50 p.m.

Auden said, 'One move, one sound, one little vibration...'

Spencer said with an unsuccessful smile, 'You'll be a Senior Inspector yet.'

Feiffer had the piece of grass in his hand. He began walking again. Auden said, 'On my own merits. No one moves me up to fill dead men's bloody shoes!' He looked hard at Feiffer and clenched his fists, '*No one.*'

Spencer said helpfully, 'Maybe it's just as everyone says and it's been left here and absolutely nothing's going to happen at all.'

Auden said, 'Sure.' He looked at Winter and Minnie and saw their faces. Auden said quietly, 'Do you believe that?'

3.51 p.m.

Spencer said, 'No.' Spencer said with a tremor in his voice, 'Eight seconds, all right? Eight seconds.'

He saw the look on Auden's face.

Auden said, grinning, 'Seven. You got it wrong. It's seven.'

Spencer said, '*Whatever!*'

He touched at the gun in his belt.

And, closing his eyes for a moment, waited.

*

Wah ... wah ... *wah* ... *wah*! ... WAH! It was rising in him: the old war cry of the warrior, growing, coming closer, reaching culmination. Minutes, seconds. It was coming, reaching fulfillment, becoming greater than the ability of his chest to hold it in—it was arriving, the moment: coming, rising, reaching pitch ... shaking at him, surging ...

He saw him. He saw the man in the park look over and drop something from his hand—grass, a piece of grass. He was coming closer, looking, searching, trying to find him, knowing he was there—walking, walking ... Morishita said ... he said ... he said ...

3.56 and a half ... It was now. The time was right. The Technician had said that ...

The uniforms were not coming.

The man walking towards him was his enemy.

It was coming. The war cry, the ultimate moment, clenching at him like a fist, constricting his muscles. On the ground next to him the furled up flag seemed to be pulsing, the hidden sun on its face beginning to burn with life like a star coming back into existence, all the painted rays emanating from its centre going blood red and shimmering ...

Wah ... wah ... *wah* ...

He was too close. He was coming, cutting across the park, his hand resting loosely near where the holstered weapon was waiting to— He was coming, too close.

He was coming, reaching, drawing nearer ...

The sun was behind Morishita. He saw the man's face. He saw him look up at the sun. He saw him move over a little to the left to cut it out. At the car the others were standing there just . . .

He saw.

He saw.

Wah . . . growing, growing . . .

He saw Feiffer see him!

He heard Auden shriek, 'Jesus Christ!' He saw the van smoking.

He heard something loud inside the van go *CLICK!*

*

The obi . . . Open, taken out of the glassene envelope, it was . . . Unbelievably, it was . . .

Owlin said, '*No—!*'

It was vanishing.

Before his very eyes, with the smell strong and pungent biting at his nostrils and making him cough, the whole thing was simply *vanishing*!

*

In the Station, O'Yee shouted at the clock, '*No!*'

On the other end of the phone, The Fireworks Man said, 'What was that?'

O'Yee shouted, 'Get here! Get here! It's happening again!'

He heard the shooting from the park.

He heard it.

O'Yee said, 'Oh, Jesus Christ!'

Too late. It was all too late.

3.58 p.m.

Helplessly, hopelessly, O'Yee slammed down the phone and said in the sandbagged, secure, safe, too far away room, 'Oh Christ! Oh, Holy Mother of God! *Oh Christ*!!'

144

Auden was running.

Feiffer shouted, 'No!' He saw the truck smoking, burning, the black oily stuff pouring out through the cracks in the rear doors. There was a burst of fire and from somewhere. Minnie had gotten hold of an Ingram and she was pouring fire at the pillbox. On the ground, Feiffer saw bits and pieces of grey masonry and dust coming off the structure in puffs. He saw Spencer out in the open.

He shouted, 'Run! Run!' and then the sniper was up again as Minnie changed magazines and a fusillade of bullets ripped tracks in the grass beside him as he got out his own gun and tried to get off a shot.

Spencer was out in the open with Auden's big, long barreled gun, firing aimed rounds through the slits of the pillbox.

There was no one inside. Feiffer saw a wedge of cement fly off as one of the bullets smashed itself to pieces again and then Spencer was shooting again, the big gun kicking high and hard in his hands. There was a crackle of dull fire as Winter got off a rapid fire clip on his Walther and then another burst as Minnie began spraying in three round series, searching, flicking at the pillbox with the big .45 rounds and tearing squat chunks out at a time.

The sniper was behind the box and not one of them could see him.

Feiffer yelled, 'Behind! He's behind the box!' He saw a flash as the sniper snapped off a shot at him from a sort of half leaning position and the air around him exploded into dirt and grass and he got his head down and tried to shoot back.

In the barrage his gun hardly sounded as if it went off at all.

Auden reached the van. The smoke was pouring out in his face. Auden said, 'Five, six, six and a half ... six and three quarters...!' The doors were stuck. The first one was a blank, always ... the first one was a blank that would blow the doors open... Auden got his hands on the handles and wrenched.

Nothing.

Spencer shouted, 'Ten, eleven!' He was timing it to the gunfire. His gun clicked empty and he got in another load with a speed loader, all six rounds at once, and snapped the cylinder closed and had the hammer back in the same motion.

He tried another aimed shot.

There was nothing to aim at.

The doors were jammed. Auden shouted, 'Bastard! *Open!*' Newton's cradle. It was inside there, burning through, getting ready to swing. Auden, wrenching, yelled, 'Open! *Open!*'

It was happening. Morishita saw the ground around the tall man detonate and go upwards like a suddenly sprouting flower. He was safe. All the bullets were hitting the pillbox and he was safe. The van was burning, smoking. He tried to get in a shot at the man wrenching at the back of it, but a burst of fire ripped across the top of the pillbox like steel raindrops and he got his head down and reached for his flag.

The man on the ground was getting up.

Morishita flicked the flag and it came out open, the rising sun on it burning with life. He saw the man on his knees shouting at someone to do something and he levelled the rifle and got a clear shot in at the man's face and pulled the trigger.

Something happened. Nothing happened. The rifle failed to kick. It was jammed, stuck. Morishita jerked back the cocking handle and the empty brass shell case came out glittering like gold and fell onto the open flag. A hole. There seemed to be some sort of tiny hole in the case and he let the bolt fly forward and chambered another round and tried to get in an aim.

The man at the van almost had it open. The doors were giving.

Where was the explosive charge? It should have gone off? Like a man shooting ineffectually in a nightmare, Morishita caught sight of the man on the grass getting ready to run and pulled the trigger again and nothing happened.

He ejected the case. They were all duds. Nothing was happening. The case came out empty and fired and the bullet had gone somewhere, but the man on the grass was still living and he was—

Tiny holes: all the ejected cartridge cases seemed to have tiny holes in them. Morishita screamed, 'Wah! Wah!' and stood up to get in a shot.

Seventeen, eighteen, nineteen... Auden shrieked at the doors, 'Come on, you bastards!' He turned like a monkey climbing a frame and saw someone standing up at the pillbox behind him—a blurred figure washed out by the glaring sun. The door was coming—he felt it give.

Spencer yelled, 'Minnie, behind! He's behind the box, not in it—behind!' He saw Feiffer standing up as the figure, lost in the sun, got up and for a moment he saw a flag and a cap and a— Spencer shrieked, 'It's a Jap! It's him! It's a Japanese!' He shrieked at Minnie, 'Kill him! Cut him in half! *Kill him!*' The Ingram's magazine was empty. He saw Minnie snap it out onto the ground and reach into the car seat for another. Feiffer was running, his gun drawn, straight towards the blurred figure. Spencer saw the flag. Spencer yelled— Winter's little automatic was popping away, but all the bullets were going low. Spencer yelled— He got Auden's big magnum up and thought— He shouted at Auden, 'It's too long! It's more than seven seconds!' and then Minnie had the magazine in and was drawing back the bolt, and Spencer yelled, 'Don't spray them! You'll hit Harry! *Don't spray them!*'

It came open. One of the doors came open. A fraction.

Then more.

And then the other one.

Something gave and they were coming open. Auden said, 'Come on, come on...' Something was holding them... 'Come on, come on...!'

It was happening in a nightmare. He was shooting, aiming the rifle, doing his honour and his duty and—and it was a nightmare. The gun was not shooting, it was simply making popping noises, like blanks, and all the bullets were going—nowhere. Morishita wrenched at the gun again to clear yet another useless case from the breech and saw in the magazine the live round come up and go into the breech. He saw the silver bullet in its end. He saw. The tall man was coming at him, running. He was twenty yards away. He had his gun out, not a military gun, but an ignoble, squat

147

barrelled little— Morishita yelled in Japanese, 'Work! Function!' and got the rifle up to his shoulder and drew a final pulverising aim onto the man's face, directly into the forehead, and began pulling the trigger. Morishita yelled—

The world exploded into bright, burning, searing light. It was a mirror. There was a giant mirror in the back of the van.

Morishita said, 'Ai!' as the light swamped him and drowned him and seemed to— The sun was directly behind him and the mirror had it all and was blinding him and burning out his eyes. Morishita said, 'Aai—!' Somewhere the man was coming at him. All the shooting had stopped. He saw the tall man for a moment in the glare turn back to the van and—

Auden shouted, 'Got you, you bastard!' and with Spencer's gun coming out in the fastest draw he had ever done in his life killed the reflected image of the Japanese sniper in the mirror with a single slot that exploded the mirror into a million fragments. Auden said, 'Oh, no...!'

The drowning pool of light was gone. Feiffer said, lost... 'Where are...' He was on the ground, rolling. He saw for an instant through the light and—

Winter shrieked, 'Auden, get out! The TNT's—'

The van was loaded with the stuff. Winter heard Spencer shout, 'No!' It was like a scene from an execution. He saw Feiffer half crouched on the ground with the sniper's gun barrel actually touching his forehead and Spencer yelled, 'No! No! No!' He saw—

'Oh, Christ...' Feiffer had a sudden picture of his father dying on the ground in Shanghai with all the gun barrels smoking and lowering like— All his breath was gone... He heard Winter shouting ... and in the overwhelming, disintegrating blast Feiffer fell backwards and thought he somehow floated away with a bloody, torn up face looking down at him and some sort of flag with a picture of the sun on it flowing all around him like a shroud, and he was drifting, hearing things, going backwards...

Spencer shrieked, 'The gun's blown up! The gun's gone up in his face!' He saw Winter out at the van wrenching and dragging Auden out of it and he yelled at Auden, 'He's blown his gun up!

It's his blood, not Harry's. He's got blood all over his face and—'

Auden shrieked as Winter pulled him off, 'I shot a fucking reflection! I've done it again and I've shot a fucking reflection!' Auden shrieked—

Spencer yelled, 'Get him over here!' He caught Auden by the shoulder as Winter grabbed him and clapped him hard on the back. Feiffer was on the grass, moving, alive. Spencer saw the Japanese stagger, his face all torn to pieces and he yelled at Minnie with the quick firing Ingram, 'Finish him! Finish the bastard! Don't worry about police regulations—shoot him before he can—'

He saw the Ingram come up. The Japanese was out in the open, starting to run, easy, a perfect target.

Spencer, out of control, shrieked, 'Kill him! Kill him! *Kill him!*' and at that exact moment the three hundred pounds of TNT The Technician had carefully placed in the van behind the mirror, a hessian sack load at a time, exploded in a single ball of blasting flame and blew him completely off his feet and onto the grass.

*

4.07 p.m. There was nothing left of the van but a burnt out chassis and, by the time the other units began to arrive—eight minutes early—no sign of the wounded sniper but his unfurled flag lying on the ground where he had dropped it next to the shattered rifle.

By his side, Auden said apologetically to Feiffer, 'Harry, I'm sorry. I shot a reflection...' He looked on the verge of tears.

Feiffer's hands were still shaking. He tried to get something out, but no words came.

Auden said, 'I'm really very, very sorry... I suppose this is the end of all my promotion chances...' He looked up sadly, like a little boy caught out.

Feiffer said, nodding, 'Yeah, I suppose it is.' He patted Auden hard on the shoulder. Feiffer said with difficulty, 'You'd be posted to another Station, you know, if you were—if you got

149

promoted . . .' He kept his hands together in an attitude of prayer on his chest and tried to stop them shaking.

Feiffer said, still trembling, 'And then, Phil, what the hell would I do without you?'

The Emergency Unit squads were running across the grass from their civilian vehicles—a motley array of totally un-believable fake delivery trucks and station wagons—coming to see the flag, but before they reached it, glistening with moisture, it seemed suddenly to fray apart and turn into a picture floating on a saucer of water like a transfer and then, as if it had never been, the flag totally and completely and utterly . . . disappeared.

For a brief moment there was a very odd smell, like decay, and then, with the flag, all at once, it was gone.

12

In his best suit, The Fireworks Man came into the charge room from the street and looked at Ah Pin. In his torn khaki shorts and holed singlet, Ah Pin was still sweeping.

The Fireworks Man asked in Cantonese, 'Did they get him?' He waited for an answer.

Ah Pin stopped sweeping. Ah Pin said with the faintest narrowing of his eyes, seeing who it was, 'No. This time he got away.'

He held The Fireworks Man's eyes for a long moment, but after all those years there was nothing that easily to be read in them and he turned away and went on with his work.

*

He had travelled from one time to another and he was free. It was like fresh air, cool and new and wonderfully light and—and he was himself, living in the time he lived in when everything was new and modern and fresh and clean. In his car by the isolated telephone box at the harbour, The Technician lit a menthol cigarette and drew in the smoke gratefully and let it out in a long, relaxed, easy stream. He closed his eyes.

His head was resting on the back of the driver's seat and he felt his lungs empty the old stale air of the tunnels and fill with the sharp tang of the sea. He had made it: he was only a few easy steps away from the end and he had made it.

Across the point, past where the junks and sampans were, he could see the pall of smoke from the furniture van turning from black to grey and then white as the last of the chassis burned down or the Fire Brigade doused it with their foam hoses.

It was over. He felt new and young and optimistic, and everything, everything was all right and linear and well-planned and certain.

One more call.

He had just one more call to make and everything would be just the way he had planned it.

Tanino, Ozawa, Morishita: they were all just memories. All dead and forgotten.

Away from the tunnels and the death and the warm, rotten air, all that was yesterday and none of it meant anything to him anymore. He had set all his charges and that was the end of all that too.

And guns and grease and oil and the stink of cordite and age and weapons: all finished, something from a war. He had returned, alive, uninjured and the war was just something, sometimes, he might think about. But it was not real anymore.

The technician said softly to himself, 'I shall be very, very rich.' He made a clucking sound and felt all the tiredness go from his body.

He felt his eyes filling with tears. 'I'll be well again. I'll be well and strong and hopeful and everything I want—' The thought was getting harder and harder to hang onto. 'It was all worth it! I made mistakes, but in the end it was all worth it!' He opened his eyes and saw his own face reflected back at him in the car windscreen. The Technician said with sudden force, 'He never did anything for me! Why should I care what happened to him?' The Technician said, 'No.' He felt encouraged. 'It's every man for himself in this world and no one ever gave me anything!' He would become one of the ever-rich, ever-young, ever-happy people he saw on television. The Technician touched at his shirt. It was light cotton. 'Silk shirts and women—anything I want! It's mine by right and whatever I did, I only did it because it was all denied to me!' He thought for a moment of the Major—The Bannin, like some sort of awful, squirming slug... Something the ever young, ever rich never thought of. 'No, it's mine by right!'

The smoke from the burning van in the park had stopped and The Technician cursed it, and Morishita who had died there, and all of them, 'Rot! Go back to dust and rot!'

There had been love between him and The Bannin. At least, he had thought so.

4.39 p.m.

No, there had been no love.

The Technician looked hard at the telephone and tried to bring his mind to his future reality by concentrating on the bright colours, the plastic and the aluminium.

One more call.

One last call and he was free.

A little behind him, on one of the cliffs was one of the entrances to the tunnels and he looked back in its direction in his rear view mirror and saw, crawling out from the time warp, *nothing*.

One more call.

Uniforms. Lots and lots of uniforms.

The Technician got out of his car and, spinning a twenty cent coin in his hand for the phone call, looked across at the horizon above the harbour and saw in it nothing but hope.

A long way behind him, at the edge of the cliffs, something moved, but he was temporarily mesmerised by the spinning object in his hand, and The Technician, in absolutely no hurry at all, did not notice it.

Dead men rising.

At the tunnel entrance on the cliff, all the dead were meeting, watching.

He saw The Technician talking to himself and grinning as he flipped the coin again and again easily and happily into the air.

The little spinning object was spinning, rising and falling, glinting dully in the light.

At the tunnel entrance all the dead were whispering incessantly in Major Takashima's ear.

The Major was listening.

. . . watching.

Nodding . . .

153

*

On the phone in the Detectives' Room the Commander said, 'Either he was a genuine bloody seventy five year old hold-out soldier or he wasn't! You saw him. What the hell was he? Didn't you see *anything*?'

Feiffer said, 'No! I saw a bloody great flash when the mirror got the full light of the sun and I saw a rifle muzzle and I saw— All I saw was about two seconds left before he blew the top of my head away and then after that all I saw was his face covered in blood. For all I know, it could have been anybody!'

'Did he at least *move* like an old man?'

'He was behind a pillbox. He didn't have to move at all, Neal, all I saw was—'

The commander said, 'Was the mirror flash.' He made a tutting noise.

'I'm sorry. I'm lucky to be alive. If it hadn't been for Phil Auden shooting the mirror to pieces—'

The Commander said, 'And the flag—'

'Evaporated.' Feiffer said, 'And the obi—'

'It's genuine. I've had it translated and it belonged—belongs—to someone called Private Masuo Morshita of the 38th and it's genuine, and as for the flag, according to Forensic it was just so old and rotten and dry that it just—fell to dust.' The Commander said, 'Harry, it can't have been a bloody real, live Japanese! Any seventy year old man taking the full force of an exploding gun would have had a heart attack and died on the spot!' The Commander said, 'Why? Why wasn't the van set up the way all the other situations were? Why the hell if someone had gone to the trouble to steal a van with a bloody great Victorian dressing table mirror set up in it, why the hell didn't he point it at his enemies instead of at his friends?'

'Why the hell didn't the uniformed people who were supposed to be sealing off Beach Road catch him?'

'I don't know! Because he didn't come through.' The

Commander said at the end of his patience, 'Because like his fucking flag, he just disappeared into thin air. Because if he is some bloody Jap who's managed to survive here for forty years he's like a bloody ghost and—' The Commander said, 'Have you had your follow up phone call yet? Maybe, the way things are going, you're not even going to get one!' The Commander said hopelessly, 'Harry, what the hell do these people want? If it was just a sniper job or even a few hold-outs I could understand it, but there are these phone calls as well. And evidently, someone who wants to kill the so-called Japanese snipers in the bloody public parks even more than we do. And these calls: one lot from someone pretending to be what? A political terrorist? And the other—from whom? From a Japanese speaking what?' Lost, he demanded, 'Someone tell me what the hell's going on!'

'I don't know what the hell's going on.' Feiffer said, 'We've got a Japanese interpreter here, but if he doesn't ring then I don't know where we even start to make sense of it.' Feiffer said, 'So far, we've had three full attacks and the one in the park and we're at bloody bedrock.'

'The Japanese arsenal must be at fucking bedrock! There isn't any Japanese arsenal! It would have been found!' The Commander said, 'Have you got anyone working on it at all?'

'I've got Owlin at Archives trying to—'

'Him? You mean the tree-nut?' The Commander said, 'Is that the best we can do?'

'No, the best we can do is take the names of the soldiers we've got from the obis and feed them into the Japanese Defense Department computer in Tokyo and then feed that into the US and British War Records computers and then, when the names come out—'

The Commander said angrily, 'And do what? Get onto all the still living relatives of bloody dead men—all the people in the photos—and say without getting them too upset, "Excuse me, but if your husband or son who died in 1942 might happen to be still alive in a bloody arsenal in Hong Kong have you any idea which particular arsenal it might be?"' The Commander said, 'And what then? After we've calmed their bloody hysteria—get down on our knees and beg them not to give the story to the newspapers?' The Commander said, 'No. Like hell we do.'

'Then we're still at bedrock.'

'I don't like it Harry. It's happening too quickly.' The Commander said, 'Put it all together and it's been happening so fast we haven't even had time to take it all in. It's almost as if—' The Commander said, 'No, I just can't believe it's a lost section of soldiers—and this other person, this one who rings up in Cantonese, the anti-colonial terrorist or whatever he claims to be, who the hell is he?'

Feiffer glanced at The Fireworks Man sampling some of O'Yee's Constable Yan made coffee and said nothing.

'And why did this man Morishita's gun blow up? Does anyone know?'

'Sands has got it for examination—what little there was left of it.'

The Commander said, quoting, ' "The uniformed forces of colonial repression." What uniforms? There wasn't a uniform in the park anywhere and still he started shooting. And who the fucking hell made a report to the Vice Squad and why?' The Commander said, 'No, it's not right. It's not how the Japanese Army used to do business. If they wanted you dead then they didn't mess about, you were just dead.' The Commander said, 'No, it's this other fellow, this one who rings up.' He asked, 'Have you got a trace set up for his call? If he makes it.' He answered his own question, 'Yes, of course you have.' The Commander said suddenly, 'The Japanese computer thing, no. We can't—not just yet.' He seemed to think for a moment.

The Commander said, like everyone else, at bedrock, 'Jesus Christ, bloody Johnny Appleseed Owlin! *Is that really the best we can do?*'

*

4.52 p.m.
The Technician looked at his watch.

Whispering, hissing, whispering: the voices were insistently rustling in the Major's ear.

The Major was listening, nodding.

His eyes were blank.

The Major—The Bannin, the watchman—

He was listening to the voices.

*

He had it. He looked at the residue on the desk where the obi had disintegrated and he had it at last.

He knew at last how to find the arsenal. There was the faintest smell of something old and bitter in the air-conditioned room and Owlin, staring down at the desk and grinning, knew exactly where the thing had come from.

Owlin Family: Records Of Tree Plantings On The Island Of Hong Kong, 1853 To—

He knew that smell.

Owlin said, 'Oak.'

A barren rock with scarcely a tree upon it. That was how Hong Kong had been described after the Opium Wars when the first of the ships had sailed to it from Macao and the first of his family to establish himself there had sent for seeds and nurtured them and walked the length of the island in search of good ground from which to grow—*oak*.

Owlin Family: Records Of Tree Plantings On The Island Of Hong Kong, 1853 To—

Owlin said in victory, 'Got you, you bastards. After all these years, my family has got back at you and I've got every record of every tree ever planted here and I know where your dirty little obis and your dirty little guns and your axes are—I know just how to find out where you stored them!'

He was the last of the line. After him, there would be no more members of his family in Hong Kong.

He knew that smell.

Firedamp.

157

What miners called firedamp.

Methane, slightly impure, mixed with—

All the crosses on his big map went nowhere. They just meandered and wandered around the circumference of an unfindable circle and they—

The obi came from the centre of that circle and it smelled of firedamp.

The reason he had been unable to locate the centre of the system was that he had been expecting straight, man-made lines when in fact the tunnels were built around natural fissures in the granite and the smell about the glassene envelope and the obi it had contained came from—

The question was not where the Japanese Empire forty years ago built an arsenal in Hong Kong to store their weapons; it was simpler than that.

It was, where had the Owlin family a hundred years ago, out of love and hope for the future, planted their oak trees?

Owlin smiled.

It was almost unncessary to go back into the Archives to look.

It was his life.

He already knew the answer.

*

On the phone in the Detectives' Room, Inspector Sands of Ballistics said, 'In case you're feeling you've had your entire life's supply of luck doled out in one glob you haven't. The rifle was sabotaged to blow up.'

Feiffer said, 'How?'

'By the simple method of drilling little holes in three or four of the cartridges in the magazine and draining off a proportion of the powder, then following them up with a live, undrained round.' Sands said, 'The first round fired and jammed the first bullet about fourteen inches up the barrel, then when the second followed suit and fused itself to the first and then the third did the same what you had inside that barrel was a pipe bomb. Then, when the next live round came up with a full load of powder, its bullet couldn't get out and the whole bolt assembly got blown back and the receiver sides just disintegrated like tissue paper.'

Feiffer said eagerly, 'So he's hurt? Seriously? The sniper?'

'Maybe. I've recovered most of the bits, including long splinters of wood from the stock that went up in the bang, but it's possible that a tiny piece of metal got him—but unlikely.' Sands said, 'The general idea, I think, was that the bolt itself would be blown back into his face like a spear, but with a hand-made gun, particularly one designed to handle experimental pressures—'

Feiffer said angrily, 'His face was covered in blood! He *must* have been hit!'

'Maybe. Or it could have been gas blast, or burned varnish from the stock, or some other part of the gun—the blueing—or maybe even—'

'Or maybe even what?' Feiffer said incredulously, 'Are you saying a bloody rifle blew itself to pieces and the man behind it didn't even get a goddamned *nosebleed*?'

'I'm saying it was a very good rifle!' Sands said, 'And before you bother to ask me about fingerprints—'

Bedrock. Everything was barren, worthless, valueless, useless bedrock. Feiffer said, 'Who the hell are these people? The fucking *Samurai Immortals*? All this stuff you're telling me is useless!'

'You're bloody lucky one of the samurai immortals decided he didn't like the other one or the only way you'd be shouting at some poor bastard doing his best to help you would be via the goddamned Celestial Phone Box! It's not my fault. I was the one who told you about the guns in the first place! What the fuck do you think I was doing while you people were being shot at in the park? Sitting on my hands? I was ready to go. Bloody Headquarters stopped me! It wasn't my idea, it was theirs! I'm an Inspector, not a bloody Commissioner. When I'm standing there in civilian clothes next to my bloody civilian car ready to go and I'm told I have to dress in civilian clothes over the next hour and then spend another forty minutes looking for a civilian car I don't say "What the fuck are you talking about?" I say, "Yes, sir!" I would have been there! I was ready to go! Bloody WPCs shooting Ingrams!' Sands said angrily, 'That's my fucking job! I would have been there.'

'Yeah.' Feiffer said suddenly calmed, 'Yes, I know you would. I'm sorry.' Feiffer said quietly, 'Look, have you got anything else at all?'

There was the slightest of pauses.

Sands said sadly, 'No, not a thing.' He asked, 'How about you?'

4.58 p.m.

Feiffer said, 'No.' He fell silent for a moment then put the phone gently back on its receiver and saw The Fireworks Man looking at him curiously.

*

4.29 p.m.

At the entrance to the tunnels, his eyes never leaving The Technician, The Bannin waited.

The voices beside him had all stopped whispering.

The Bannin touched at his face and found he had Morishita's blood on him.

5.00 p.m. exactly. From somewhere behind him on the headland, The Bannin heard a siren howl to signal the end of a work shift. He saw The Technician look at his watch and then get back to his car to wait.

The Technician had been spinning a little coin up in the air over and over. It had glittered dully.

The Bannin also had something made of metal in his hand that glittered in the sun.

Brightly.

He felt its sharp edge and narrowed his eyes.

*

At the door, Ah Pin looked hard at The Fireworks Man at a desk near the sandbags and then to the tape recorder and tracing extensions on O'Yee's desk. O'Yee looked up and smiled at him and Ah Pin, his eyes still on The Fireworks Man, nodded back.

It was a minute after five, past his quitting time.

Ah Pin, drumming his fingers out of sight on the door jamb behind him, hesitated.

O'Yee, still smiling, said lightly in Cantonese, 'You know, my grandfather lived to be eighty nine years old and he'd be with us still if it hadn't been for the overwork.' He looked pointedly at the clock and, in case Ah Pin was waiting for permission to leave, nodded at him encouragingly.

The Fireworks Man's face was bland.

All so long ago . . .

The Fireworks Man's suit was expensive and well cut.

At the door Ah Pin smiled back at O'Yee and then, after a moment, went back into the charge room in his torn shorts and singlet, to go home.

*

Running across Hong Bay, directly through all the overlaid crosses and marks on the map, there was a natural tunnel in the granite.

In the centre of it, long before there were detailed geological maps to be had, Owlin's family had planted a forest of ash trees.

In their deep, dead, decomposing roots, those long dead trees now grew Japanese obis and methane gas.

He was the last of the line.

In his silent room, Owlin ran his finger across the coloured strata of time and change and looked for where the tunnel, linking generations, came out into the present.

*

5.05 p.m.

By his car The Technician closed his eyes and tried to focus dreams.

161

One more call.

Behind him, the siren was still howling, running down and he thought that in less than three hours it would all be over.

He tossed his coin casually onto the bonnet of his car and it made a tinkling sound as it struck, rolled a few inches, then, losing momentum, lay flat in front of him, waiting.

13

The two nickel-plated balls in Auden's hand went click-click-click... Auden caught The Fireworks Man looking at him and opened his hand to show the man what he held. Auden said, 'They're lead balls, plated.' He drew an imaginary filament from the balls with his fingers, 'They hang on strings from a central point and when you hit one against the other they click. It's an executive toy. It's called a Newton's Cradle.'

The Fireworks Man was sitting at O'Yee's desk. In front of him was the telephone with a tape recorder and extension wires attached. The extension wires ran to Feiffer's telephone and the one on Spencer's desk. The Fireworks Man looked first at that and then at the sandbags and the bullet proof vests. Auden had been speaking in English. He thought the man had not understood and began again in Cantonese.

The Fireworks Man said, 'I understand English. It's a pendulum device invented by Sir Isaac Newton.' He seemed worried. He watched as Auden smiled and nodded at him and then went back to clicking. The Fireworks Man said quietly, 'Like most things they are originally a Chinese invention.'

Sencer looked at Auden and shook his head. The sounds were clearly upsetting The Fireworks Man. Spencer said in explantion, 'It's part of the device used to set off the rifles.'

The Fireworks Man said, 'Originally, it was designed as an amusement. Gunpowder was originally designed as an amusement!' It was warm in the Detectives' Room and The Fireworks Man took out a white handkerchief from his inside coat pocket and dabbed at his face. Feiffer was at his desk going through photographs and folders, getting something ready. The

Fireworks Man said with a trace of desperation in his voice, 'I don't know that I even remember the sort of Japanese soldiers speak. It's not the same as commercial Japanese—'

O'Yee said, 'You'll be fine.' He connected something from the telephone into the tape recorder and touched a button to test it. A light came on on the recorder and he switched it off again. O'Yee said, 'All you have to do is keep him on the line. The last time I tried Japanese on him it gave him such a shock that he was stunned into total silence for about thirty seconds and—'

Feiffer had a folder assembled. He brought it over and put it on the desk in front of The Fireworks Man. Feiffer said, 'Here's everything we know about them—the names, everything.' He waited, but The Fireworks Man went on looking into his face. Feiffer said gently, 'There's no problem about your good character. I've told you you can have it whether you do this or not.'

The Fireworks Man's face seemed to be melting. The Fireworks Man's mouth formed a word, but nothing came out. Behind him, he could feel the invisible presence of Ah Pin in the charge room. The Fireworks Man said, 'What did he tell you? Ah Pin. The executioner? What did he tell you about me?'

Auden said, 'The what?'

Feiffer said, 'Nothing. He told us what I told you.' He pushed the folder a little closer, 'You're our last chance.'

'*Why* am I your last chance? I don't ask you to do my job for me, why should you ask me to do yours?'

O'Yee said, 'We can't get anyone else. There's no one else who can speak the Japanese slang of that period and—'

'*How in the name of heaven can they be Japanese soldiers?*' The Fireworks Man said, 'Look at me! I'm their age! Can you imagine me with enough courage to go into battle now?'

'No one's asking you to go into battle.'

'Why am I doing this? To convince a cleaner after forty years that I was a loyal Chinese?' The Fireworks Man said, 'Look at me, I'm rich! Why should I have to convince him of anything? I—I was standing there in my—in my best suit and he in his dirty, ragged—and he—' The Fireworks Man looked down at the folder and pushed it away. The tape recorder and extensions were on the desk in front of him. All of a sudden, The Fireworks Man said, 'No!' He shouted at Auden, still clicking, 'Stop intimidating me! It's all over! It's finished! I was tried and it's all over! Why should I lose any more?'

Feiffer said, 'There are people dead!'

'There are always people dead!' The Fireworks Man said, 'All right, I believe you: you're an honest man. You're the only honest man I've met in almost eighty years on this Earth—you said I could have my good character for my licence renewal whatever I did—all right, I'll do nothing—now give me my good character!'

Feiffer said, 'At least read the file.'

'You said I could have it! I want it!'

'At least look at the names! At least give us *something*—'

The Fireworks Man said, 'No!' He shook his head. 'No.' He challenged Feiffer with a look, 'You said you'd give me my good character, now give it to me! I won't have anything more to do with this and you can tell your cleaner that if—' The Fireworks Man said, 'No!' Give me the character! Let me finish my life and sell the whole filthy factory for the peace of my soul! *Give me the good character!* Let me be rid of myself!'

Spencer came forward to rest his hand on The Fireworks Man's shoulder. Spencer said gently, 'Look, you're just a little upset—'

'You *boy!* You fresh-faced, stupid, unknowing *boy!*' The Fireworks Man demanded, 'What's the worst thing you've ever done in your life—*stolen money from your mother's purse?*' He saw Feiffer's hand on the folder and he swept it away, 'I don't want to see the names! I don't want to have to read them! I don't want to have to remember! I don't want to even—' His hand closed around the folder to fling it to the floor, but Feiffer's hand was on his wrist.

Feiffer held him. Feiffer said suddenly, 'What the hell are you holding back?' His face had gone hard. He looked down at the folder and then back into The Fireworks Man's face. Feiffer said over his shoulder to O'Yee, 'Give him his good character. Type it

165

out and sign it.' The Fireworks Man's wrist in his hand was surprisingly strong. Feiffer said with his eyes still on The Fireworks Man's face, 'You know something. Don't you?'

'Nothing. I know nothing!' The Fireworks Man wrenched his hand free. He turned his eyes to Auden, 'You, playing with your little toys and telling me—' He looked at O'Yee, 'And you, you *Eurasian*, you with your little wires and your—'

Feiffer ordered him, 'Read the names!'

'I know the names!'

'Read them!'

'I know them!' The Fireworks Man grabbed the folder and held it up in his hand, 'Who have you got so far? What have you got— their thousand stitches obis? You asked me in my office if I knew what a thousand stitches obi was. Yes, I know what they are! I knew the people who wore them! I was married to a Japanese girl who made one! Yes, I know what they are!' He turned to Spencer, 'You, is your family rich?'

Spencer said, 'Well, no, of course they're not—'

'Are they poor then? So poor that they steal from garbage bins to stay alive? So poor that they sell what they steal rather than eat it themselves? So poor that—'

Feiffer said, 'Nobody is suggesting that during the Occupation—'

'I wasn't poor during the Occupation! I was rich! Being poor was a choice! I had no choice! I had a Japanese wife and I had no choice at all!' The Fireworks Man said, 'Even now I have no choice!'

'You have a choice! You don't have to do this.' Feiffer said evenly, 'But if you know something and you're holding it back—in a murder investigation—then God help you when—'

The Fireworks Man said, '*Tanino*! Am I right?' He looked down at the folder, 'Sergeant Quartermaster Seichiro Tanino of the thirty eighth division in Hong Kong. Am I right?'

Feiffer said in astonishment, 'Yes.' He had thought the man had meant only that he knew the names figuratively. He had thought— Feiffer said, 'Yes, he was the one in Cuttlefish Lane—'

Auden said, 'And the boat?'

The Fireworks Man said, 'Corporal Sakutaro Ozawa.' Tears were beginning in his eyes. The names were coming out like old unhealed wounds. The Fireworks Man said, 'Private Masuo Morishita.'

Feiffer said, *'How do you know all these names?'*

The Fireworks Man looked hard at Spencer's unlined face. The Fireworks Man said quietly, 'And their leader, Major Quartermaster Juzo Takashima, called by those who knew him well or those who loved him, "Bannin", Watchman—because he once, during his student days, took a job where he—' The Fireworks Man said quietly, 'You see I know all the names already. I know them. I know every one of them—and some of the others, some of the others who were temporarily attached to his section, but who—' The Fireworks Man said in a sudden explosion, 'I don't have to look at your file! *I know all their names already!'*

Feiffer demanded, 'How? How do you know all their names?'

Spencer said softly, 'My God, they really are Japanese soldiers!'

The Fireworks Man said with the faintest of bitter smiles, still looking at Spencer's face, 'Yes, they really are.' The Fireworks Man said quietly to Feiffer, 'I know the names of every one of them. Even after all these years, every one—'

'*How?*' Feiffer demanded, 'How? How do you know their names? How? After all these years, *how* do you know their names?'

Ah Pin was long gone, but The Fireworks Man still felt his presence behind him and the invisible presence of other things. His best suit was merely a sham: an old man dressed up. He touched at it and felt his eyes brim with tears. The Fireworks Man said, 'How? How do I know all their names?'

There was silence in the room.

The Fireworks Man said quietly, 'Because almost forty years ago, one night, September the first, 1942, I, not the bombs, but I ... I killed them.'

5.17 p.m.

As, on the headland, The Technician got out of his car to make his call, The Fireworks Man looked at all the faces in the stilled room in Yellowthread Street and said softly, 'The Bannin—Major Takashima—was my wife's brother. The Resistance ordered me to kill him to save her and I did.' He touched at his suit and shrugged, 'But then, because she was Japanese, after the Liberation, they killed her anyway.'

The Fireworks Man looked down at the telephone in front of him.

The Fireworks Man asked the room, 'What do I say to a ghost?' Tears were running down his face. The Fireworks Man said almost inaudibly, 'That I'm—that I'm *sorry*?'

*

JAPANESE SOLDIERS IN HONG KONG?

Persistent reports reaching this newspaper that recent shootings in the Hong Bay district were carried out by hold-out Japanese soldiers from World War Two were again denied by the police in a statement issued late this afternoon.

The Press Officer at the Japanese Embassy in Hong Kong, Mr Michael Okuno, when questioned by reporters from this newspaper, refused to confirm or deny that recent police investigations had centred around nationals from his country, but said that, following a request from various sources, his Embassy would be releasing a statement aimed at clarifying the situation sometime tomorrow morning.

Mr Okuno refused to be drawn on what the contents of the statement might be.

*

Outside, dusk was coming. Feiffer said quickly, 'Then where the hell's the arsenal now? If that's where you killed them, then where the hell is it now?'

The Fireworks Man said, 'I don't know and that's the truth. That night, when the bombers came I went in and planted charges along the passage that led from Wyang Cove, but Wyang

168

Cove isn't there anymore. When the bombs fell and the charges went off there was nothing but rubble.' He looked at O'Yee and held out his hands in a gesture of helplessness. 'Wyang Cove isn't even there anymore. Not even by name. After the war when the Public Works people sealed off all the old air raid shelters and the tunnels the entire area was covered as part of a reclamation scheme and Wyang Cove became part of the new Beach Road.' The Fireworks Man said, 'The next morning when the Japanese inspected the damage they thought it had all been done by the bombs and they never even once suspected—' The Fireworks Man said, 'My brother-in-law, The Bannin—Major Taka-shima—he was never involved in the torture and the exe-cutions, but the Resistance decided he was one of the few Japs they could kill and get away with it and they were trying to impress the Communists and the Nationalists to send them arms and money and they needed to show that they'd at least killed somebody.' The Fireworks Man said, 'They needed confirmation that a real live Japanese with a name and a family had died—and they got that from me—someone they trusted—they let me go on working for the Japanese, because he was a—' The Fireworks Man said, 'And then, after the war, they killed my wife and they— *Because they never knew which side I was really on!*'

Spencer said anxiously, 'Whose side where you on?'

'Don't ask me that!' The Fireworks Man said, 'I was on the winning side! Can't you tell? Look at me! See how prosperous and happy I am? I was on the winning side!'

Spencer said after a moment, 'And which one was that?' All of a sudden he no longer felt fresh faced and young. Spencer said, 'Which was the side that won? The one that lost the fewest people it loved?'

The Fireworks Man said to Feiffer, 'I don't know where the entrance to the arsenal is. There were many. It was one giant system. All I did was destroy one little part of it.' The Fireworks Man said, 'I don't know. At first, when nobody was purposely hurt—on the building over there—when only one man was accidentally killed according to the newspapers—I thought it could have been children and then, in the papers, it hinted that it was some sort of anti-colonial terrorist gang and then—' The Fireworks Man said, 'I waited to hear about a flag.' He looked at Auden. Auden had the two balls in his hand. He looked down at them and put them gently on his desk. The Fireworks Man clenched his hand, 'Before their last hopeless battle, before they all committed suicide, the Japanese always burned their flag to stop it falling into enemy hands, but I—I haven't read about flags so I—' He asked, 'Has there been a flag?'

O'Yee said, 'Yes.'

The Fireworks Man said, 'Then they've come back.' The Fireworks Man closed his eyes. The Fireworks Man said quietly, 'Hanabi San: Mr Fireworks.' He smiled, 'My brother-in-law—Major Takashima—that's what he called me.' He said quietly, 'The Bannin—The Watchman.' He looked down at the telephone and said quietly, 'My brother-in-law—The Bannin—he's come back for *me*.'

*

He had had to go. It was obvious. He had had no choice in it. It was obvious. At the telephone, The Technician paused, gazing out across the harbour. *It was obvious and he should have no regrets about it because it was obvious!*

The Technician said quietly, 'Bannin...'

It was obvious and he had had to go.

An inch. All he had had to do was miss a few people by an inch and everything would have been all right and all this Japanese shit would have been— The Technician gripped the telephone receiver in his hand in a fury and cursed, 'Damn it! All you had to do was just what you were told and you could have had half! But no, you had to have all this Japanese shit and—'

—and sooner or later everyone would have been caught and it would have all been for nothing. An inch, just one inch. All he had had to do was—but no, that was too straightforward for a goddamned Jap and he had to start shrieking Banzai and killing

170

people and—and Morishita had died in the park in the set-up and all The Technician hoped was that his face had been so thoroughly shot to pieces by the cops that it was just a pulp! The Technician said, 'Curse you! You could have had half!'

'Divine mission to eradicate all the uniformed forces of colonial repression. . . .' Would they still wear it?

They had to. It was too late to change. It might just last long enough until . . .

The Technician, hesitating in the phone booth said in a fury, 'Damn him! He deserved to die!'

The 38th Division of the Japanese Imperial All Conquering Army in China—it was the goddamned methane gas or marsh gas or whatever it was down there. It had sent him insane. The Technician said, 'I had to kill you! I had to!' The Technician said to the plastic and aluminium telephone, 'You could have had half! I found the tunnels and I found you and you could have had half with all my blessings!'

He said in a fury of frustration at the telephone, *'Fuck you! You could have been my brother!'*

By now, the first of the incendiary charges would have gone off.

The Technician put his finger to the dial and began ringing the number for Yellowthread Street.

A hundred yards behind him, his face covered in blood, a ghost from forty years ago stood up at the cliff side.

The Technician had his back to him in the phone booth, dialling a number.

The long, razor sharp bayonet flashed in the ghost's hand.

His boots made no sound on the grass as he went forward.

*

The Fireworks Man said helplessly, 'No, you don't understand! If it's him . . . If it's the Major . . .'

Feiffer said desperately, 'Please, just one word . . .'

All the tracing apparatus and the recording devices were attached to the phone. The Fireworks Man said, pleading, 'If it's him come back—'

Feiffer said, 'People are dead! We've got nothing! All we've got is you!'

The phone was ringing.

Feiffer said in a final appeal to the Fireworks Man, 'Please . . . *please*!'

*

The final map in his collection was a geological chart of the Hong Bay region, complete with seismic soundings and surveyed, accurate strata formations and—

And he found it.

The tunnel went—

He found it.

Maltby Point. It came out in at least eight places on the cliffs and under the—

Owlin said softly, 'Got you!'

He had found it.

At least one of those natural tunnel exits would have been used by the Japanese engineers, possibly two or three, and at least one of those exits was still there because the Public Works Department, after the land had been sold, had only given cursory attention to the sealing up of old craters and—

He had found it.

He flipped back the canvas backed chart and overlaid it with a modern street map and stopped.

One of the tunnels, if all the maps and his calculations were right, came out under the—

The tunnels were filled with what? With guns. Shells? Explosives?

The Keeper Of Secrets stared hard at the street map and then flipped it back to expose the survey chart.

One of those tunnels came out directly under the—

It went right past where the old oak forest had been, directly under—

172

Owlin said, 'Oh, my God!'

One of those tunnels packed with guns and dynamite and TNT and God knew what else—one of the tunnels the Public Works Department had missed—came out directly under— Under the modern, fully operational Maltby Point fireworks factory.

Owlin said softly, again, 'Oh, my God . . .'

He flipped back to the first map again to make absolutely sure he was right.

*

Feiffer said in a whisper with his hand on The Fireworks Man's shoulder, 'Please, just one word . . .'

The Fireworks Man said, 'I mined the entrances and the air vents. The Resistance knew the bombers were coming and I had a pass to move around at night and I—I mined the spot where Major Takashima and his men were asleep and they—' The Fireworks Man said, trying to make someone understand, 'It was me! It wasn't the bombers, it was me! I killed them—my own brother-in-law, everyone—the whole eleven man section! I killed every last one of them!' The Fireworks Man said, 'No! It can't be true! *They're all dead*!'

*

He was coming. Across the grass, the Major was coming. He touched at his face and his hand came away bloody and black with the burned powder from the exploded rifle. The bayonet was in his other hand, held low. He looked down and saw his cracked leather boots crushing at the grass as he walked. The Technician was ahead of him in the phone. The Major said softly, over and over, 'Traitor . . . traitor . . .' He lifted up the long steel bayonet and it glittered in the sun.

The Technician had his back to him. His muscles tightened against his white shirt as he held the receiver hard to his ear, listening about to speak.

All the voices of the dead were whispering in the Major's ear. They came as wind in from the sea, coming across flat water in the dying light.

They were whispering, cajoling, working on him, hinting, entreating. The Major felt his breath coming in hard gasps. The Technician was in front of him. He saw the muscles in the man's back flicker as he moved in the booth and cocked his head slightly against the phone receiver to say something.

The Major's boots made no sound on the grass.

The Technician was moving, leaning closer to the phone, readying himself for his lies and dishonours and his—

The Major said softly, 'Traitor . . . *traitor!*'

He raised the bayonet and it flashed in the light.

The Major's hand was tight and hard on the haft. His arm was full of life and power. He felt his bicep tremble with anticipatory force.

His boots made no sound on the grass as he approached.

*

On the phone, O'Yee shrieked, 'Who the hell are you? *What the hell do you want?*' He heard Feiffer snap, 'Christopher—!' and O'Yee shouted, 'You lousy bastard, what the hell do you want?'

'I have a divine mission to—'

'Bullshit! Bullshit!' O'Yee saw the Fireworks Man's face and shouted, 'What the hell are you doing to my people? What the hell do you think you're doing to everyone? You're killing people! You lousy, rotten, stinking bastard, you're killing people!'

'—*divine mission to eradicate the uniformed forces of*—'

'No!' The Fireworks Man said, 'No! It's him! I know it is!'

Auden yelled, 'Pick up the extension!' He thrust it into The Fireworks Man's hand and The Fireworks Man pushed it away. Spencer said desperately to The Fireworks Man, 'Please, just one word! Just hold him long enough to—' He was already on the other phone dialling the number for a trace. Spencer said, 'Please, wouldn't you just—'

'—divine mission to eradicate—'

O'Yee shouted, 'No, I don't want to hear it!' He glanced at Spencer. Spencer was through to the exchange and he was reading off the number to them to get the engineers working. O'Yee said quickly to Feiffer, 'I can't hold him—' He looked hard at The Fireworks Man.

The Fireworks Man said—

'—colonial repression and I have—' He stopped. Behind him, The Technician heard something. In the phone booth he turned and saw death. The Technician said in Japanese, 'Bannin! *No!*'

He heard it. From across the room, he heard it. The Fireworks Man said, 'No, it can't be—' Auden still had the extension in his hand. The Fireworks Man said—

Auden thrust the phone into his hands and ordered him, 'Talk! Say something! Hold him until we can—'

'Bannin! Ie! *No!*' The Technician said hysterically, not knowing which way he was talking, 'I have a divine—Bannin! No!— mission to eradicate—'

O'Yee shouted, 'Who are you? *Tell us who you are!*'

Spencer was onto the engineers. He was saying, 'Yes, yes ... yes ...' as they narrowed down the call street by street. Spencer said, 'Yes ... yes ...'

Feiffer shouted at The Fireworks Man, 'Damn it, don't kill anyone else! Help us!' The Fireworks Man had the phone loosely in his hand. Feiffer gave him a shove in the back that almost sent him crashing against Auden's desk, 'Talk to him! Talk to him in Japanese!'

The Technician said, raving, '—uniformed—' The bayonet was glittering in the Major's hand. The Technician said, '—to eradicate all the—' He heard another voice on the other end of the line say in Japanese—

The Technician said—

'*Kwan Yu!* Kenneth!' The Fireworks Man said, not in Japanese, but in Cantonese, 'It's you! Kenneth, it's you! *Isn't it?*'

'It's Shozo, father, it's *Shozo!*' The Technician said, losing power, fading away, 'It's Shozo ... they were all Shozo.... I ...

it was...' The Technician said, 'It was mine! My birthright! I didn't do any of the things you did and it belongs to me when you're dead, not your soul!' The Major was standing next to him in the phone box, cramped close, his breath on The Technician's face, smiling, his eyes lightless and blank. The Technician said, babbling, 'Father, it was all mine ... you had no right to ... you have no right to ... to ...' He saw the bayonet come up, 'No right to deny me my .., my ... *my*....' He saw the bayonet come up. The Technician, The Fireworks Man's son by his second, Chinese wife, shouted in extremis, 'Father, *help me*—!'

Spencer said, 'Maltby Point! The call's coming from Maltby Point!' From near the—!' He looked hard at The Fireworks Man, '—from near the fireworks factory!'

There was a silence. At the other end of the line there was nothing but a silence.

The Fireworks Man said, 'Kenneth? Kwan Yu? *Kenneth?*'

He heard someone breathing.

He heard a hissing sound.

It was Shozo. It had all been Shozo...

The Fireworks Man said into the phone, 'After the war started I got you out, away—I got you away to Japan to stay with your mother's family ... I did right!' There was only a silence from the phone.

The Fireworks Man said, 'I thought it was the one good thing I ever did! I thought it was the one good thing—' The Fireworks Man said, desperately, changing to Japanese, 'I didn't want to kill him! *I had to!* It was either that or your mother and then, after the war, they killed her anyway!' The Fireworks Man shouted desperately at the son he had never wanted back, 'I got you away to Japan when you were just a baby! I thought it was the one good thing I ever did!' The Fireworks Man begged, 'Shozo! *Answer me!*' The Fireworks Man said, pleading, 'You were my first born son! Understand what I did for you! And then, after the war, I thought if they ever found out I had a Japanese son still living they'd take the factory back! Everything I had! I thought you wouldn't ever want to see me again after I killed your mother's brother and

176

your—I thought—' The Fireworks Man begged into the phone, 'Please, Shozo, *please!*'

O'Yee said quickly to Feiffer, 'I can't follow it all, but it's his son! It's the son of his first marriage to a Japanese woman! It isn't a hold-out at all, it's his son! It's someone from now—it's someone who's come back and made some sort of alliance with the other son, the Chinese one, and—'

The Fireworks Man shrieked into the phone, 'Where is my second son? What have you done to Kwan Yu? To Kenneth? *Where is my second son?'*

'*Here!*' The Major's voice said in a sudden old man's croak, 'Here! With us! With all the men you killed! With me! With The Bannin! Your son is here! *Hovering!* Waiting! *Rotting!*' The Major said, 'Your son—all your sons—all your family, everyone you ever touched—they are all—'

The Fireworks Man heard his second son say in a gasp, '*No. . . .!*' There was a terrible thump.

The Bannin said, 'Dead! Where we all are since you murdered us! All—long ago . . . all of us—*dead!*'

*

It was burning. The first of The Technician's charges had gone off in the underground testing chambers and the fireworks factory was beginning to burn.

*

5.45 p.m.
In his office in the Archives Owlin tried for the third time to ring the Station.

There was no one there. The phone just went on ringing and ringing.

Above him, in the streets, he had no idea whether it was night or day and he had to look up the times of sunset in an almanac before, drawing a breath to venture into the outside world, he

177

knew that there was at least an hour and five minutes before the city became dark.

*

It was burning. The factory was burning. All his enemies were coming. At the entrance to the tunnel on the cliff The Bannin heard the sound of sirens and klaxons as, from all over Hong Bay, uniformed men came to consecrate the last battle of the 38th Division of the Japanese Imperial all-Conquering Army in Hong Kong with their deaths.

The factory was burning.

5.59 p.m. The factory on Maltby Point was burning.

In the coming dark the flashes and detonations lit up the sky.

The sirens and klaxons were coming.

The Bannin was ready.

He went to inform his men that their victory, at last, was momentarily upon them.

14

In the car Auden shouted above the roaring of the engine and the blast as one of the wooden fireworks storage rooms went up, 'It's The Fireworks Man! He was after The Fireworks Man! He was going to kill him under cover of shooting at bloody uniforms in the fire so he's got to have a set-up still in there!' The locked wire gates to the compound were racing towards him. He saw a pothole in the road, swerved to avoid it, and saw the night shift running along the grass inside the fence looking for a way out. The wire gates were padlocked. There was a man trying to climb it and Auden wound down the window and shouted in Cantonese, 'Get away from the gate!'

Spencer yelled, 'He can't hear you!' The man was half way up on the wire like a monkey, trying to fling a leg over the top. Spencer yelled, 'Hit the fence! Hit the fence a little way down from the gates!' Auden hit a pothole and Spencer went flying inside the car and grabbed hold of the dashboard to steady himself. A fireball exploded low and racing across the compound it ignited a second wooden shack. It burned for a moment, then, as the flames caught, the gunpowder stored inside disappeared in a flash and a billowing blast of grey smoke. It was like an old black powder cannon salvo: the smoke rolled and turned white and got in the open window of the car.

Behind him, Spencer could see the Commander's car coming to a skidding halt at the telephone box and then the Commander, in full uniform, was out with Feiffer and O'Yee waving the fire engines to a stop and ordering someone to take cover. Another blast roared out from the factory and incinerated first one, then another of the small shacks, then like giant's footsteps, the

179

explosions erupted in a steady line. Spencer yelled, 'Mind the people at the—' and Auden hit the wire fence with the front of the car and smashed it down. One of the shacks went up and rained down sparks. Spencer shouted to the running men inside the fence, 'Get out! We've brought the fence down! Get out through the opening!' They didn't have to be asked twice. Spencer, out of the car, bent double against the heat, yelled, 'Through here!' and ducked to one side as the workmen went past him running for safety. Spencer yelled, 'They're clear! Get the car started!' He saw Auden get out with his big gun in his hand and yelled, 'He's dead! He's up by the phone box! We've got everyone out—'

A shack detonated and almost blew him off his feet. Auden yelled back, 'He was after The Fireworks Man! He was going to kill him before he sold his land! Look at all the bloody uniforms up there! There's goddamned fire and ambulance and the cops and—' A small storage shack of maroons and rockets went off like machine gun fire and sent burning powder cascading fifty feet into the air. Auden shouted. 'He's left a set-up in here! He's set his bloody little executive toy and his bloody little guns to get The Fireworks Man when the uniforms came in to stop the fire!' Auden looked around and saw the administration buildings fifty yards in front of him, still unburned, all the windows glinting in the last rays of the setting sun. Auden shouted, 'It's somewhere opposite the offices! That's where The Fireworks Man would have been helping with the hoses or—'

Spencer yelled, 'So what?' All the workers were safe and running towards the police and the fire brigade. Spencer yelled, 'He's dead! So what if he's—'

'He's fucking shot me once and made me look stupid twice!'

Spencer yelled, 'So what?' A shack went up and staggered him with the blast. Spencer shouted, 'This place is turning into—' He saw Auden's face, 'Phil, he's dead it doesn't matter any more! The Fireworks Man isn't in his office—he's safe! Back there! With Harry!' All the words had no effect. Spencer yelled, 'Safe! Harry! All right? Everything's—' He saw Auden's glazed eyes. A shack went off in a fountain of yellow and white sparks and rolled a billow of smoke down and covered them. Spencer heard Auden shout, 'Just once! Just once I'm going to—' and then there was a secondary blast that cleared the smoke and when Spencer looked Auden was gone.

One, two, three, four seconds ... five, six ... He saw Auden running towards the administration building with the giant gun still in his hand. Auden turned for a moment with a fierce look on his face, then staggered as a blast caught him sideways and spun him around. All the buildings were wood: a shower of planks and splinters came down at Spencer and ricochetted off the car and smashed through the windscreen. Spencer yelled, 'Phil—!'

Auden mouthed something. It could have been, 'Nine seconds...!'

Spencer shouted back, 'Seven, goddamn you! It's seven! Seven! Seven!!'

All the workmen were safe. The fence was down. All the buildings were wooden. Spencer yelled—

Spencer yelled, 'Seven, curse you!' and began running after him into the fires.

*

At the telephone, the Commander roared through his bullhorn, '*Nobody*! Nobody enters that compound!' He heard an engine start as one of the firemen decided that the time had come to earn his money. The Commander thundered, 'Nobody and that's an order! The first man, fire brigade, ambulance or cop who moves one millimetre farther forward will be on charges!' The engine stopped. There was a steady roaring coming from the fireworks factory. The Commander shouted, 'Everybody stays here until the fire is out!' The engine started again and he wrenched the Chief Fire Officer next to him by the shoulder and shouted, still through the bullhorn, 'Is that place sited safe to burn, yes or no?'

The Chief Fire Officer said, 'Yes!' He looked at the fires with longing. The Commander's grip on his shoulder turned into a vice, 'Yes! It's safe! It's sited safe. We can let it burn!'

There were uniforms everywhere. The Commander ordered everybody, 'Nobody moves! Everybody stays here! Let it burn—nobody gets shot! And that's an *order!*' He saw the Emergency Unit counter sniper platoon setting up behind a fire engine, unlimbering their guns and looking for something to counter snipe at, and the Commander, turning the funnel of the amplifier on them, ordered them, 'Set up here! If there's someone around here who thinks he's a goddamned Jaanese soldier set up here and protect these people!' If there was someone around who thought he was a Japanese soldier then he was well hidden. There was nothing but grass and cliffs and smoke. The Commander thundered out, 'Keep your eyes out for a tunnel!'

*

At the phone box, The Technician had taken a single thrust through the throat. There was no trail of blood—he had gone down and died without a twitch where he had been hit. Feiffer, with his hand on The Fireworks Man's shoulder demanded, 'Where is it? The tunnel? Is it in the factory?' The Fireworks Man was on his knees over his dead son, his hands moving above his face gingerly, afraid to touch him, too late for love. Feiffer demanded, 'Where? Where is it?' Behind him he heard Doctor Macarthur say to Sands, 'It's an obi. I can read a bit of it. It says Major—something—Takashima of the—' and Feiffer shook at The Fireworks Man's shoulder and rapped at him—

The Fireworks Man said, 'I don't know! It's here! It used to be here! It used to be everywhere—all over the island! It used to go from the beach right through here and come up—but it's all been bombed or filled up or—' He tried to touch his dead son's face, but his hands were trembling too much. The Fireworks Man said, 'I don't know!' He heard a gigantic rumbling explosion as one of the underground testing chambers caught and detonated, and he shouted, 'I don't know! I should have been in there! At this time of day when the shift starts I'm always in my office doing the accounts! All this is for me!' He looked down at his son's face and

182

it, dead, reacted not at all, like wax. The Fireworks Man implored at him, 'I did it for you! It's all bad joss—all jinxed, ill-fated! I did it for you!' He looked up at Feiffer and tried to make someone understand, 'It was all tainted—all the money! I thought during the war that the things I did to earn this place were all worth it, but they weren't! I learned that in old age!' He looked back to his son and it was all too late, 'You could have made your own way! My money was tainted!' The Fireworks Man implored Feiffer, 'Understand! I wasn't being hard! He was only my second son and I—' The Fireworks Man's face was running with tears and soot from the billowing, acrid smoke. The Fireworks Man said, 'He did all this for the money! He was going to kill me so the land could all be his!' He looked down at his son with desperation, 'He was just like me! He did it all for the money!'

Sands said suddenly, 'Jesus Christ, it's gone!' He had a piece of the obi in his hand and it was decaying literally before his eyes. Sands said, 'Doc, what the hell's—'

Macarthur touched at a piece of the material and it crumbled. He saw Feiffer looking at him. Macarthur said, 'It's dry. It's desiccated, like—' He looked down at his hand and the material had gone to dust. Macarthur said in a whisper, 'Where the devil has it been kept? *In an Egyptian pyramid?*'

Wrenching at The Fireworks Man, Feiffer said again, desperately, 'Where the hell is the *tunnel?*'

*

In the main compound, Auden shouted, 'Here! Here it is! That's it, isn't it?' A fountain of exploding sparks burst out from one of the shacks fifty yards away and fell fizzing to earth around him. The two storey office building in the compound was the only one in the place still undamaged. All the wooden framed windows were still intact. Auden yelled, 'That has to be it! That has to be where The Fireworks Man had his office!' He looked around quickly and avoided a piece of burning wood that threatened to set fire to his pants leg. Auden said, 'Look, what was supposed to

183

happen was that we'd all turn up and use the compound here as a base and we'd form a picket line here and The Fireworks Man would have—' His brain was working overtime, 'And we'd keep him back here and then the set-up—' Auden looked around. The compound was full of what looked like old derelict wooden barns and storage shacks, 'And then the set-up would start opposite here—there! And kill the bastard!' The stopwatch in Auden's brain was going like a Swiss chronometer. Auden said, 'There! One of those shacks there! He must have set up in one of those shacks there to catch him in the line of fire!' He began moving. Spencer said, 'So what? It's all over! The Fireworks Man is safe and—' and Auden shaking his head, said with an evil grin on his face, 'And the smoke hasn't even started yet so I've got all the time in the world!' He went quickly to the first wooden shack and kicked the door down and dashed in.

It was wrong. The logic was all—Spencer glanced around the compound and tried to see how everyone would have placed themselves and it was all— Spencer said, as a blast from a far shack erupted sky high like a volcano and showered him with sparks, 'No! Phil! It's all wrong! It's too easy! How could he have actually hit anyone—?' He saw Auden come out of the shack looking disappointed and he shook his head and said again, 'Phil, it's all wrong!'

Seven seconds. No little puffs of smoke. No trick mirrors. No blanks to make you fall down clutching your chest and thinking you were shot on the roofs of buildings. No—

Spencer yelled, 'It's all wrong! It isn't the way it would have been done!'

Auden ran to the next shack and, the fierce grin still on his face, turning bright red in the glow of the burning shacks, kicked the next door down with a look of pure delight and anticipation.

*

At the phone, Feiffer said, 'I don't know. I don't know where he is! For all I know, he's nowhere or fifty bloody miles away!' The

184

counter sniper unit had lowered their rifles and they were watching the fire and enjoying the show. Feiffer said, 'I know he's here, but I dont know how to—' He saw the Commander's face. Feiffer said, 'I don't know! *Under us*! He's somewhere bloodywell under us and I haven't got the faintest bloody dog's idea where to even start sniffing!' He saw O'Yee grab one of the fleeing workmen on his way past and spin the man around to ask him a question and Feiffer demanded, 'Christopher, where the hell are Auden and Spencer?'

O'Yee was questioning the man in rapid-fire Cantonese. O'Yee said, 'They're still in there! They left the car and went in to get—I don't know!' The workman shook himself loose, ducked as a gigantic explosion lit up the darkening sky and got free of O'Yee's hold on him. O'Yee called out to Feiffer, 'They've gone in to look for more people—I think!' The workman ran towards an ambulance, found it closed and himself uninjured, and just kept on running. O'Yee yelled to the Chief Fire Officer, 'Is there anyone else in there?'

The Chief Fire Officer was ticking off numbers in a notepad as the workmen came by. The Chief Fire Officer said, 'Two more.' He saw them running towards him. He ticked them. The Chief Fire Officer said, 'No, that's everyone!' He saw the Commander's face set, 'Sir, when the hell can we go in and put out the fire?'

The Commander ignored him.

The Chief Fire Officer said, 'Sir! Commander—?'

The Commander was looking down at the ground. In a Japanese arsenal, below ground, packed with war material...

The Chief Fire Officer said again, 'Sir, when the hell can we go in and put the bloody fire out?'

The Commander said, 'Harry, where the hell's that goddamned *tunnel*?' He saw the Chief Fire Officer about to open his mouth again and he snapped at him, 'Shut up! Just shut up, will you!'

Feiffer said, 'I don't know. *I don't bloodywell know*!'

*

All, all for nothing. By his dead second son, The Fireworks Man was crying quietly. All, all for nothing.

He should have let someone, a long time ago, kill him.

All, all too late.

The Fireworks Man looked at the waxen, set, dead face and shook his head.

All, all too late.

He couldn't even remember what the boy's voice sounded like. He had never heard it.

He touched at the blood on the neck and it was still warm and he fell down over the body and wept.

*

'*Phil*!'

Auden shouted, 'Let go!' He spun around and got Spencer's hand off his collar. Auden said, 'This is it! This is the one! Look!' He stabbed a finger in the direction of the two storey office building. 'I've got it taped! We would have all been there and The Fireworks Man would have been—'

'We've got to get out of here!' Spencer ducked as a series of explosions rumbled at first deeply beneath his feet, then cascaded up through one of the far shacks and detonated in an ear-splitting crack, 'This is all just small stuff! The big stuff could be going off any second and for all we know the entire administration building could be wired and that's made of concrete!' Auden's mind was somewhere else. Spencer yelled, 'Phil!' Spencer said, 'The bloody Japanese tunnels are under here somewhere! They could be full of bloody TNT!'

'*No*!' Seven seconds. He saw another shack. Auden said, half mad with delight, 'No! This is the one! Time me. I'm going to—'

Spencer shouted, '*What*?'

Auden said, 'Time me! Time! All right? Eight seconds, is it? Just watch this!'

'Seven! Seven! It's bloody *seven*!' Spencer shouted as another storage shed went up and filled the compound with thick white smoke, 'What am I doing?' He reached out for Auden and caught only smoke, 'What the hell am I doing arguing with you?' Spencer yelled into the smoke, '*Are you out of your goddamned mind?*'

Auden kicked down the door and yelled something.

Auden yelled, 'Got them!'

They were there, inside in the half blackness, glinting at him: the guns—all set up to go, the first with a phosphorous or fragmentation grenade to blow the door down, the other six with naked muzzles, one at the back with yet another grenade set on it, and behind, in rows, satchel charges to blow the whole place to pieces when the guns' work was finished. It looked like a death sentence in steel. Auden, delighted, said with triumph, 'Got you!'

Just like Christmas, he had exactly what he wanted.

He had an urge to sit down on the dirt floor amidst his prizes and, gurgling happily, have a little game with them.

*

At the phone, Feiffer said urgently, 'We have to go in and get them, Neal. They could be down—'

The Commander said, 'No. Nobody goes near the place until we find the sniper and his tunnels or until we find—'

Feiffer looked at O'Yee. O'Yee was up on the bonnet on one of the Dennis fire engines, scanning the area with field glasses and trying to see through the smoke.

Feiffer said, 'Neal, look—please...'

The Commander, like stone, said firmly, 'Harry, *no!*'

*

It was all wrong. It simply didn't look in real life the way it looked on the maps: it was all different, turned around, not flat, but undulating, and the green on his maps was not green at all, but grass and the contour lines were all—

Behind the farthest ambulance, Owlin craned his head to see

the cliffs on the other side of the burning factory. You couldn't see the cliffs. The factory was in the way. On a map, it was all flat and easy to read, but in reality, in the outside world, it was confusing and wrong and—

The world was not constructed properly. It should have been made the way the maps said it was: laid-out and readable and seen with a God-like eye, one dimensional and— Owlin said in annoyance, 'No! It shouldn't look like this at all. It's all wrong!'

He had his folded up map in his hand. He looked down at it quickly and touched at the cross he had made where the tunnel entrance was and found absolutely no correlation between that— the truth—and reality.

He saw something lying by a phone box with darkness all over its throat and neck and he realised with a start that it was a dead body.

He clenched his fist and looked down hard at his map to try again.

*

'*Where the goddamned, bloody hell is that tunnel?*' At the phone box, the Commander said, 'I have to clear the area. I don't know where the hell it is other than that it's probably underneath us and I don't know what the fuck is in it, but I have to clear the area!' He saw Feiffer wince as a series of explosions from the compound sent planks and wood splinters sailing and spinning up in a cascade of sparks, 'I'm sorry, Harry, but I—' The Commander ordered the Chief Fire Officer, 'Start to move everyone out! We're going to have to evacuate everyone along Beach Road and set up a defensive fire perimeter in case—' There was a giant roar and then a blast of hot air as one of the bigger shacks along the cliff edge towards the harbour must have ignited, 'Harry, if your people haven't come out of there by the time the main storage sheds go—' There was an overwhelming blast as one of the main storage sheds went. The Commander said urgently, 'We can't go in and get them!' He called out hard to the Chief Fire Officer, '*Start to move everyone back!'*

*

In the shed, Auden said, 'Heh, heh, heh . . .' It was too easy. He cut through the first burning fuse and let it fall to the earth floor with a chuckle. It was all too simple: the last ball in each of the Newton's Cradles was held back by nothing but a single piece of string and that was tied off with nothing more difficult than a single spluttering fuse. The fuse burned through the string, the string let the ball fall, the ball hit the next ball and then the next and then the last hit the upside down rifle right on the trigger. Too simple. The trigger guards of each of the rifles had been taken off to give a clear fall to each of the little balls and each of the little balls . . .

Auden cut through the next fuse with his penknife and went, 'Hey, heh, heh . . .' The fuses were all nice and long. He said, shaking with pleasure, 'Ha, ha, ha . . .' and cut through the next.

He looked at Spencer next to him, looking worried, and yawned. Auden said, 'Ho hum, too easy . . .' He cut another fuse, the one with the grenade set onto its muzzle, and took time out to stretch.

Auden, bored by the childish simplicity of his task, said languidly to Spencer, 'If you'd like something to do, old son, you can cut off some of the fuses on the satchel charges.' Auden cut another fuse. Bloody executive toys.

Soon-to-be Senior Inspector Phillip Auden, the saviour of the world, said happily, 'Hey, heh, heh . . .' He looked at Spencer's face and snapped, 'Oh, for Christ's sake, smile a little, will you?'

An explosion rocked the shed and Auden, drinking it all in, said, 'Ha!' He saw Spencer with the first of the satchel charges designed to blow the whole shooting match to pieces when it was done and Auden, all-knowing, said, 'Oh, the fuses on those will be a bit longer, so if you—'

Spencer held up one of the satchel charges and opened the flap.

It was empty.

The fuse was tied into the canvas bag attached to nothing and when it burned through...

Auden said, 'That's a bit odd.'

It would have burned through and ignited... Nothing. Auden said, 'I don't know, maybe he had another method of blowing the place up.' Auden cut through another fuse. He looked over at Spencer. Spencer was looking out anxiously through the open door at the glinting windows of the administraton building opposite. Auden said, 'Um, you don't think, do you, that...?'

Auden began rocking a little, like a mourner. Auden, with the last cut fuse in his hand fizzing away into nothingness, said in a strange, sad, strangled voice, 'Oh, no, Bill, they wouldn't do it to me again, would they?' Auden said, 'Not, not *again!*'

*

The Commander said, 'Harry—!'

Feiffer said, 'No!'

'You go with everyone else!'

'I can't!' He's here! I know he is!'

'Then tell me where the hell that bloody tunnel is!'

'I don't know where it is!' Feiffer, looking around, saw the fire engines and the ambulances starting to back up. There was nothing but grass and rocks and cliffs and the smoke pall from the burning factory. Feiffer said, 'I just don't bloodywell—know!!'

*

There was a bang and the centre window in the office block was gone and falling in glittering shards through the smoke. Auden said, 'Oh, no.' He looked at Spencer. Auden said, 'He worked for his father, didn't he. The second son?' None of them was a question. Auden said, 'He did, didn't he, and he had an office up there, didn't he, and all this was just a little too easy to find, wasn't it, and because it was such a simple set-up—just fireworks fuses and—' Auden said, 'We would have got The Fireworks Man to defuse it and he would have been standing in here looking up at that window as it broke and—and I've done it again, haven't I?' He was rooted to the spot, disappointed on unwrapping all his Christmas presents. They had been shoddy, bought at a five and dime and once you had played with them they just fell to pieces and—Auden said heartbroken, 'Aw, gee—'

There was a bang and Spencer shouted, PHIL! GET OUT OF HERE! IT'S A—'

It was a grenade.

For an awful moment, Spencer thought Auden was going to hold out his hands and catch it and put it in his pocket. He was in mid air and so was the grenade. Simultaneously, as the grenade hit the earth floor and buried itself fizzing, he connected with Auden and drove him hard into the corner of the shack and, protecting him, got his hands onto the back of the man's head and, in Auden's wandering sad mind, as a punishment for being naughty, shoved his nose deep into the dirt and held it there.

*

They had stopped. All the explosions had stopped and there was only the hissing of fires burning on bits and peices of destroyed shacks and on the roofs of the other empty buildings in the compound and inside the downed fence. White billowing smoke began dissipating back and forth with the slight wind in from the sea and Feiffer heard a siren a long way off from a ship and then there was nothing . . .

Silence.

Feiffer looked down at the grass under his feet. It was still, unmoving. Beneath him, the rocks and stratas of the earth ran in all directions and if there was a black, dark tunnel under there—

There was nothing but silence. All the engines of the fire brigade and the ambulances were still off.

It was growing dark. Long tentacles of blackness were there in the sky, stretching out from the sun and under the ground— It was becoming night and all the recognisable features of the land were going and becoming nothing but lines and contours on a map.

It seemed like hours. It was only seconds.

The tunnel. Where the hell was the tunnel?

*

He heard it click. The grenade made a clicking sound. Under him, Auden said through the dirt, 'God—fzzipple—damn!' It felt like hours. It was only seconds.

Pressing harder, Spencer said over and over, 'No ... no ... no ...'

*

Owlin said again, 'There! I'm telling you, it's there! The old oak forest was there! The old roots are rotting and giving off marsh gas!' He had Feiffer by the shoulder and he was pulling him towards the edge of the grass. Owlin said, 'It's part of a natural granite tunnel! It's there. It's on my map! *There! The entrance to the tunnel is there!*'

Over the edge of the cliff, Feiffer saw it. It was ten feet away. It had been there all the time, a minor entrance, nothing: a hole in the side of the stone worn away by erosion. He saw the Commander look in his direction and start to come across. In the last failing light, Feiffer could see the blackness of the hole. It was big enough for one man. Feiffer ordered Owlin, 'See that man in the uniform with the megaphone? Tell him!' He saw the Commander point the bullhorn in his direction and draw a breath.

It was moving. The ground was moving. All the explosions in the fireworks factory had weakened something and the ground was moving under them. At the fire engines and ambulances men looked down at the ground as it shook and heaved under them.

It was moving. The earth was changing, subsiding—

The Commander, using his bullhorn, shouted, 'Out of here!

192

Pull back! It's going! Pull everyone out of here *now*!'

Feiffer yelled to the hesitating Owlin, 'Go to him! Tell him! Get the hell out of here!' and before either Owlin or the Commander could reply or react he was scrambling down the cliff face and, swivelling himself like a rock climber, slid into the black deep entrance of the tunnel and was gone.

*

Auden said, 'Damn it, it isn't going to go off!' He tried to get his head up and Spencer shoved it down again. The earth was rumbling and groaning against his ears. Auden said, 'This is another bloody humiliation! The dead bastard hasn't even got the bloody grace to finally bump me off! After everything he did to me while he was alive he didn't even have the goddamned fucking grace after he was dead to finally bump me off!' He got his head up, 'He didn't even have the—'

There was a click from the grenade.

Spencer said, 'It's going to go—!' He felt the earth move in readiness.

Auden said, 'Goddamn it, he—' and then there was the most brilliant flash he had ever seen in his life followed by a shattering, grinding blast that he thought killed him where he lay, and suddenly, as the concussion from the half buried grenade blew the earth floor and the supports under it to dust, the ground opened up to him, and he and Spencer, tumbling over and over like two Alices disappearing into the rabbit hole, fell down and down and down a long way into blackness and were, instantly, somewhere else.

15

The ground beneath his feet was shaking. An earthquake was coming. Beneath his feet O'Yee could feel the ground heaving and moving. All the cars and ambulances and fire tenders were going: above the roar of their engines he heard a series of sudden popping sounds as the earth subsided in giant footsteps and tore through the grass covering and devoured it. There was a brilliant flash that lit up the sky and the administration building had gone, then a series of deeper, throatier blasts as the single charges hidden away in its construction against rafters and structural walls exploded one by one and set the building to burning with a fierce yellow light. Below him, a little way down the cliff face, the tunnel entrance was changing, closing in on itself like a camera aperture. O'Yee yelled, 'Is that it? Is that the one?' The entire top of the cliff moved and began to give way.

All the lights of the vehicles were going. There was no one left. Bits and pieces of burning wood and plastic were falling down in parabolas from the burning building and setting more buildings on fire. There was another gigantic blast and the ground heaved again and sent a jet of white steam and foam out into the sea at the base of the cliffs and set the water boiling and foaming.

There was no one. Everyone was going. O'Yee had his gun out but there was nothing to do with it. Under him, the ground was moving, sliding. He pulled Owlin away to get to firm earth, but everything was moving inexorably. O'Yee shouted, 'There has to be another entrance! Where's the other entrance?' and a storage shack went up in a series of rapid fire explosions and drowned him out. O'Yee shouted, 'Think! Where's the other—'

Bits and pieces of burning paper from fireworks were falling onto Owlin's hair and onto his shoulders. Owlin shouted, 'I don't know! There aren't any!' He was a log-roller: the ground under him span off to one side and he overbalanced, 'I don't know what's happening! I thought you got him! I saw him at the telephone! He was dead!' In the yellow light he tried to see O'Yee's face. The ground under him rocked as something deep within it changed and moved and exploded and he grabbed for O'Yee's coat and shouted, 'I want to go back! I can't take this! I want to go back to where I'm safe!'

Nothing to do. Nowhere to go. Under him, Feiffer was— O'Yee, hopping from one foot to the other and starting off and coming back again, said in desperation, 'That dead bugger was only trying to kill his own father! This bastard is trying to kill *everyone!*' The ground rocked and erupted under pressure like a great boil and then subsided again. O'Yee shouted uselessly, 'Find something! Find somewhere! Find me some way to get in!'

'How? There isn't anywhere!' Owlin said, 'I can't think! You're not leaving me time to think—!'

'There isn't any goddamned time to think! This is war!' He tried to grab for Owlin, but the man pulled away, 'All we have to do is stop him! There's nothing to it: no brainwork, nothing. Simple, like a war—all we have to do is find him and kill him!' He saw Owlin's face in the yellow glow, this thick glasses glinting, looking like a huge, dumb, un-understanding rabbit. O'Yee yelled above the detonations, 'Fine me somewhere! You're a scholar! Find me somewhere!' He tried to remember what The Fireworks Man had said. O'Yee yelled in sudden victory, 'The old air vents! Find me the old air vents!'

Owlin said, lost, 'I don't know. I don't know where I am in relation to— They'd all be covered up by grass! They'd be all—'

Nowhere to go. Nothing to do. Everyone had gone. O'Yee, hopping from one foot to the other, yelled at the top of his voice above the noise, *'Find me the old air vents before he decides to blow all the goddamned tunnels to bits!'*

*

195

They were sliding, falling, coasting. They were sliding on moving earth. There was a giant ramp of falling earth building up and making an enormous slide into the blackness and they were sliding down to its base, going over and over. Auden managed to get his head up to see the sky and the hole above him closed in as the sides collapsed and cascaded him with pebbles. He was hurt: he felt pebbles rip and tear at his clothes and lacerate his arms and spine and then he was rolling over and over onto soft dark soil and all the pain was being cushioned. Auden shouted, 'Bill!' There was nothing but blackness. He felt Spencer next to him, still falling over and over and he reached out and caught the man by the sleeve and almost wrenched his arm off. He called out into nothingness, '*Bill!*' and then Spencer seemed to go over the edge of an abyss and Auden was falling with him, still being cushioned by the soil, still falling away into nothingness.

Spencer called out, 'I've stopped!' He had his hand around something and was hanging on. It was a rock or a pebble—in the blackness it was impossible to see. Spencer shouted, 'I've got my penlight,' and then whatever it was he had hold of gave way and he was still falling. He got his finger onto the switch of the tiny flashlight and shot the beam up and over to the left, illuminating rock and shale and blackness. Spencer called out into nothing, 'Phil, are you—' He felt Auden crash over the top of him and then stop and he landed a little to one side of him in shale and stopped falling, gasping for breath.

Auden said, 'The light! Shine the light over here!' His face was in water. The water was coming along the stone floor of a tunnel and filling up. Auden shouted between gasps, 'Water! There's water coming in!' He saw the light waver and then stab out into the darkness and he was in a tunnel with a foot of water in it and there was a shadow at the end of it and Auden shouted, 'The light! Turn out the light!' It was him: The Bannin. Auden yelled, 'For Christ's sake turn out the light!'

It wasn't The Bannin. It was shadow. Auden said, 'It's—' and then a terrific blast somewhere behind him threw him hard against a wall and the water came sluicing down behind him and spun him off onto the other wall. He was sliding again, all the ground giving away beneath him, the ramp breaking up and re-forming. There was another deep rumble and then a creaking sound as something gave way and then, cracking like a giant egg, a sharp report that sent a cascade of foaming water into his eyes and nostrils and swept him deeper into the maze.

Spencer had his torch held high above his body. He was lying full length like a surfer, being propelled along by a wave. All over his body he was hurting in pinpricks as the stones and shale on the floor cut through to him and scraped him full length. Spencer yelled out, 'They're behind us! The explosions are behind us!' and there was another deeper blast and a hail of biting, cutting seawater picked him up and drove him at a wall. His torch went under: he saw its light flicker for an instant and then turn grey then it came out again, strong and white. Spencer reached out for Auden and connected with nothing, then saw the man's feet being bumped and bounced along in front of him. The water was receding like waves in a bathtub, not deep, slowing. Spencer yelled, 'Phil, it isn't deep. Get up and—' and then there was a shock that swirled the water back again past him and he was talking under water with his mouth full of salt and the smell of the sea.

Auden yelled, 'The flashlight!' He saw for an instant something illuminated in the bobbing beam and he reached out for it, let his feet go past him in the surge, and then, at their full length, jerked hard and pulled and managed to get himself upright.

The smell in the tunnels was awful: dead things and gas. He saw bubbles foaming under the water near Spencer's face and he reached down to get him as Spencer brought his head out of the water streaming and the bubbles still kept going on and on. Auden said, 'Marsh gas! The place is full of—' and then, far away, there was a heavier, deep rumbling and the water foamed briefly and then became a cascade.

The Bannin was blowing up all the lower galleries. Auden shouted, 'There!' and wrenched Spencer's flashlight hand to the wall and saw the fissures forming in the granite and streaming water. Auden shouted, 'He's blowing it all up! We're below sea level!' He saw a gigantic fault line form like a sudden tear and he grabbed Spencer's wrist and pulled, 'Run! Run!' There was nowhere to run. The hole above them was closed, fallen in, or drowned. Auden shouted, 'Run!'

'Where? Where?'

There was only one place left. For a moment Auden caught sight of a hole in the roof of the tunnel, leading up into another gallery. Auden shouted, 'There! Up there!' The gas was bubbling in the water and rising to the surface and breaking. All the methane gas was going upwards. Auden shouted, 'Up there! To the next gallery! There's nowhere else!' He saw something move in the half light and he called out, 'It's him!' He had Spencer's wrist hard in his hand. Auden shouted, 'Up! We have to get *up!*'

*

It was all going like an old mineshaft. Behind him, Feiffer could hear the roof collapsing in the tunnel and driving the dust and debris down after him. His penlight was minute: it threw only a circle of yellowness on the earth in front of him. Through its rays he could see the dust rising and falling in anticipation as the roof groaned and moved above his head. His own running footsteps activated it. He looked up and the roof above him was creaking and moving: he saw it begin to go and ran hard towards the end of the tunnel. There was no end to the tunnel: it curved and then went deeper and he was running along a dark, stinking passage towards more darkness and stench. He stopped. He heard the roof behind him come down in a crash and then, deeper down, in the lower level, there was a rumbling and then a sharp, crashing explosion as a satchel charge went off.

Through the walls he could hear the sea boiling. All the walls were being weakened and holed and the sea at full tide was rushing in to fill the vacuum.

He heard a voice and then another crack and he shouted,

'Auden! I hear you!' and then behind him there was a brilliant flash of blue light as a pocket of marsh gas ignited and all the air seemed to go in an instant from his lungs and he was gasping and burning. He smelled sea water. Somewhere below him he heard it come crashing down a tunnel like storm torrents and the smell of fresh air and salt came up to him and filled his lungs with pure air.

Feiffer yelled, 'Auden! I hear you!' The roof above him groaned and he ran on, holding the torch and his gun out in front of him like a blind man's white stick. Under his feet the rocks were slimy and wet with the moisture. For an instant, on the wall, he saw an old electrical flex that had been fixed there for some long dead power connection and as the light and the water vapour got to it it fell to pieces in front of his eyes and seemed to fall to the ground as dust.

White, pumice-like, dry dust. It seemed to be coming from the roof in clouds. He smelled the methane gas. Desiccated. Everything was bone dry and desiccated, ready for destruction.

He heard another, deeper blast a long way off and then, in series, another and another, and then, at the extreme range of his light at a junction of two tunnels he saw, for an instant, Auden and Spencer.

Feiffer called out, 'Phil!' He saw a flash of light as Auden and Spencer moved their lantern and he thought—

What goddamned lantern?

Feiffer said, 'Christ!' a moment before The Bannin's light disappeared in a gigantic white flash and the bullet roared past his ear and tore off a chunk of rock and ignited all the marsh gas behind him in a brilliant sheet of blue flame.

All his air was gone. Feiffer, tripping on something, felt water at his elbows and then the flash was there again. He heard the bullet whine off a rock and tear a chunk of rock loose from the water and then, in a suddenly released stream, water was coming in and all the air was back.

Feiffer yelled, 'Auden! Spencer!' He saw two drowned looking figures in his torch light suddenly appear at the entrance to a smaller side tunnel and he went forward and dragged at them to

199

get them moving in the right direction.

Auden yelled with relief, 'Harry!' Feiffer saw Spencer looking drowned and breathless. He still had his issue penlight in his hand. Feiffer yelled. 'Move! Move!'

The Bannin at the end of the tunnel was gone. Feiffer could hear his boots ringing on the hard rock higher up as he ran. The two penlights together lit the tunnel for a distance of more than twenty feet and illuminated a rain of thick falling white dust and what looked like broken cobwebs.

Feiffer yelled, 'The whole place is bone dry and the water's making it fall to pieces!' He saw Auden looking at him dumbly in the light. The man's face was covered in scratches and lacerations. Feiffer shouted, 'Have you still got your gun?'

Auden said, 'Yes!'

'Bill?'

Spencer said, 'Yes!' He was bleeding through his wet coat, like a wounded hard hat diver. Spencer said, 'The place is full of marsh gas!'

He heard The Bannin running. There was a terrific explosion deep down in the catacombs and then the sound of roaring, rushing water. Feiffer shouted, 'Get after him!'

Spencer shouted, 'Harry, the place is full of marsh gas!'

'To hell with the goddamned marsh gas!' He heard the running sounds, magnified and echoing in all the tunnels. In the echo it sounded like an army. Feiffer yelled, 'The place is full of goddamned Japanese!' He saw Auden stare at him. Feiffer, pushing them both to start, shouted, 'For Christ's sake, don't you understand? He's running for the bloody *magazine!*'

*

On the surface O'Yee said, 'Where? Where the hell would the centre be? You're the bloody scholar! Where would the bloody redoubt be? The core of the place?' He jerked Owlin around to face the direction of the sea, 'There! That's where Harry went in'—he jerked him the other way—'And there, there's the other

200

sea front and there's the bloody point—now where the hell would the centre be? In the bloody middle or where? *Where?*' He saw Owlin in the glow of the fires shake his head and start to say something. O'Yee demanded, 'Would it be in the deepest part of the natural rock formation or what?'

Owlin said, 'Yes! Yes! It would be!'

'It would be *what?*'

'In the deepest part of the rock formation! Where the natural tunnel was deepest and—'

'*Which is where?*' He saw Owlin looked dazed. O'Yee said, 'Come on, you're the expert! Where the hell is the deepest part?'

'I don't know! Even if I found it how could you get down to it?'

The administration block was still burning. Bits and pieces of tar paper and fabric were still falling, alight, all over the compound. There was a series of rapid bangs as one of them must have gone straight through the open roof of a damaged storage shack and set off more fireworks. Owlin said, 'There! The deepest part is there under the hump on the grass!' It was hopeless. In the light he could barely see it and whatever was under it was at least fifty or sixty feet of solid rock. Owlin said, 'There! It has to be there! What good does that do for you?' He saw O'Yee pace out the distance and then look back in the direction where Feiffer's tunnel entrance had been. Owlin demanded, 'What do you think? That there's some sort of wheel with a central hub? Even if it was, the tunnel entrances radiating to it could be anywhere!' He saw O'Yee make for the cliff side to leeward along the imaginary line from the imaginary core of the imaginary hub and he shouted out, 'This is ridiculous! This isn't research—this is ridiculous!'

O'Yee was scrambling down the cliff face, grasping and yanking at rocks to get a hold.

Owlin shouted, 'Don't do that! That isn't the way to descend a cliff face!' He got over and grabbed O'Yee's hand and pulled him back up. Owlin said, 'No, that isn't the way! If you're looking for a tunnel entrance or a cave what you have to do is work out the structure of the rock strata and the—' He saw O'Yee's face with a look of contempt on it.

201

Owlin said with a snarl, 'I read a book about it! All right?' A hundred feet below him he saw the sea. It seemed in the sky-glow of the factory to be boiling.

Owlin said, 'All right! I'll find your goddamned second tunnel!' He saw a flash as something else in the factory suddenly ignited and then there was a heavy rumbling under his feet and below him, at the sea, a jet of boiling steam came out from the cliff base as the fiery blast hit the water and evaporated.

Owlin said, 'There! There's your evidence! It's there! Down there!' In the glow, the sea was phosphorescent. Owlin said, 'Right there! Where the sea's on fire! If you want a way in, *that's it!*'

*

In the maze of man-made tunnels leading off from the natural shaft all the wooden roof supports and braces were falling to bits in the beams of the flashlights. Thick strong beams of oak and juniper, they were disintegrating without reason and falling with the dust from the roof as splinters and shards of material no thicker than tissue paper. Mould was forming on them: in the absence of the methane gas the beams were going furry and white, then collapsing and floating down to the ground without weight. Behind them, in the lower levels, the water was rising: it came in great surges as the tide changed, pumped it in through holes and shattered rocks and seeped it through splitting fissures and faults. The smell of decay was overpowering. Spencer stopped, tried to clear his head, and almost fell over. He felt Feiffer grab him and propel him past a beam on the point of destruction, and then, as the beam fell in a curious absence of sound, he was around a corner and the smell of methane was gone and the air was fresh again.

Auden saw someone move. At the end of the tunnel, for an instant, he saw a shadow in Feiffer's flashlight beam and then the figure was gone. There were chambers at the end of the tunnel. Auden said, 'Harry! Ahead!' He heard a scuffling sound and then a click and he flattened himself against a wall and waited for the shot. It came, lighting up the methane in a sudden intense blue light, and Auden, getting his own giant gun up two-handed, let fly in the direction of the source. He heard the bullet whang off something hard, striking sparks, and then the blue sheet was there again, racing down the tunnel, burning all the methane pockets and he saw a figure.

Spencer said, 'I see him!' He got his own short barrelled gun up and it barked hard in the confined space and brought a shower of desiccated powder down. There were no sparks. The soft lead bullet ripped into a collapsing A frame support thirty feet ahead and tore it to pieces.

The Bannin was running again, moving. Feiffer heard his boots ringing on the floor. Spencer said, 'Harry! You said *Japanese*—how many of them are there? I thought there was just—' He saw a shadow and Auden's gun went off next to him and almost deafened him. The figure moved again: a shadow, and there was a brilliant flash and a ringing detonation as he fired back and went around a corner. By the corner there seemed to be chambers or rooms, all darkened. Auden saw at an acute angle something in one of the rooms and called out, 'Another one!' and got a single shot off that sparked and popped as it ignited pockets of methane near the roof.

The figure inside the chamber was either unreal or it had been killed or it was already dead.

They heard a click.

Feiffer yelled, 'There's a charge in there!' and as Auden let fly with another round to cover them, they ran past, flicking their torches into the room as they went by. Whatever was in there didn't shoot. For an instant Auden saw him in the periphery of a beam: a single figure sitting waiting with a rifle in his hands and he gave it two more shots as he went by and saw the figure fly to pieces as if it had been hit by a bomb. Auden said, 'I got him!' He felt his head start to swim and he slowed down, let everyone else go by, and decided to walk back in the darkness and ask the figure exactly where the bullet had gone.

Auden said, 'I just want actually to ask him if I got him, because the last time I was out in the range I was shooting really high and I thought that this character wouldn't mind if I check up whether—' He felt a grip of iron grab him by the collar and pull him forward and he said, 'Look, I don't think he'd mind. I mean, I've already killed him so I think he'd . . .' He was raving, his head full of methane gas. Auden said angrily, 'Look here, what the hell do you think you're doing pulling me around? Don't you know who I am? I'm Senior Inspector—'

Whatever it was inside the chamber went click and then there was a sort of soft fizzing sound and Auden said drunkenly, 'What the hell are you doing pulling me around?' He was being jerked by a total of four hands. He felt his knees give way and he was being dragged by the collar. His legs gave way. He felt his backbone turn to rubber and he was being—

The explosion from the chamber turned the tunnel bright white. Auden said, 'Now they're throwing depth charges at poor old Lew on his boat and they're—' He felt something acrid burn his lungs and he yelled, 'Phosphorous! It's a phosphorous genade! We have to get out of here!' but it was too late, he was already out into the next tunnel and Auden, somersaulting over in mid gasp and getting a face full of dust from the roof, shouted in protest, 'I'm all right! I'm all right! You can let me *go!*' He heard a series of deep thundering explosions a long way down in the galleries and then the roar of the sea and he yelled, wondering for a moment where he was, 'What's happening? I can hear the sea! What the hell's happening?'

He heard footsteps running.

Auden shouted, 'I shot him! He's dead! I can hear him running! How many of them are there!'

*

'There!' In the phosphorescence and the light from the burning factory, the sea was coming out from the sides of the cliffs like giant faucet flows, draining out in foaming cascades and falling back into the surf. Owlin said, 'There! Below the top fall—you can see the hole opening up! It's a tunnel!' The entire cliff face seemed to be going critical, becoming porous, springing giant leaks. Owlin shouted, 'It's coming in below sea level and filling up the galleries and then it's flowing out with the pressure!' The cascades were turning the darkness light with a fine white vapour. Owlin scrabbled for a hold on the cliff and got his hand to O'Yee's shoulder and pummelled him to get his attention, 'There! You can see the level of the flooded galleries and we can get in above there where the walls are collapsing with the pressure before the water rises!' He was no commando or policeman or rock climber: he was a researcher. Owlin said, 'You! You can get in!' The pressure holes were opening up all over the cliff at about the level of the roots of a good sized tree, an oak or a juniper or a— It wasn't possible that after all these years there could still be— He thought for a moment he saw the blackened roots of an ancient tree flow out with the sea.

Owlin said, 'There! There's a big hole opening up! There! At tree root level! There! We can get in there!'

*

Spencer yelled, 'It's on fire! The gallery is on fire!' He looked back and the entire tunnel behind him was bathed in a bright blue glow, banging and popping as the burning phosphorous ignited pockets and corners of gas and set the beams falling and burning. A long way off down the tunnel he heard a deep bang as an entire passage must have gone up. It was burning away from them, going deeper, looking for the heavier concentrations of gas. Spencer said, 'It's all right, it's—' and then the gas half way down his tunnel went up in a solid rolling ball of flame and the fires were moving towards them. The air was gone. He ran after Auden and Feiffer and turned a corner and he could smell the sea again. In Feiffer's flashlight beam there was a figure. It seemed to be standing watching him. Feiffer yelled, 'Look out!' and then there was a flash and a gunshot merged in with the sea and the roaring fires.

The figure was gone. It seemed to be leading them somewhere. Feiffer's flashlight went out and he flicked at it and it came back on. Feiffer shouted, 'Up! We have to get up to the next level!' Below him, literally under his feet, he felt and heard the vibration as tons of sea water came in through a suddenly collapsing gallery wall. The ground shook. Dust was falling down like white rain and getting in his nose and throat. It felt dry and old and then, suddenly, as the water vapour got to it, it was at once wet, then dry again, and then it had disappeared entirely.

The figure in the chamber. All the beams turning to powder. Flags disappearing. Feiffer said suddenly, 'Christ, I think I know what the hell's in here!' He came to what looked like stone steps cut in the end of the tunnel and he pushed Spencer ahead of him and yelled, 'Up! Up!' They were fifty feet below ground: they could have been fifty thousand. He heard the sea come crashing in in another gallery and then there was a series of explosions and the blue burning flame was behind him in the tunnel and he got up the stairs and saw it pass by.

Auden said, 'Footsteps! I can hear footsteps!' He saw something in a chamber and got his gun out to kill it. There was an instantaneous flash of white light and the chamber was gone. There was no smell of burning flesh. It was all the stink of powder and mould and old, wet wood. The explosion had seemed minute, muffled. He heard a hissing sound, a cracking, a groaning, and then the water came in and he followed Spencer and Feiffer quickly up higher on the stairs and got into the upper gallery and almost passed out.

The stench was awful. Spencer said between gasps, 'God Almighty!' He felt a gag reflex start in his throat and he thought he was going to be sick. He reached out and saw Feiffer with a handkerchief up to his face. Above the handkerchief his forehead and hair was white with rock dust. Spencer said, 'What the devil is it?' He knew. It was the latrines, the old, ancient, decaying excreta still swirling methane and nitrates. Spencer said, 'Harry, what the devil is it?'

They were in Feiffer's torch beam—great collapsed sections of the tunnel showing a strange changing colour in the yellow light. Staggering, Feiffer looked up. All the roof beams were perfect, preserved, bright and strong, as intact as they had been on the day they had been cut. He saw a chamber going off to one side and in the beam he saw the boxes of rifles and ammunition all pristine and oiled and mint. Feiffer said, 'It's here! They were all kept here! This entire area is a time lock!' He faltered and felt his head swirl with the gas. 'All this methane and the dryness has preserved everything intact.' He got the beam onto the holes in the gallery where the tons of still reacting muck were giving off their foul odour. One of The Fireworks Man's bombs must have blasted through somewhere near here and set off something and sucked all the air out in the implosion effect, and everything in here—' He could go on no longer. He saw a metal door at the far end of the gallery with white dust all over it and he shouted, 'There! He's gone in there! If there's anyone still alive in here, he's in there!' He knew what he would find. He saw Spencer stagger and Auden's eyes start to dilate in a mad drunkenness again and he got his arm around Spencer's shoulders and pushed him towards the steel door. He saw Auden get his gun out and he grabbed him too. There were pumice, talc-like marks all over the door, hand marks. The dust had come from the other galleries. He got his hand onto the handle of the steel door and from the room inside heard a crash as something hard and metal struck hard: a great re-inforced door slamming. The door came open easily and they were in the war room, moving towards the last steel door to the core of the arsenal.

There was a crash as Spencer slammed the door to the smashed latrines closed behind him and the air was warm and clear with the faintest breeze coming in from somewhere, tinged with the smell of salt water.

Feiffer said, 'There!' The beams from his and Spencer's flashlights were dying fast. He knew what he would find behind that door. Feiffer, cocking his gun, pulled at it and got it open with a single jerk.

The room behind was lit by lanterns. It was enormous. It was a cathedral, a place of reverence, and in it the last survivors of the Quartermasters' Section of the 38th Division of the Japanese Imperial All-Conquering Army in Hong Kong all awaited them.

All one hundred and three of them.

All dead.

All intact.

All preserved.

They were mummies.

Their faces, above the intact, tattered uniforms and the high polished cracked leather boots, were all covered in cobwebs.

16

It was Pompeii. They were all there: Tanino, Ozawa, Morishita, all dead for a very long time, dead the instant the bomb forty years ago had torn out all the air in the tunnels and burned their lungs away like paper, dead, twisted, uniformed, all their skins turned to leather by the dryness and the methane, their hands outstretched, clawed, their uniforms in tatters, their boots cracked and gleaming dully in the lantern light. Dozens of them, scores of them—they were everywhere: in mounds, in lines, in groups huddled together for protection in that awful millisecond, the hair all gone from their heads, their bloodless lips drawn back over yellowing animal teeth, all dead, all preserved, all there. Auden said, 'God Almighty, they're—' He saw something move in the light: a figure, a shadow and he yelled, 'Bill, look out!' as something behind a shadowy structure stepped out and turned the room into daylight with a muzzle flash. The bullet went past him and smashed itself into pulp on the steel door. Auden yelled, 'Look out—he's in here!' He saw Feiffer go for the ground with his snub nose revolver up and pointing at the flash and Auden, bringing his magnum up, got off a round that detonated like a cannon shell in the room and set everything vibrating.

There was a figure. It was standing up. Spencer said, 'There!' He saw something glint in the light. It was a rifle. Next to him, Auden's great gun went off again and the figure seemed to expand like a slow motion explosion then blow apart into dust. It was one of the corpses. Spencer yelled, 'No! They're already dead! He was all of them!' and the dust was falling down behind the shadows and spreading out towards him.

He had been all of them. Tanino, Ozawa, Morishita—The

Bannin had been all of them.

Spencer yelled, 'It isn't him! He's behind the other—' and for an instant he saw something with hair on its head—its face all blackened and burned by the exploding rifle—and let fly two quick shots that drew sparks off something metal and whined up to the roof. All the beams on the roof were wood. They shook, then changed, then collapsed. Spencer saw them coming down one by one as shards of wet black cardboard. Spencer yelled, 'There's moisture getting into here from the sea! They're all decaying!' He saw Feiffer on the ground behind a corpse and then a movement and Feiffer was shooting rapid fire at something on the back wall as it went towards a tunnel entrance.

There was something fizzing. Spencer rolled over and went on top of an outstretched claw hand that bit into his backbone. He rolled back and the dead, eyeless face was next to him. It was a Corporal: he saw the uniform and the insignia of rank. Spencer yelled, 'He's near the exit tunnel!' A bullet whined past him and he rolled again for cover. There was nowhere to go. All the uniforms were khaki and in his civilian clothes he stood out like a beacon. He saw Feiffer rolling over and over getting the cylinder of his gun open to get another load in and then he had the gun forward in front of him and was shooting out the lanterns. One went and spread flame onto one of the corpses and it began to burn, twisting as the dried out skin contracted and shrivelled with the heat.

It was a Sergeant. Auden heard a shout and then there was something dark moving towards the burning figure and shooting rapid fire. The bullets were ripping off the floor in front of him and ricochetting into the corpses. They were dancing with the blasts, moving, jumping, falling to pieces. Auden got a line on a far lantern and blew it to pieces and the flame from the spirit fell down the wall and set it on fire. He saw something move. He heard a fizzing sound. Something twisting and rolling came towards him and he moved to one side as the corpse, on fire, rolled over and over, making hissing sounds like a balloon. The firing from near the exit tunnel had stopped. Spencer got to his feet and

210

it started again and he dived behind something solid and black and got his hands to it to give him support. It was a sort of long steel ledge with heavy objects on it. In the darkness, he put his hand out and found they were round.

Auden yelled, 'Where is he? I can't see him! Which one of these bastards is he?' He saw something start to get up and he poured four shots into it and it jumped and blew to pieces. Dead men: he was killing dead men. Auden yelled, 'Harry, I can't—' and then another lantern went out with a gunshot and the flames were falling down the walls and running across the floor towards more of the dead. Auden yelled, 'Harry, which one is he—?' He saw a flash as something metal moved and then a light from a spark and he turned the gun on Spencer and was about to pull the trigger.

Spencer cried, 'They're naval shells! The things on the shelves! They're four inch naval shells—hundreds of them!' He saw a blast of sparks near his hand as yet another fuse set against the shells caught and went fizzing towards the main charges, 'He's got the whole place wired up to go!' He saw a flash and then a bullet actually struck one of the shells and ricochetted off the steel into the roof and brought down a shower of dust and stone. Spencer yelled, 'Phil! *I can't find the charges!*'

There was another lantern on the far side of the wall. The fires were falling down the rock and setting the rear section of the room alight a section at a time. The Bannin was somewhere near them. Feiffer drew an aim on another lantern, missed it, and then fired twice, and smashed the object to pieces. The fire came out in a solid ball and then fell down the wall in burning stalactites. He saw a shadow and then, for an instant, The Bannin. He was naked from the waist up, wearing a thousand stitches obi—God knew whose, another of the dead men's—and Feiffer shouted, 'You! You're—' and then there was a burst of rapid fire that ripped a corpse into powder ten feet from Feiffer's face and sent bits and pieces of shredded uniform and bone into the air like shrapnel.

At the ledges, scrabbling for cover, Auden said, 'Where? Where?' He saw the sparks and got his hand in to get the fuse, but it was deep between the shells and his hand was too big. Auden yelled, 'Push it over!' He strained on the shell, but it was too heavy. Auden shouted, 'Bill, you're thinner than I am! Get your hand in and get the fuse!' Feiffer cried, 'Bannin!' He saw the man's face, blackened, lacerated, going mask-like with the dust in the room. He saw him look at the flames on the wall. Feiffer yelled, 'Bannin! You're—' He saw the man grin with victory and he brought up his revolver and pumped round after round into his shadow until the gun clicked empty. He saw The Bannin start to advance and he rolled over and tried to get more ammunition from his soaking pocket and load it into the gun.

The Bannin was hissing, grinning. Feiffer shouted, '*Phil!*' and the giant gun went off from somewhere behind the shells and The Bannin was gone, Feiffer yelled, 'You got him!' an instant before, from somewhere totally different in the semi-darkened room, The Bannin got the rifle up and poured bullets against the steel door and the walls behind the shells. Feiffer yelled, 'Get behind the corpses! He's avoiding hitting some of the corpses!' So far he had hit three. They were three that didn't count: no longer people, for some reason, no longer worth taking into account.

Feiffer said, 'Christ Almighty!'

The corpses that were no longer corpses were the ones he had avenged: the people he had already been in Cuttlefish Lane and at the launch shooting and in the park. Feiffer saw a mummified creature lying grotesquely on the ground between him and the shells wearing high boots and what looked like silver badges of rank and half ran and half crawled to it and got behind it.

It was the real Major Takashima—he had been laid reverently on the ground and someone had tried to cut his fingernails and— his fingernails were all gone, fallen out a decade ago. Feiffer saw the man's tunic open: the old leather skin drawn back over an empty chest and stomach cavity. The obi was gone. The Bannin had left it at the phone box to draw them in. He was in the wrong place totally. All the rites had been done for the Major and this was his last battle The Bannin was fighting now. There was a single blast from the rifle and the bullet struck the corpse somewhere on the shoulder and lifted it up like an empty paper

212

sack and blew it to dust. Bits and pieces of white and yellowed bone shattered in Feiffer's face and he covered his eyes and felt the dead clothes and hands and bits and pieces of uniform covering him like a shroud. He rolled away, shooting, and the pieces were still falling in slow motion and the stench as the rotted hardened skin blew apart into gas almost overwhelmed him. There was a blue flash and then a sheet of flame from the far end of the room as a pocket of trapped methane gas caught and detonated in a popping sound and through the flames he saw The Bannin with the rifle in his hand, his mouth opening and shutting in some sort of warrior's war cry.

He was enjoying it. It was his final battle. The Bannin, seeing Spencer above the shells for an instant, turned the hose of his gun onto him and fired off a complete magazine that turned the storage area into a welder's room of yellow biting sparks. The shells were too thick to be penetrated by the bullets. For an instant Spencer thought the fuse was out, but in the sparks there was a brighter, insistent flame, and he tried to get his hand in to get it and ducked as a ricochetting bullet tore past his sleeve and almost took all his fingers off. Bits and pieces of the wall behind the flames seemed to be falling into fragments. The wooden roof beams were falling. Feiffer heard the sea rushing in under his feet in the lower galleries. The place was filling with moisture and everything was rotting, coming to pieces.

Feiffer saw the fuse burning and in its glow, Spencer bent over it like a worshipper at the shrine of some sort of fire god. The Bannin was gone. He was moving around in the darkness at the far end of the room and he was gone. All the lanterns at the far end had been shattered and the fire was spreading out across the room and setting the sleeves and hands of the dead on fire. There was a terrible crematorium stench starting and a glow from burning, dead skin. Spencer yelled, 'I can't get it!' and then Feiffer saw The Bannin in the far corner trying to get a bead on the man and fired a single shot that brought down a chunk of wood from the beams and missed The Bannin by an inch. He was moving around, at home, knowing where he was, enjoying himself, his face blackened

213

and ruined by the exploding rifle in the park and the falling dust in the arsenal. For an instant Feiffer saw his eyes, wild with exultation and the effects of the methane, and he drew a steady line on his face and pulled the trigger.

The gun clicked empty.

The Bannin moved.

Feiffer yelled, 'Bill! He coming around to you!' and then Auden's big gun went off in the room and lit up all the naval shells with the flash. Feiffer got another load into his gun—his last—and lashed off a single shot at where The Bannin had been. He heard for an instant the laughing and then the sound of boots on concrete and he fired at the sound. Down below in the next gallery, the last of the satchel charges went off in a thundering roar and he heard the sound of the sea as it crashed in to fill the gap. The air in the arsenal was becoming moist and salty. The corpses were rotting, turning to jelly, deflating. He saw a grinning hairless head on the ground in front of him suddenly break lose from its neck vertebrates and it turned and seemed to look at him. It was a nightmare. The dead were all changing, burning, rotting away into nothingness. The water in the lower gallery seemed to be rushing in a torrent, going somewhere, coming up. There was a bursting sound as the pressure built up and then it came out in sudden hydrants on the floor and washed over the burning bodies and put them all out.

Auden yelled, 'Got it! You've got it!' The fuse came out in Spencer's hand, burning only inches from his knuckles. It had about four seconds left, three, maybe less. Spencer grabbed at it and said, 'I can't hold it!' At the end of the charge there were fragmentation grenades tied together like onions, all primed, set to a central charge of what looked like a cake of TNT. The fragmentation grenades, unlike bullets, would pierce the skin of the naval shells like razors, flying red hot and spinning into the central thick core of explosive and— Spencer grabbed for the fuse again and it burned him and he jerked his hand away. Spencer yelled, 'Phil, I can't—' and Auden was there with a strange look in his eyes, reaching for the fuse. Auden said wildly, 'Seven seconds, is it? Seven goddamned bloodyseconds, is it?' and then his eyes on Spencer, put his hand completely around the burning fuse and, holding it as it burned through to the bone, jerked it loose without the faintest expression of pain on his face. Auden said in triumph, 'Got you, you bastard!' He shouted out at something, at someone, in exultation, 'No bloody brains! That's me! No bloody promotion! No bloody brains! But by Christ, I'm not short on bloody *brawn!*' The fuse was out. He had it in his hand. He dropped it and tried to pick up his gun in the same hand, but it was a useless claw and he clenched it hard and gasped with the pain.

*

They were still in a natural tunnel. Coming from the other side of the headland, they were only about a hundred and fifty yards from the central core of the arsenal. Owlin said, 'Oak trees! Look!' In the light from O'Yee's flashlight he could see old blackened roots and bits and pieces of dead, fossilized leaves and branches hanging down. Owlin said, wrenching at O'Yee's shoulder, 'Look, that's what they did! *Look!*' The stink of methane was strong in the tunnel, coming up. Owlin shouted, 'Look! Look! *Look!*'

'*Shut up!*'

'Look! *Look!* That's what they did to my family! Look! They cut them! All of them! They cut all of them— They didn't leave even one!' Tugging at O'Yee's shoulder, hearing the gunfire, Owlin shrieked, half mad with the methane, 'I'm the last of the line and they didn't even leave me just one!' The dead remnants of the trees were everywhere. Once it had been part of a great, wonderful, growing forest. Wrenching at O'Yee as the man went quickly down the tunnel wih his gun out and ready, Owlin, his eyes wide and staring behind the thick glasses, yelled hysterically, 'Look! All I've ever been— Nothing! Nothing remains of the past! Nothing! Just nothing left!'

There was a second tunnel in the room, a second way out. The water was rising, putting out all the fires on the floor and swirling the bodies around as they broke up and separated. There were papers appearing, photographs, notebooks, floating around the raft corpses. The fuses on the shells were out. The water was coming up in sudden fountains, bubbling up from invisible pipes and flowering in the lantern light and then subsiding and washing across the floor. The bodies were all floating, bumping into each other, their parts becoming detached, turning into skeletons. In the necropolis Feiffer saw The Bannin making for the tunnel across the boiling water, his rifle still in his hand. He saw him turn and pull the trigger and then, looking down at he weapon, bring up a fresh magazine from somewhere and click it in quickly and expertly. The Bannin was naked from the waist up. Feiffer saw the thousand stitches obi around his waist suddenly turning another colour, all the writing and the wishes for success and victory written in ink suddenly starting to flow and melt and run. He saw The Bannin look down at it and make a grab for it before it decayed to nothingness and Feiffer fired a single, precious shot at him and missed. He saw The Bannin look up. With even the last remnants of the obi he was still invulnerable.

He saw The Bannin reach the tunnel exit and disappear into darkness.

He came to what looked like a rockfall. It was thin, only pebbles and a rotten beam down across the tunnel and O'Yee, pushing at it, got it to one side and got through. The stench in the tunnel was awful. He felt his eyeballs drying out in the gas and the powder. Behind him Owlin was raving about something to do with trees.

O'Yee heard a single shot, then a burst of rapid fire, then Auden's big gun going off, and then there was the thick smell of the sea and salt as something heavy gave way deep down and there was a roaring thundering sound as the sea broke through

216

completely at the base of the cliff somewhere and came pouring in.

Owlin shrieked, 'More!' There were dead roots everywhere in the roof. Owlin shrieked, 'There were trees all over here! It was on my map, but I ever knew there were so many!'

O'Yee yelled, 'Harry!' He heard footsteps, running, boots on rock or cement and he flashed the beam of light as far as it could carry through the dust and yelled at the top of his voice, 'This way! There's a way out! *It's this way!*'

*

The Bannin was in the tunnel. At the shells, Spencer was down on his knees trying to get Auden's hand underwater to stop the burning. A body floated to him and he punched it to one side and the body turned over. The Bannin was out, running. His flag was burned and he had all the dead to avenge once he got out.

No more uniforms. This time he would kill anyone he saw. Feiffer yelled, 'Christopher! We're down here! He's in one of the tunnels!' He heard The Bannin running on dry stone and got up in the swirling water and slipped down again. Feiffer yelled, 'For Christ's sake, don't let him get out of here!' He heard O'Yee shout, 'Harry!' as if he hadn't heard and Feiffer, fighting the water to get upright, snapped open his gun and saw only a single live round left there. Feiffer yelled, 'He's in one of the tunnels! He could be coming your way!' He heard the footsteps, 'He's going up! He's got another way out! He's going up into the city!' He heard O'Yee yelling louder, 'Harry! Harry!' as he fought at some obstruction somewhere to get in through solid rock and, moving fast towards the tunnel, Feiffer shrieked at the top of his voice, '*For Christ's sake, don't let him get out!*'

*

The tunnel was collapsing. O'Yee yelled, 'Help me!' and a rotted oak beam, filled with moisture from the sea, fell down around him like soaked cardboard and felled him. His gun was gone. For an instant, O'Yee saw the roof move with a vibration

217

and then glisten with moisture and then the rocks above him were creaking and groaning as, deep below or in the place where Feiffer was, something gave way. He heard footsteps. O'Yee yelled, 'Harry, he's coming this way!' His light was pointing up at the roof. He tried to reach it but it was too far away. Owlin was pushing past him from behind. He was stuck fast. He heard footsteps, boots on dry land. 'I can hear him coming!' The light flickered for a moment and he saw Owlin over the top of him, the glasses glinting. 'Stop him! Don't let him get past us!'

'*Those bastards cut down every tree my famly ever planted!*' Owlin was in a pocket of methane. His eyes were staring, his face shaking. 'They left me nothing! They turned me into something less than every member of my family who ever came before me!' He had O'Yee's gun in his hand. It was wavering as he ran. Owlin yelled into the deep blackness of the tunnel, 'You! Tree-cutter! If you're a shadow of forty years ago, *so am I!*'

*

He was at the entrance to the tunnel with his penlight held out in front of him. There was only one cartridge left. Feiffer, ducking his head to get in, flashed the dying beam ahead of him and saw only blackness. Maybe it was the wrong tunnel. He heard the running footsteps. They seemed to be everyhere, echoes, an army of ghosts running through a nightmare, coming closer, their eyes blazing. Feiffer called into the blackness, 'Christopher! Is it the right tunnel? Are you—'

He heard O'Yee's voice come back, 'Yes! There's a way out onto the cliffs!' There was a deep rumbling and then an explosion and from behind him Spencer's voice shouted, 'It's going! The water's coming in and putting out all the fires, but it's going!' He shouted in apology, 'Phil's almost out with the pain! I can't leave him!' There was a deep movement of the earth, 'The shells are safe!' Spencer yelled, 'All the bodies are breaking up! They're—'

'Christopher!' There was a confluence of two tunnels, both with beams filling up with water and starting to fall to pieces. The decay of decades—the pumice-like stone and the methane—was free and swirling around. Feiffer yelled, 'Christopher, I've lost him! He's taken one of the tunnels and—'

'He's coming! I can hear him coming!'

'*Shoot him!* Bring him down! Shoot him! Kill him if you have to, but for Christ's sake, bring him down!' He saw a flash and then a shattering blast raced at him up the left hand tunnel and Feiffer yelled, 'He's to my left! Can you locate my voice? He's to my left!' He heard a voice say 'Yes!' and he shouted back, 'Who the hell is that? Owlin, is that you?' There was a hissing sound and then another and Feiffer yelled, 'Christopher, are you with him? I can hear Owlin!'

'He's got my gun! I can't move! I'm stuck here in the—'

'Owlin!' One bullet left. Feiffer, running, yelled, 'Owlin! That bastard can see in the dark! He lives down here! Do you hear what I said? *He can see in the dark!*'

'He cut down every one of my trees! Every one! He left me nothing!' The voice changed. Owlin yelled not at somewhere, but at some*one*, 'Every one! You left me *nothing!*'

He was there: The Bannin, his chest heaving, naked, his breath coming in short hard gasps. He was hissing. He was in the dark, looking at the glinting glasses and the man facing him and he smiled and made a chuckling sound in his throat. He reached down to touch his invulnerable obi and with the other hand, seeing in the dark, brought the muzzle of the rifle up to sweep Owlin away with contempt. The Bannin said in a whisper, 'Causes. Great causes and victories. Great...' He looked at Owlin in the dark and made a chuckling sound. He saw Owlin look up at something on the roof of the tunnel, something insignificant: a tree stump, some remnant from nothing more than a tree. The Bannin, ready to die for great glories, tensed in readiness.

There was nothing to a gun. He had once read a book on the subject and all it meant when you had thoroughly researched it was that it was nothing more than the simplest flint tipped weapon and that, like a spear, you only pointed it at someone and then you simply, unimportantly, without difficulty or thought—

Owlin, another man from below ground and from a long time ago, seeing clearly in the dark, raised the muzzle.

Great glories, victories—

The Bannin raised his rifle. Something in the faintest reflected light from the falling white dust glinted in his hand. It was the stock of his rifle, varnished wood, made, a long time ago, from what had once been a living tree.

Owlin looked up at the murdered ravaged stumps all around him. The ruins of his life were there and he stood beneath them. He saw the wooden stock glint, the stock of the last tree the last member of his family had planted, the last, single great tree left in the world, ruined, put to a shoddy, cheap use, not left to grow and blossom and inspire, but simply to—

The Bannin said in a whisper, '*Victory!*'

The revolver was pointing between the hissing man's eyes.

The Bannin said—

There were no words. Owlin closed his eyes and felt them full of tears.

All, all too late, All . . .

He wondered.

He wondered. He wondered what he might have been.

Like the Bannin, he would never know.

Owlin said softly, 'No . . .'

He said sadly, shaking his head, 'No.'

In the darkness, in all his adult life never having once wanted for its own sake to see a morning coming, out of a sudden, strange, unaccountable pity, Owlin pulled the trigger.

*

Into a clear blue sky . . .

At dawn they began bringing the remains of the bodies out one by one. Beneath the sheets on the stretchers, as Feiffer and O'Yee and Auden and Spencer watched with others, the shapes changed in the air and became different, ancient and timeless, and before they reached the line of ambulances waiting for them on the grass, like memory, without reason, decayed totally and were gone.

220